Flashing Swords
#8

Edited by

Robert M. Price

Cushing Publishing

www.cushingpublishing.com

Cushing Publishing

P.O. Box 38

Middlesex, NC 27557

Contents

Introduction

The Past Returns with a Vengeance

Sword and Sorcery fiction marches bravely and indefatigably on! A new generation of tale-spinners and lore masters have felt the call of the ancient gods and heroes to carry on that noble tradition! For some, this is a summons to chronicle the adventures of new characters cut from the same coarse cloth as their forbears. These would include Skar the Barbarian, Ansell of the Dream Lands, Boscastle the Huguenot, Varla of Valkarth, and Tonga of Lost Lemuria. Others obey the whispered commands of the classic heroes such as Duar the Accursed, Elak of Atlantis, Simon of Gitta, Thongor of Lemuria, Ki-Gor the Jungle Lord, and Tara of the Twilight! Like a barrel of Sarn wine, this eighth volume of *Lin Carter's Flashing Swords* is fairly bursting with intoxicating excitement! If you know what's good for you, you'll hasten to agree!

There are other tidings to share with you heroic fantasy fans, news that attests to the revival of interest in this terrific genre! Not long ago, *Sorcery Against Caesar*, an expanded collection of Simon of Gitta's exploits, adding a couple of my own pastiches, appeared from Pickman's Press. Adrian Cole's collection of his excellent Elak pastiches, *Elak, King of Atlantis*, was published by Pulp Hero Press in 2020. Michael Moorcock, a mighty raconteur indeed, has added a new novel to his canon of Elric masterpieces with *The Citadel of Forgotten Myths*.

My own posthumous collaboration with Lin Carter, *Thongor Conquers the Underground World*, has recently emerged from Ramble House. Here's what Charles Hoffman, an expert on Robert E. Howard's work, wrote about the book:

> In *Thongor Conquers the Underground World*, Robert M. Price, working from an outline by the late Lin Carter, takes us on two journeys back through time. The first trip is to the raucous decades of the sixties and seventies, when Edgar Rice Burroughs and Robert E. Howard ruled the paperback book racks. Thongor was Lin Carter's love letter

to both Burroughs and Howard, with a Conan-like hero in a setting not unlike John Carter's Mars. The second time trip is back to the lost Lemuria of Thongor. The Thongor tales are set 500,000 years ago; at this time in reality, the Pleistocene epoch, modern humans had yet to appear. But this is when Carter placed all the lost continents men have envisioned; Atlantis, Mu, Hyperborea, and Lemuria. Since these were home to advanced civilizations—Thongor's Lemuria has flying machines—it makes sense for a writer to place them so far back that the planet has had time to erase all traces of them. Now Robert Price has created a worthy addition to Carter's Thongor saga. His new novel is an engaging blend of fantasy, horror, science fiction, adventure, and even teen romance. Added to this mix are elements of Howard's Kull stories and even Lovecraft's "The Rats in the Walls." A pre-eminent fantasy scholar, Carter crafted his own fiction with an enthusiast's heart. Price manages to replicate Carter's jovial tone, crafting an exuberant, high-spirited narrative with plenty of zip-and-zing. This makes *Thongor Conquers the Underground World* a rousing good read.

Thongor also appears alongside King Kull and others in the pages of the comic series *The Mighty Barbarians* from Ablaze Publishing.

I admit, as an adolescent, I was attracted to the Sword and Sorcery paperbacks initially by their wonderful cover art by the likes of Gray Morrow, Frank Frazetta, and Jeff Jones. Today, as an editor, I am honored to carry on that tradition with wonderful artists like Bebeto Daroz, whose perfect portrait of Lin Carter's Tara graces the present volume. Conan, Thongor, and others have also been treated very well in comic books by artists like Barry Smith and John Buscema. In our own pages, Clayton Hinkle joins them in heroic glory!

Happy Magic!

Robert M. Price
Hierophant of the Horde
June 9, 2013

A Witch-King is Born

Michael A. Turton

THE LEOPARD JUMPED lightly out of the forest and sauntered onto the stone-stubbled trail as if to say it could have pounced but merely chose not to. It sat on a piece of slate, its black-mottled tail swishing slowly from side to side, watching Kaloan as he ascended. Gray-skinned, its body covered with cloudy patterns of black and reddish-gray, it was half as long as a man is tall. It was lovely, a thing of art, he reckoned, set by the nameless gods to grace the forest.

It regarded Kaloan with hooded eyes, weighing him.

Kaloan stopped, crossing his arms. The animal was no threat to him, nor would he kill it, for he took no pleasure in killing, but it was beautiful, and looking at it was a good excuse for a rest. The two regarded each other for a time, then the cat dipped its head at him, rose to its feet, and vanished into the underbrush. Kaloan waited for a while, then started climbing again. He still had a couple of hours of hiking, and he wondered what he had just seen. He shook off the thought as pointless, focusing on setting one foot in front of the other.

The sun was setting fire to the plains below when he finally reached the cave. He had started on the trail just before sunrise, hoping to be at the cave before the mid-morning sun seared the mountainsides with late summer heat. A prudent man, given to pessimistic estimates and careful planning, he had surprised himself by achieving his goal. He took it for a positive augury of the future.

The trail, carefully camouflaged and studded with man-traps, spikes, pits, and other defenses the hill tribes had evolved in their perpetual struggles with each other and the Zan invaders, was known to every Sasayat. The cave was a sacred site, where Lolokan and his sons had committed suicide after their long rebellion against the Zan had ended in defeat and the destruction of their entire clan.

He devoutly hoped *that* wasn't an augury of the future.

Still, the boy-not-a-boy's choice of this cave proved to Kaloan that he was a Sasayat, since only his own people knew its true location. Yet Kaloan knew he was also a Sihayan, a member of the hated ruling class of the Zan invaders, who had stolen the plains from his people and turned the easygoing lowland farming clans into fierce, squabbling mountain tribes. And as a Sihayan, he had powers . . .

For the hundredth time Kaloan wondered if the meeting location were some kind of coded message. He shrugged to himself. If it were a signal, he couldn't read it. Sometimes he felt as though he lacked the subtlety for this level of politics, a game in which he was outplayed as soon as the pieces were set up on board. Given the choice, he preferred to bash things with the sword that hung at his side. Like most people, he flattered himself that he was like a sword, simple and direct. But he was not.

The mouth of the cave, a mere slit recessed in the mountainside behind a curl of gray rock and hidden by bushes, was announced by the presence of a bright, well cared for sword and dagger with a curling snake worked into the hilt resting against the gray rock. So the boy-not-a-boy knew! The sacred cave must not be profaned with weaponry. Nodding his approval, Kaloan undid his pack and extracted his pair of well-worn long knives, removed the small dagger from its boot sheath, and stood his sword against the rock. He slipped into the crack, scrapping his leggings against the rocks. And halted.

The cave was inhabited by a monster. Teeth like flakes of obsidian, red eyes, scales, and a lashing, spiked tail. Facing it, Kaloan crossed his arms and began to laugh. "Is that how you kept people away? With these outlandish illusions?"

The creature vanished.

"You're a day late," said a voice in Sasayat.

"There was a delay," he replied. "I was followed by four Yapi."

"Did you kill them?"

"Of course." The voice was silent for a moment. "Come in, then." Kaloan felt the light touch of Sihayan power, that psionic capability that marked them as a breed apart, brushing with etheric fingers across the surface of his mind, probing, testing. He formed a shell, fended it off with ease, though he was rusty in using that power. The ghostly feeling of being probed remained, however. The boy-not-a-boy was powerful.

"You have Sihayan blood," said the voice, registering surprise. "I was told you were merely the war leader of the Sasayat, their greatest swordsman." Laughter echoed cavernously. "A Sihayan posing as a barbarian war leader? A clever subterfuge. Who would suspect?"

Kaloan shrugged, his eyes adjusting to the half-light. He was in no mood to banter. "Usually it's easier to settle matters with a sword," he replied. He sighed wearily and reaching out with his own mind, set a light on the ceiling, partly, he admitted to himself, as a reassuring demonstration of his own more limited powers. It was good to openly exercise his own powers, like stretching a long-unused limb. The darkness skittered away, leaving a brightly lit, egg-shaped cave with a clean, high arching roof of gray-brown rock. The air stank of heat and stillness, but at least it was cool inside. He noted the seven sitting stones of Lolokan arranged around the sacred fire in the center of the cave, the sitting stones representing the sons who had been killed.

Sons who have been killed? What kind of omen is that? he wondered.

They stood, blinking at each other in the sudden glare. They were mirror images, Sasayat warriors both, brown skinned and flat nosed, with narrow brown eyes and square heads and shortness stopping just short of squatness. Both wore whitish deerskin jackets and leggings, worked with red and black diamond patterns representing stylized snake scales, a Sasayat specialty. Kaloan was the taller, a warrior in his prime, with broad, well-muscled shoulders and thighs like boulders, while the boy still sported the leanness of youth, longer-limbed and obviously quick. Kaloan knew, though, that his counterpart was decades old. Many Sihayan still practiced the ancient art of arresting their aging to appear less threatening—or more so—as necessary. This was obviously a being of immense power. What other powers might this one have? A coldness traveled down his limbs: he was alone, and weaponless, and the other was much stronger.

The boy studied him, noting his discomfort, then grinned warmly. "We could almost pass for brothers. That could be useful," he mused.

"Useful?"

The boy motioned at the circle of stones. "Come, sit. Food? Drink?" When Kaloan ritually refused, he continued. "You are Kaloan son of Egea, right?" The boy did not offer a name nor, in typical Sasayat fashion, the name of his father, Kaloan marked. Why not? Kaloan did not like any of the possible answers to that question. "Let me tell you why I called you here."

Kaloan ambled over and plopped down on a stone seat, arms dangling. He was glad enough to sit down after hours spent marching in the morning. "I heard you needed an army and thought I was the man to give it to you," he said.

The boy sat down and nodded, shifting to face him. "You follow Zannai politics?"

Kaloan laughed genially. "Seldom. It's enough work just keeping track of the problems between our own people." The probing continued, and he hardened his shell to stop the boy from reading him. In fact, he knew perfectly well what the boy was going to tell him, but he wanted to see how the boy understood things.

"There was a civil war last year in Zannai between the Sihayans over the status of our land. The Sihayan domains here on the plains declared independence from the Zannai Empire. It was inevitable. Most of their trade runs to the north, to Ponjan and to Yukuru, and south to Chelsya and Pili-pili and the islands beyond. The Sihayans and Zan colonists have been here for generations and are no longer like the Zan in the empire proper. They have interbred with the mountain peoples and picked up many of our habits. The split is permanent, they claim, and the local Zan will no longer send tribute or have their children educated there."

Kaloan mulled this. "How is this possible?"

"Zannai is weak. The long wars with Wueh and the Shevan Empire have drained its resources. That is why no new Zan colonists have crossed the water in a generation even though the plains along the southern mountains are still sparsely populated. So the Sihayans here decided the time was ripe and banded together. For once." The boy-not-a-boy leaned over. "You see what this means. The local domains can no longer draw on the Empire for new colonists and troops and financial support. They must rely on local resources. They are vulnerable. And they are already squabbling amongst themselves."

"How does this involve me?"

"I need an army."

"A Sasayat army."

"Indeed. An army I can trust. It is said the warriors will come if you ask. The Atya too, and the Turungi. And others. You have led them before."

"Aye, they might, if sufficient loot is offered and the attack looks easy enough." Kaloan peered at the boy, intent, wary, remembering how old he actually was. "What is your plan?"

"They say you are both patient and clever, full of trickery."

Kaloan laughed uneasily, not liking the flattery or the way the boy put off a direct question. He waved a hand in the air. "Me? I can post the troops where I like, and am first into battle, but getting them to follow me or listen to commands in the heat of battle when they would rather be stripping the dead or celebrating a kill, that is the only time I am patient and clever. As for trickery, well, beaten men will make any excuse for their failures."

The boy-not-a-boy snorted, one side of his mouth twisting up. "I know my people. They are good fighters, but you can't build an empire out of them. They are focused only on the here and now."

Kaloan sighed. "They are good only for raiding and looting. That is why the Zan always win in the long run."

"Not this time," the boy declared. He leaned forward. "What I have in mind is a raid, perfect for the mountain people."

"Say on."

"You know, every year, at the harvest festival in Kaigi the Chukulungu Witch-King must perform the Autumnal rites in one of the city temples there on the night of the first full moon of the season. The rulers, after all, must nod to the religion of the ruled." He looked thoughtful for a moment, as if just realizing something, and then continued. "That means that in thirty days the Witch-King will be in Kaigi, just there, just below the mountains, accompanied by his court troops, his picked guards, and his courtiers. He is the most powerful Sihayan in the land," the boy continued. "Simple. We come down out of the mountains that night and attack Kaigi, you leading the warriors against the city militia and the Witch-King's retinue, me to fight him."

"You?" The outburst echoed in the cave.

"Me. You of all people know how old I really am. For many years I have been hiding among our people, studying, practicing, cultivating my powers. It is easy to conceal one's identity in the mountains."

That last is true, Kaloan thought, recalling how he had done just that. He raised a skeptical eyebrow. "Can you really defeat the Sihayan Witch-King, who has sat for over a century on his throne? And his Sihayan priests? And how do you plan to breach the city walls? Our people will not build siege machines. They will not remain in front of the walls for more than an hour or two. Even I will not be able to keep them there."

"I will break those walls," the boy said. "As for the priests," here he waved a hand dismissively, "even you are more powerful than any of his priests."

Even me, Kaloan thought, once again disturbed. *This one is arrogant, maybe mistake prone.* Mistakes offended Kaloan, who made few, and was always careful, watching closely for weaknesses in himself and others.

Sensing his doubt, the boy stood, held a hand to the mouth of the cave. "Come, you must see and believe, because you must tell others."

Kaloan dipped his head and followed the boy out of the cave, snuffing the light he had set. They began climbing.

The sun was arcing towards midday, and Kaloan once again appreciated why Lolokan had chosen this spot to make his final stand. From the ledge above the cave mouth to the east almost all of Chukulungu could be seen. Just below them lay the market town of Kaigi on the Kun, a spider's web of roads surrounded by the fields of rice, sweet potatoes, and green vegetables. Tiny storms of dust and smoke rose in the air from fires and farming. Winding its long, lazy way to the sea, the Kun glistened in the late morning sunlight. Leagues beyond Kaigi, at the mouth of the Kun, lay the Port of Chukulungu, visible only on the best of days.

They followed the merest hint of an overgrown footpath among the trees to the top of the ridge. A few minutes of steady hiking brought them to the top, where the trail dropped onto a broad shelf of rock with staggering views over the mountain ranges to the west. Sharp blue peaks blotted with streaks of white marble were backed by higher ranges. He knew that on the west side the high ranges rushed down to the open sea like giants tumbling over each other to jump into the water, leaving a line of sea-cliffs half a league high in their wake, lined with beaches of gray stone and seashells. Lolokan must have stood in this exact spot, Kaloan thought, planning his attacks, brooding on his defeats.

The boy-not-a-boy stepped lightly onto the shelf of brown rock and gestured. "See that peak? Where the marble outcrops at the end of the ridge?"

"Of course." A high peak, and where its slopes fell to blend with the ridge half a league away a long belt of white and black marble pushed out like a bit of skin from a torn glove. A sight that Kaloan had admired many times.

The boy smiled ferally. "Watch."

The last thing Kaloan saw was the boy putting out his hand. There was no sound. Suddenly the universe turned to white light, filling space, burning a white afterimage across his eyes and flooding his mind with a vast torrent of power. He blinked, steadied himself. The boy gave a harsh laugh and he felt the power, the surge of triumph, through the boy's touch on his mind. He opened his eyes, adjusted back to the world.

The marble ridge was gone. In its place was a perfect half-circle of nothing, as if some Brobdingian predator had taken a bite out of the mountain. For minute the mountain overhung the space, then Kaloan watched bits of rock, then bigger rocks, then the whole slope, begin to slide, forming a vast avalanche that would bury the gaping wound.

"This shelf is not strong," he warned, springing backwards, elbows in the air. "The rock is rotten. It could collapse if the mountains shake."

The boy turned and together they leapt back to the trail and scrambled over to the other side of the peak. They stopped and stood, panting, admiring the view over Chukulundu in silence, as the broken mountain behind them rumbled and quaked the trail beneath their feet. Kaloan felt the sun beating down on his shoulders, heating the soft cloth that hung over his upper body. Yet the pressure on his mind had subsided. The effort had weakened the boy-not-a-boy considerably.

Or he could be bluffing, hiding his true strength. Unease washed over Kaloan. There were too many things he did not know.

The noise had subsided a bit, and Kaloan tilted his head at the boy-not-a-boy. "If you kill the Sihayan, you will become the next Sihayan Witch-King. The local Zan will all follow you."

"Yes. The Zan are sheep, to be herded at will." The boy looked away, out over the vast checkered plains. "Usually the position falls to the eldest son, who also subsumes his powers. The Sihayan . . . accumulate their power. They are leery of having sons, since the eldest may one day try to supplant them. But the Chukulundu Witch-King has no children. Any sufficiently powerful Sihayan can take his position from him and rule in his place. I will." The boy turned his face to look up at Kaloan. "I will be the next Witch-King, and you will be my general, my right-hand, my second-in-command. Your word will be law, after mine."

Kaloan's eyebrows rose. Power itself held no attraction for him, but he couldn't deny it was useful for getting things done.

"What about our people?"

"They will have Kaigi to loot."

Kaloan shook his head and stretched a hand out over the plain below. "The northern county of Kaigi was once Sasayat land from Deerport to the headwaters of the Kun. Give it back to us. Move the Zan off, we will occupy it. The Atya and the Turungi can have the looting of Kaigi."

The boy considered, then nodded decisively. "Wise of you. That will be better for our people." He suddenly smiled. "The Kun is navigable by ocean-going ships all the way to Deerport."

Kaloan grunted. "We were once a sea people, trading with Zannai, and Pili-pili, and faraway Suanz. We will be again."

"And taxes to me?"

"Will be paid."

"That will be a new thing for the mountain people." They both chuckled. "You want nothing for yourself?" the boy asked, in a softer tone.

"One day I will retire and have a farm along the Kun. I will grow mangoes, and smoke *dama*. Maybe I will travel a bit. See Zannai with my own eyes."

"So my general is an idealist."

That made him laugh. "If laziness be idealism, then I am the most idealistic man you know!"

The boy-not-a-boy chuckled. "How came you by your powers?"

"I do not know. My father left my mother when I was a babe to find work in the Port of Chukulundu, I never met him. But somewhere in his line, there was a powerful Sihayan."

"Yes, even diluted by several generations, the power is there."

Kaloan continued, aware of the heat, aware that the light pressure on his mind had returned. He hardened his shell. "When I was a lad my mother fostered me out to her cousin, a Sasayat, from Three Lakes. Her husband was a Zan, a merchant at Kaigi. They sent me to school in Kaigi."

"You were fostered? And went to school?"

"Aye," replied Kaloan, his eyes glinting with humor. "It was held that I had promise,

though it doesn't seem to have come to much."

The boy cocked an eyebrow at him. "So how did you come to be an itinerant warrior with no property of his own, if you're the educated child of a wealthy Zan Merchant?"

"My foster father dealt in camphor wood from the Hills. He was at Fort Ruhai when the Yapi raided it. He and his wife were both killed."

"He left you nothing?"

"Foster children cannot inherit if there are true children, by Chukulundu law, if they are mountain people." He spat, mouthing an old curse. "My foster brother cast me out. Gave me a sword and some coins and told me to go." Even after so many years, Kaloan felt the pain of that, fresh as yesterday. There was a great hole in his life, left by the loss of his foster-parents and then the loss of his family. He had not chosen of his own will to become a loner, concealed from others. "For some Zan, the mountain people are not really people," he finished.

"So you have some reason to hate the Zan."

"If a cow gores you, do you hate all cattle?"

The boy considered this. "I do."

Kaloan laughed at this conceit, for he considered hate a useless emotion, dangerous and misleading. "And you, Sihayan and Sasayat both?"

"A similar story. My father was a powerful Sihayan. He killed my mother, a Sasayat from Laiji, after I was born, meaning to take me for his own. But my mother's family hid me in the mountains. I was raised by my mother's parents in the hills above Laichi."

"What's your name, boy?"

"Duha will do for now. Names give power. Even false names."

Kaloan grunted. It seemed a weakness, to believe that superstition. Suddenly he felt that uneasiness return. So much riding on this boy's ability. What were the boy's other weaknesses? What other strange beliefs did he hold?

"You have thirty days, Son of Egea, to make your case to our people. I will say your name among the Atya and the Turungi. They know me of old. Perhaps they will come. Where should we gather them? Goshala's Rock?"

Kaloan considered this, running fingers through his hair. After a moment, he said: "No, that's too strong a sign that our goal is Kaigi. Do you know the meadow below Aruru where the Great Creek has that wide waterfall?" The boy nodded and Kaloan continued. "The Witch-King will be in Kaigi for the first full moon of autumn. Have the warriors gather in that meadow three days before the full moon. It is a longer march to Kaigi, but close to Deerport. Tell them we are assembling for a raid on Deerport. Who knows, if word gets around, it may even draw off some of the garrison from Kaigi."

The light pressure on Kaloan's mind ceased altogether and the boy clapped him on the back. "I will. Good hunting to you."

Kaloan nodded in return. He picked up his weapons and slung his pack over his shoulder, then began to descend the path. He felt the boy-not-a-boy's eyes on his back for a while, until he disappeared into the vegetation far below the cave. Behind him the earth rumbled with the agony of the mountain's collapse. Duha was powerful. Yet even the smallest arrow could slay him, Kaloan told himself, like any other man.

Powerful?

My father was a powerful Sihayan. The boy's words echoed in his mind as he pushed his way between the trees. There was only one Sihayan who could be his father. Only one who had dealings with the Sasayat. He remembered: *the son subsumes the father's powers when he dies.*

Kaloan shuddered. The sun was an avalanche of heat, burying him under its weight. Catching a glimpse of the peak, he looked back over his shoulder at where Duha should be.

He thought: *This can only end in betrayal.*

* * * * *

He had been two days on the side trail up to Three Lakes, the more or less central settlement of the Sasayat people, when he encountered the hunting party. He had sensed them passively for a couple of hours before they ran across the trail—he never actively probed for other minds since it might reveal his possession of Sihayan powers, but minds intent and focused were easy to sense. They were descending through the orchards that sprawled across the slopes, moving at a fast pace, obviously chasing something, obliterating the presence of other Sasayat, old women singing as they tended their fruit, old men bringing up water from wells, children squealing at play, other people on the move.

"Son of Egea!" said a voice, both astonished and glad, as the group moved onto the trail. There were six of them, young warriors of his people, heavily armed with bows, swords, and daggers, dressed in nothing but a loincloth, shields slung on their backs. They were covered with sweat though the sun was still low in the morning sky.

"Sende, Son of Tonna," Kaloan replied equably to the speaker. He pretended to study them as they clustered around him. "Food and drink?" he asked ritually, extracting some jerky from a pouch. They refused.

"Where are you going like this, armed for battle?" he asked, as he shoved the jerky back in its pouch. "Who are you chasing?"

"There's a party of Zan troops coming up the Fanlu Trail from Left Camp," Sende replied, breathlessly.

His eyebrows rose. "Up the Fanlu trail? How many? How armed?"

"Forty, maybe more. A few crossbowmen, spearmen mostly," answered another. "I saw them with my own eyes, War Leader."

They looked at him eagerly, like puppies.

"And how many are we?" he asked casually.

"Ten of us wait by the trail. Yesterday they sent me—Alay, Son of Moro—back to fetch more men."

"So with sixteen you were going to ambush forty well-armed Zan troops." Kaloan shook his head. Stupidity like this was why so many women in the hills had no men. The party of warriors all studied their feet. *At least they have the grace to look sheepish*, he thought.

"Now we are seventeen, War Leader," one of them pointed out.

Kaloan gave him a sour look. Inwardly he hoped the ten camped out along the trail hadn't become impatient and tried their luck with an ambush. *And the boy-not-a-boy thinks we can take Kaigi with these!*

"Well," he said at last, shaking his head. "Let's go take a look."

* * * * *

"Taking a look" took several hours of marching on a side trail in the midday heat, it turned out. The heat had baked the forest to stillness, and they encountered only troops of monkeys hooting challenges at them, and a solitary boar that ignored them as it dug by the roots of a tree. They arrived at the Fanlu Trail and took up a position on a low ridge overlooking the trail, which ran along the Nonogulat, a tributary of the Kun. Alay ran off to find his compatriots tracking the Zan troop detachment while Kaloan and the others rested.

They'd had one piece of good luck, stumbling into a party of Tuga'a toughs descending to the plains to take heads at one of the tiny farming communities located at the base of the hills. Eleven more fighters had been added to their number when Kaloan had promised them a large share of the loot. He had a low opinion of the Tuga'a, whom he considered little more than looters and murderers of helpless farmers, but they could stop a spearpoint as well as anyone. Besides, tattooed and painted like demons, they looked terrifying.

This part of the lower slopes was a no man's land marked by temporary, shifting fields and small trading posts where Sasayat and Zan traders mingled foods and goods and bloodlines. The Nonogulat with its wide, shallow, graveled riverbed and network of associated trails was a highway through it when the water was calm, pointing like an arrow into the heart of Sasayat mountain country. Indeed, the Sasayat jade mine at Fongton, the only one in the land and a key source of Sasayat wealth and influence, was located just off one of the Nonogulat's own tributaries, many leagues up. Sooner or later, if they pushed up the river, the Zan would discover it. Then they would never stop coming until they had the jade.

The Zan troop soon hove into view, and they were joined a few moments later by the remaining Sasayat fighters. His heart rose when he saw the Zan troop. There were indeed forty, mostly spearmen, clad in cheap leather jerkins and helmets that protected their noses and ears. Some were dragging the butts of their spears in the road, clearly exhausted from the day's march. Most of them were quite young. A pair of them were unarmed, probably engineers, Kaloan thought. He sensed no Sihayans and wondered why. Usually an expedition like this had a priest or two in tow. He also noted several large carts clanking along behind the troop drawn by mules, full of sharpened bamboo stakes that were obviously intended to form a palisade.

The Zan weren't very competent at anything, but they were very methodical about everything, Kaloan knew. The palisade would be followed by a fort, which would be followed by a crude dirt road, cut through the forest by laborers from the mountain people, and paid for by the vast corruption that marked Zan administration. Then a plank road, and finally, a stone-paved road. Then settlers would arrive and another piece of Sasayat land would fall to the Zan. Kaloan sighed. This would have to be dealt with.

"Look, they have mountain guides," someone said.

"Yapi," scowled a voice. "The Yapi are treacherous."

A pair of his Sasayats scuttled up to him as the group watched the Zan trudge up the trail.

"The Tuga'a are cowards," someone quietly rasped at him. "Why must they fight with us? They will run at the first sound of battle."

"No, they are warriors. They can fight," the other, younger, insisted. "Is that not so, War Leader?"

Kaloan readied wry agreement with the first speaker, then stilled his tongue, suddenly thoughtful. *They are warriors. They can fight.* All the mountain peoples had been one people long ago, speaking the same language, sharing the same hearths. In the mountains, divided by difficult terrain and differing lifestyles, their languages had begun to diverge. And the fighting erupted, the constant, man-draining fighting . . .

Suddenly he felt light-headed, as though ill. He groped for support, clutching a nearby tree. The sound of a million bees filled his mind, a feeling of vastness so great he could sense only the merest hint of it. For the first time in his life a vision, a true seeing from the nameless gods— he knew without being told—poured into him, flooding his mind the way an overwhelming torrent quickly fills then overtops a weir, a vision of a superstate of all the peoples of the land, all the mountain peoples. An end to the pointless fighting between the mountain peoples. Yes, and an end to fighting with the Zan too. He saw ships crewed by Zan and mountain people alike, laden with trade goods plying the routes to Shevan and Suanz and Pili-pili, wealth flowing out of the mountains to the sea, wealth brought back from abroad, spices, cloth, tools, machines, the tilling of pleasant fields and the tending of mountain orchards, peoples living side by side. And a Witch-King who could bridge both peoples.

That was something worth fighting for. Worth dying for. Worth living for.

"Quiet," he commanded, trying to get his bearings as his mind returned to the situation at hand. The men were staring at him, uncertain. The vision had shaken him and he was already becoming keyed up about the coming fight. "The trail widens out to a flat area not far ahead. See those stakes? They will camp there and set up a palisade. We need to get moving." Once the palisade was up, he knew, the Zan camp would be invulnerable.

Quickly he laid his plans.

* * * * *

When Kaloan stepped out of the trees into the open everything seemed to pause. The Zan troopers, roughly half of whom were busy shoving bamboo stakes into the ground, all stopped to look at him, first in disbelief and then, in growing amusement. A single savage coming out to challenge their whole troop?

Kaloan stood, his back to the forest, his feet wide, the Zan soldiers spread out in front of him a spear's throw away. He had stripped to a simple loincloth into which he had shoved his sword and a long knife, and his skin was fired bronze in the setting sun. Soldiers who had been relaxing on the ground were coming slowly to their feet, and heads were poking out from under blankets. The crossbowmen sitting on the cart straightened up and peered at him incredulously, feeling for their weapons. Men looked up from campfires, smiling unkindly. Behind them the river burbled and murmured along its gravel banks, as if excited to witness the coming events. Beyond the river the trees rose in rank upon rank up to the steep walls of the gorge, dark and unreadable, an audience.

"*Aiyi, Aiyi!*" he shouted, and in flawless Zan added: "Die, Zan pigs!" He drew his sword with deliberate unhurry, and pulled out the dagger for his left hand. He was in a state of exhilarated nervousness, every muscle crackling with energy, his mind filled with power.

Someone barked an order and the crossbowmen sitting on the carts unleashed their bolts.

Then the Zan discovered why Kaloan was accounted the greatest warrior of his people: he cheated.

To the people watching it must have seemed that Kaloan had almost superhuman skill in dodging. The bolts slid harmlessly past him as he twisted his body, because he had touched them with his mind, ensuring they would miss. He then reached out with his mind and snapped the bow strings. The crossbowmen would attribute that to the usual corruption of Zan administration, he knew, if they survived to explain to someone what had happened, stammering: *But sir, they sold us bad strings!*

That was his secret: he worked his magic only on inanimate objects, never actively on human minds, never revealing himself.

The officer yelled another order and a group of five spearman made a rush for Kaloan. The rest remained at alert, readying weapons and watching the forest. The Zan officer was taking no chances. That command, however, was enough to trigger the first part of his plan: the ten Sasayat fighters he posted to his right had strict instructions to kill the officer the moment they could identify him. Sure enough, arrows flew out of the forest, taking the man in the thigh and the arm. He went down and dismay rippled across the troop. The Zan resolve melted and several troopers began to shift nervously backwards towards the river. Kaloan scowled to himself as a couple of arrows zipped over his head at his attackers instead of at the officer. Well, he couldn't fault them for wanting to protect him. They were young, after all.

Behind him the Tuga'a warriors began shouting and screaming. Another volley of arrows flew out of the trees. A Zan fell, but only one. The Sasayats were fierce swordsman but indifferent archers.

He stepped forward, raising his weapon in defense. Time seemed to come to a standstill. Spears flew at him and he dodged them, again pushing them aside with his mind. His attackers were on him and spears and swords were flashing on him right and left. To his left he was dimly aware that the Tuga'a had rushed out of the trees, earlier than he had wanted. This meant that his Sasayats . . . yep, they had followed suit, anxious not to lose honor to the despised Tuga'a. On either side the Zan soldiers nerved themselves for the clash, then rushed in, screaming and waving their spears.

Kaloan dodged the thrown spears easily, and then cut down the first man to reach him—the poor fellow had no idea what he was doing with his sword. Another slashed at him from the right and Kaloan beat aside his sword and then took the man's hands off at the wrists. Blood gushed over his forearms. The two men to his left had easy shots at his exposed left side but somehow managed to miss—with a little nudge from Kaloan's mind. He pivoted, beat their swords aside, and took one in the gut with his dagger. The dying man staggered back, meeting Kaloan's eyes in mute appeal, and then opened his mouth in a soundless scream. Falling, he tried to kick Kaloan, but missed. The remaining two stepped back, awareness dawning that they would not survive an encounter with Kaloan. One turned and ran. Other Zan ran forward pell-mell to help, to fight, to their deaths. They were the worst kind of soldiers, he thought, both unenthusiastic and incompetent.

He strode forward into the melee, where the grass was smeared crimson and the air stank of blood and sweat. A Zan screamed at him, helmet askew, and rushed at him, spear held ineptly at his waist. Kaloan smiled, shoved aside the point, then hacked at the man's arms. There was a scream and the man collapsed on the ground, groaning in pain. A man rushed past and Kaloan slashed at him, but his sword skidded off the leather armor, the shock traveling up his forearm. His shoulder ached as he evaded the return blow. Swing. Dodge. Raise his sword . . . Kaloan found himself falling into that eerie trance state of slash-recover-repel, striking quickly at exposed body parts as he ran past, deeper into the fight, pushing aside spear and sword points aimed at him, trying to ignore the shouts and moans of pain and screams of the dying. It was incredible how much noise a few dozen men could make.

He struck down a man, and another. A crossbow bolt thudded into the ground next to him, and he cursed and reached out and snapped the strings *again*. But his mind was elsewhere for a moment and he missed a spear point coming at him. It drew a long cut along his sword arm. Yelling in pain, he buried his sword in the guts of its owner, his dagger blocking another sword. He threw the man off with his left forearm and raised his own sword. His heart was pounding and it seemed like there wasn't enough air in the whole world to fill his lungs.

Suddenly, in the midst of all that endless noise, came a high-pitched scream that filled the air, obliterating all other sounds.

"Aiiyee!!!" it rang out in Zan. "The savages are behind us!"

Kaloan smiled in grim satisfaction. At least one part of his plan had actually worked. Earlier he had sent six of his Sasayat bravos up the river and instructed them to ford it and come back down to the shelf where he expected the Zan to put up their palisade and attack as soon as the fight began. They had rushed out of the water, killed a couple of the crossbowmen and were now hitting the Zan from behind.

Fear magnifies the number of enemies, he knew, and his compatriots had struck at just the right moment. At the rear of the Zan, they seemed like a thousand, killing as they went.

"The savages are behind us!" Several voices took up the cry. "The savages are behind us! Run, run for your lives!" The Zan began looking around fearfully, edging back, throwing down their weapons and running for the trail. The officer might have been able to reverse things, for the Zan still outnumbered his own little force, but he was down and presumably dead, and their morale collapsed. Several more were killed as they turned to escape, but roughly a dozen ran pell-mell down the trail. A couple of the Sasayat tried to pursue, but Kaloan called them off. He did not want any more of his own killed in stupid reckless attacks. Besides, he wanted time to think.

He collected his wits and carefully checked his own body for cuts, but though he was covered with blood there were none save the gash in his arm, still bleeding freely. The grass was strewn with bodies, some writhing or crawling with desperate urgent slowness toward the river. The repeated, odious sound of *thunk!* told him his warriors were already about, finishing the wounded and looting their bodies.

Kaloan shrugged and went down to the river to wash, counting his men as he went. Six of the Tuga'a had survived, along with thirteen of his own. Over twenty Zan lay dead in the grass. He should have felt pride, but the sight sickened him. The dead were so young. And for all his power he could do nothing to heal them. The mind itself may be vulnerable, but it automatically protected its own body from intrusions of other minds, even when they were trying to repair damage. It was as if everyone were gifted with Sihayan power, but only a few were actually aware. He sighed, hating the waste, brooding over other battles, other dead . . .

One of the Sasayats approached him, softly, as if sensing his mood.

"War leader."

"Yes."

"The mules?"

He grimaced, bracing himself. "Give them to the Tuga'a," he answered.

"The Tuga'a! But——"

He glared at the boy. "They fought well and lost half their number. If we treat them with respect, they may ally with us in the future. If we treat them badly, we will make an enemy. How many more enemies do we need?" The corner of his lip turned up. "Besides, do you really want them?"

The other stared at him for the moment as if to say *But it's loot*, then sensibly replied: "No."

"Well, then. Go and explain to the Tuga'a how to take care of them. I don't think they know anything about mules."

The lad grinned, white teeth like porcelain cups under big brown eyes.

"That will be funny. They're just going to get frustrated and eat them anyway."

They both laughed a little, there among the dead, as the evening fell softly around them.

* * * * *

The mountains were alive with Yapi, crawling over the slopes like beetles on a rotting log. The Sasayat and the Yapi abutted one another across the ranges, one side flowing into the other the way a river meets the sea, creating a murky, free-flowing area full of life that changed composition with every shifting tide. But now the Yapi were in flood.

Kaloan had killed a small party of six that intercepted him on the trail. He had avoided a larger party, costing him two days of extra walking. Staying overnight in one of the gray slate houses at High Tree village he heard tales of sadness, the woman weeping because the Yapi had killed her pigs and torn up her fields, another lost her son in an ambush, still another, her soursop orchard raided and the trees burned or poisoned. Two days later he encountered the mutilated bodies of a group of young men near the sacred rock below Laichi. The Yapi had ambushed them.

Something was amiss in the mountains.

One evening, just before making camp for the night, he found a string of footprints, of a beast he had never seen before, with three giant claws on a foot that was like a withered oak. The holes left in the trail by its claws swallowed his hand. It had savaged a deer before wandering off, and Kaloan shuddered at the gaping wounds it left in the poor animal. He camped far from that place. Another night, lying just inside a cave, he was awaked by the sound of screams overhead. An object thudded to the ground next to his firepit. In the morning he saw it was the remains of a child's thigh.

Something was deeply amiss in the mountains.

A ten-day after the battle Kaloan found himself in the long hall at Three Lakes, crammed with dozens upon dozens of angry, worried, and sad Sasayats. The meeting had been called for midday but in fine mountain style nobody showed up until late in the afternoon. Warm greetings came his way, men gripping his wrists as if to check whether he was real, women throwing their arms around him and rubbing noses and cheeks with him. Children slithered through the throng, snatching up eatables. The hall, made of gray slate and cedar wood with a waterproof roof of clay tile in imitation of Zan practice, smelled of roasted pork and wild rice, and ferns cooked in olive oil. Someone thrust an areka nut into his hand and he chewed on it, meditating. It was good to be home, he thought.

"Son of Egea, we heard you killed an army of Zan a few days ago," a voice said across the hubbub, and Kaloan felt a thrill of pleasure as the crowd hushed to hear his reply. Nothing, not his prowess in battle, his Sihayan powers, his language skills, or his ability to read and write, made him as proud as his status among his own people. This was a thing he had earned, an acceptance that he had because of who he was. And now, if everything worked out, he would be able to give back to them. Once again a million hornets hissed in his mind, the vision channeling through him, a torrent of dreams, closing the walls on him, calling him out of his body. He shook his head to clear it. *Nameless gods, please, I need to concentrate on the here and now . . .*

The pressure instantly vanished. Stunned, he sent up a prayer of thanks.

"Well," he replied to the speaker, feeling the areka spread heat through his body as he squatted, arms on knees, "it wasn't much of an army." They listened intensely as he described the battle, stressing the importance of the cooperation with the Tuga'a. One of the elders recited the names of the dead, blessing them. Finally, when he was done, they all started shouting at once.

"If only it had been Yapi!" Someone yelled.

"Yes! Those Yapi! We have to do something."

"Treachery! May the gods spit on them!"

One of the old men poked the air with a bony finger, summoning silence. "Son of Egea, what do you think we should do about these," he spat, uttering a curse, "Yapi."

The hall quieted.

"The Yapi are not our problem," said Kaloan. He looked around the crowd, meeting eyes in a clear challenge.

The hall erupted in a thunderous roar of protests and denials.

"*Ai-yi!*" It was Anei, Mother of Toluot. Her youngest clung to her, still baby-chubby, peering suspiciously at the crowd, thumb in mouth. She was a tall woman, nearly as tall as Kaloan, not yet middle-aged, with a strong jaw and broad shoulders. She was accounted wise by the others. "Didn't any of you thickwits listen to the Son of Egea? And before him, to the Son of Mutu? The Zan killed by the Nonogulat and by the Son of Mutu were all young, untrained. No real soldiers among them. No Sihayan priests either. And now the Yapi! *Ai-yi!* Think! Did none of you ask yourselves why the Yapi are attacking us now?" She mashed a fist against her head, implying that her listeners had less than the proper amount of brains.

Kaloan watched, grinning quietly, admiring her wit and passion, the way she made the men quail. The Zan, who kept their women cloistered and away from important affairs, marveled at the women of the mountain people who sat in council with the men and helped make key decisions, headed households, sometimes even lead men in battle. No woman in the mountains was ever married against her will.

She continued as the talking died off to a murmur. "The Chukulundu King is pushing the border up into the mountains, using local gentry militias, those bravos the gentry use to fight among themselves and bully local farmers. Those dead boys bore his sigil, but they knew little of fighting. The priests are being held back in the cities, along with the real soldiers, because the Witch-Kings are all fighting amongst themselves now that they have split with Zannai. They need real soldiers, the priests for that!"

The silence was absolute. She spun her head, meeting every eye. "The Yapi have made a bargain with the Witch-King of Chukulundu. He has made a game of them, to keep us occupied while his officers push the border a little further into the mountains, eating us little by little. We Sasayat are the target!"

She swept a pointing finger round the crowd. "And you! Clods of earth! You hold a war council and jabber about attacking the Yapi! You are doing the Witch-King's work for him!" She thrust out a hip and then rolled her eyes, as the young girls did to indicate a man is undesirable.

Hoots and guffaws greeted her. Several men made lewd offers to her, to which she responded with playfully obscene gestures. More laughter.

"But," she said, waving them to silence again, "the Son of Egea sits among us, and it's certain he, the great planner, has a plan. Can we hear it?"

There were shouts of agreement. "Let him speak! Let him speak!"

The crowd quieted in anticipation. Mother of Toluot eyed him expectantly.

Kaloan spat out the remains of the areka and spoke. "Thank you, Mother of Toluot," he said gravely. Her eyes glinted with answering humor. He described the Sihayan Duha who was also a Sasayat, his powers, the plan to take Kaigi, the broken mountain, the reward of territory for his people. He asked them to fight for him.

He kept the vision of the future of the land to himself, but it was there beside him in the crowd, palpable.

Out of respect, there was a period of silence after he spoke. Then the crowd broke up into little knots of people, arguing and gesticulating at each other. After a long discussion, they would arrive at a consensus, probably after half the group was drunk, he calculated. He found a bowl of rice wine sitting on a stool and stole a sip, since talking was thirsty work. Then he sidled up to one of the knots, a group of old men. One was speaking, impassioned.

"Eh, who does the work in the Port of Chukulundu? Eh? The laborers are mostly Yapi and Sasayat. We fight here, we work together there, strange, eh? The other Sihayan kingdoms all use Talogot, Ilokan, and Aya, pay them in useless coins and give them trash to eat. Where is their pride, eh? In the tanneries and slaughterhouses and ironmongeries of Chukulundu the hard work is done by mountain people, young people, the mountains are being drained of their young people, eh? Look at my family! My grandnephew speaks Zan and the port polyglot, but he can't even greet me in proper Sasayat, eh? His brothers have never even met me! Another generation or two and there will be no mountain people. We must send the warriors now, take back our land! I will go myself. I can still swing a sword!"

Another added: "Aye, a merchant told me once that was Sihayan policy. Dispossess people of their land, and they have no choice but to earn their food with their backs, laboring. Then they quickly lose their own identity, which is centered on the land. Then how can they resist the encroachments of the Zan?"

"But the Yapi!"

"Damn the Yapi!"

One group at the far end of the hall slowly unwound and took up dignified stances around the center. It was obvious they intended to speak. The leader moved to the center and faced Kaloan.

"Son of Egea. Your story is hard to credit. This Sihayan is a Sasayat and will reward us with land and territory? And he smashed a mountainside? And promises to break the walls of Kaigi? And for this . . . tale . . . you want us to fight? And ignore the Yapi?"

"I saw it with my own eyes," said Kaloan evenly. He knew what was coming.

"If he truly is a Sihayan, how do you know he didn't . . . influence your thoughts." The words were obviously a compromise to avoid direct insult. The subtext of *You have to be delusional or lying* was clear, however, to everyone in the room.

Kaloan shrugged. He could hardly answer that question without revealing his own power. "What do you suggest then, Son of Loglon?"

"See the priestess. The gods speak to her. If she says you are telling the truth, then I and my clan will be your right and left hand in the attack on Kaigi."

There were slow nods of agreement, then voices, rising to a clamor. "Let her decide. The priestess! The priestess of the nameless gods! The priestess!"

Kaloan bowed his head, accepting the verdict, but inwardly he was grinning. His plan had worked once again. He really must thank the Mother of Tuluot with a rich gift of cloth.

* * * * *

Dusk was casting long shadows down the mountainside when he set out from the long hall. Looking back over the hall, he saw the neat slate and cedar houses of Three Lakes nestled against the ridge, and further down, the sun glinting on the waters of the lakes themselves, in a basin ringed by high steep peaks. The village was already lit by cooking fires, and the sound of conversations floated up to him, carrying his own name.

The priestess lived in a ramshackle house a short walk above the village. He had just turned up the path and was lost in thought, considering Duha and all he implied, already planning the next few steps in his campaign, when he saw the leopard. He had almost walked right past it, its gray-mottled skin like a piece of the land itself. It was watching him impassively from under a bush, sitting with its tail curled round its legs, head tilted. In the half-light of the fires its eyes glowed at him.

Kaloan halted. He regarded it serenely for a moment, then dipped his head to it and moved off by a side path. The leopard studied him, then turned, and was swallowed by the night.

There was no mistaking it. Once might be a coincidence. Twice? That was a message.

His feet arrived on her doorstep. He stepped inside the house of slate and thatch and cedar, soundlessly.

The wood in the hearth burst into flame when he entered, and the room lit. He took in her dwelling, filled with the detritus of years: porcelains from Zannai and Ponjan, the shrunken dried heads of plains dwellers, human and animal bone, stacks of fur, dried plants of every description, wooden bowls and baskets, clay pots, ropes and strings, chunks of obsidian and jade and marble, pieces of day-old pork lying on the small table to the side. There were even some paper playing cards traded up from the plains on a shelf hanging off the wall, she knew not what they were but she had kept them because they were of a material outside her ken.

He found her squatting by the fire. She was old, the oldest person Kaloan knew, with brown skin like scales made of dry leaves that hung on her bones as if by living long she had slowly used up all her flesh. She was so old her name had been forgotten by her people a generation ago. She wore only a loincloth. Her face was heavily tattooed in the fashion of her youth, long since abandoned by the mountain people because the Zan brothels paid more for tattooed girls. Her teeth had fallen out an epoch ago, and she was busy scooping rice from a worn bowl made of green marble, mashing it with her fingers, and then shoveling into her mouth. She looked up when he came in, and her mouth opened wide with astonishment and pleasure, the rice dripping out of it.

"Kaloan!" She rasped, setting the bowl down and wiping her fingers on her loincloth. "So long since I've set my eyes on you. One of my girls told me you were here."

"Oh? Training up another one to take your place?"

She considered this. "The gods will not talk to her. They are keeping me alive for some reason, what reason they won't tell me." She frowned at him, as if to insinuate that the gods were peevish. She peered at him. "This long life is no gift, I tell you, no gift."

He nodded distractedly and squatted in front of her. "There is a thing I want to ask you." He licked his lips, hesitating. Suddenly he was a child again, awkwardly asking about the gods, expecting to be punished for ignorance or insolence or both. The Zan had gods and demons for everything, for doors, for trees, for food, wealth, machines, books, all with names and titles, a confusing welter of beliefs that all had to be memorized and worshiped in the proper temple… the Sasayat too had gods, but they had no names. They could be worshipped anywhere there was stillness and quiet.

He came out of his reverie.

"I think the gods are sending me messages."

She squinted at him. "What did you see?"

"A leopard. It appeared on my trail. Twice."

"Not walked beside you, or led you?"

"No, it just sat, then moved off."

She looked down at her bowl for a moment. "I know that message," she finally said. "That is a heavy message." In the broken light he could see her eyes suddenly shining with tears. He arched his eyebrows at her, as if asking a question, but she shook her head. She placed an areka nut in his hand, and Kaloan chewed slowly on it. They sat together for a long time as the night came down like a felled tree and darkness engulfed the village, listening to the cicadas and the frogs and the night birds.

At last she said: "Is he the one we wanted?"

"You already knew that when you sent me to him."

She considered that, nodded. "The nameless gods give it to us, their servants, the knowing of things—the weather, when avalanches will come, names that are hidden, the uses of plants and animals, the future. To you men, come other powers. The Sihayan powers."

A lecture he had heard many times. What he really wanted was to understand the leopard. The unclarity of the gods exasperated his clean, orderly mind. Nevertheless, he asked: "What is his name?"

"He is Inogai, son of Sharrin, the Witch-King of Chukulundu."

So the boy-not-a-boy had lied to him, Kaloan realized. The Witch-King had a son.

Egea paused, peered at him in the darkness. "So you agree he is the one we have been looking for."

"Aye, that he is, if I am any judge. But he is powerful."

"Powerful, he is? What kind of powerful?"

"He is the most powerful I have ever seen. He will crush the Sihayan in Kaigi. You chose well."

"And then?"

"I will do what I can. But . . . you know this can only end one way."

She nodded, spat. "In betrayal." She stared at him, blinked, as if seeing him for the first time.

"Will our people get the reward he promised?"

She squinted again, looked off through the doorway into the darkness. "The nameless gods say yes." She tilted her head, continued.

"I have seen that, in a vision," she rasped, eyes afire. "The whole island, united. A single domain. The Witch-King of Chukulundu King over all the land. And the ships . . . the ships . . . ," her voice faltered.

"I have seen that vision."

"Then, you know what you must do. It is for our people."

"Yes."

In the evening cool there was a sudden, palpable heat that filled the little house. Her voice shriveled to a whisper, like the sound of grass rustling on a hillside in a stiff breeze. "The nameless gods send you a warning. There have been . . . summonings."

"Summonings?" His blood ran cold. He had an inkling of what she meant.

"Ask Inogai. Ask him to explain it to you."

They fell silent for a moment. Finally, he leaned forward, intent.

"What does the leopard mean, mother?"

She reached out and drew him toward her. Then Egea, priestess of the Sasayat and mother of Kaloan, smiled sadly and kissed her son on his forehead. "It means I will not see you again, my son. Not in this world."

She turned away. "Send the son of Loglon to me tonight," she rasped. "You will have your army in the morning."

* * * * *

Men, streaming out of the mountains in little rivulets, arriving by drips and drops at the meadow below Aruru to form an army. They camped placidly in a string of meadows while Kaloan tore his hair out just trying to find food for them. He had never managed so large a body of men. Within two days they had scoured the nearby forest clean of game, and men were already wandering off to fill their stomachs or grumbling about waiting. The only good thing about it was that the Yapi had ceased their raids on the Sasayat, apparently convinced that the massing of men was aimed at them. Kaloan, canny as always, encouraged the men to say this, and he further confused things by telling the men several different destinations for the army, knowing they would spread the conflicting stories far and wide.

But other, more ominous stories reached him.

A group of men descending past a burnt-out hamlet strewn with bodies at night, glimpsed a monstrous creature in the glow of the house fires, maggot-pale and feeding on the bodies of the dead. One weeping warrior told Kaloan of another with many arms, each like a mass of slugs, that left a trail of phosphorescent slime in its wake. In wee hours of the morning on some paths the men were tormented by the sound of women screaming in torture, but no women were ever found, and men disappeared in twos and threes trying to rescue them. One group beat off attacks by a winged monster with flights of arrows. A party of warriors was found, every man dead but bodies untouched.

Inogai met him on the evening of third day, descending out of the mountain like one of the nameless gods, trailing followers in his wake. He appeared to have aged in the ten-day they'd been separated.

"Kaloan!" he called. Behind him Atya and Turungi warriors crowded round the pair, grinning. "Loka!" They called, using his Atya name, clustering around him, touching his clothing, patting his shoulders, and clutching his hands. "Long time! Long time!"

"Long time!" he echoed, grinning back. He refused offers of food, studied Inogai, one eyebrow cocked. The Sasayats, who had been resting in little knots of men among the trees to escape the afternoon heat, rose to greet the newcomers with shouts of joy and recognition. Many of the warriors had brought their hunting dogs, whom they considered brothers. Barks of joy and menace filled the air.

"Inogai."

"Kaloan."

They clasped each other's hands, and he felt again the light brush on the surface of his mind. Once again his shell went up. "What's going on in the mountains?" he asked. "What are these monsters everyone is seeing?

What is a summoning?"

Inogai laughed. He was in a bright mood. "Well . . . my name. I see you've been talking to your priestess."

Kaloan grunted, and the other turned serious.

"Let's get the warriors moving. I will explain on the way."

They roused the men, and after much grumbling, arguments, and pleading for friends out tracking down something to eat, the warriors began to stumble down the mountainside along the river. Kaloan made a rough estimate of the size of their little army and was impressed: over five hundred men, Sasayats, Atyas, Turungis, Tuga'a, and a smattering of other peoples. He felt a quiet sturdy pride: his name had worth. And the mountain people had unity for a moment, even if it was around the idea of loot.

Inogai fell in alongside him as they stumbled through the evening, shortly after moonrise. With the moon near full there was plenty of light and the men, all experienced at moving through the forest in the dark, soon realized that it was better to be moving in the cool of the night. With that, the grumbling eased and the little army focused on the steady business of putting one foot in front of the other. Even the dogs quieted.

"Inogai. Tell me about these summonings."

Out of the shadows Inogai spoke, his voice low. "Some of the Sihayans have cultivated the ability to pull creatures from other . . . worlds. Most of these creatures are like fish on dry land. They quickly die, because they cannot live in this world. But some . . . do not."

Kaloan contemplated this. "How? How can they do that?" There was no inkling of this in any of his own powers. A chill went up his spine. *How can we fight such power?* "These are the creatures we have been encountering in the mountains?"

"Yes." Inogai paused. "It requires tremendous amounts of power, more than any single mind can generate. So they drain the minds of their slaves, even priests, to power the crossing of the gulf between worlds. Afterwards the poor slave is broken—a body with a vacant mind, unable to even care for itself. They usually have enough power to bring across a single creature. They dare not bring more, it is said, because they cannot control them once they are here. They also fear that if they bring over too many, they will breed, and make no end of trouble."

Who said? Kaloan thought, but he set the question aside. "So they open a gate between worlds and use them to terrorize us." He paused. "But I saw them before I talked to anyone about my plan." *Except you, Inogai*, he mentally added.

Inogai frowned as if he had picked up the thought. "The Witch-King knows we have assembled an army, of course. But I think the Witch-King wanted to have them appear with the Yapi, to further terrorize us."

"They probably scared the Yapi away, in that case."

Both men chuckled. Watching the files of men ambling slowly along, Kaloan called for a rest.

The command rippled up and down the line, and in twos and threes the men sat or squatted to rest, setting down their gear and sharing food and gossip. Kaloan looked up and down the line of ghostly forms in the dark, filled with pride and worry. He was already considering how to handle the march across the farmlands to Kaigi on the morrow, calculating how many men he might lose. Not to the Zan, of course, but to looting: many would satiate themselves pillaging the farms, ponder the walls of Kaigi, and quietly return to the forest. He was still lost in thought when the monster ran out of the forest.

He caught a glimpse of a dark grayish body suspended on two tall legs far above the humans, looking for all the world like one of those giant wasp nests hanging from a tree. Then it was on his men, or rather, his men were on it. Kaloan rose to his feet, snatching up his sword, but he was far too slow. Warriors born and bred, his Sasayats had already slashed through its legs and feathered its body with spears.

It fell heavily, like a slab of rock sliding drunkenly off a mountainside, landing with sigh on the riverbank not far from where Kaloan stood watching, sword in hand. Half of one leg was still stuck upright in the earth next to the trail, fixed by its massive claws, an absurd monument to its death. Kaloan joined the cluster of gawkers and barking dogs around its body.

The beast was not quite dead. It lay in the water, its half legs thrashing uselessly in the current. It had no neck or head, and a huge hole in the side of its leathery, quaking body gasped regularly, as if breathing. Kaloan could make out no teeth in that hole.

A stab of pity shot through Kaloan. The poor creature! To be torn from one's roots and thrust into a completely different world, powerful, but with every man's hand turned against you and no hope of return? What a terrible way to live, and then die, he thought. No wonder it staged crazed attacks on everything it encountered. He shuddered, watching the beast fight to live.

After a time the beast lost its struggle, and slowly the warriors turned away from the sight, returning to the task at hand. Kaloan quietly issued commands and the men retrieved their gear and fell into files, working their way down the mountainside as the night deepened.

* * * * *

Dawn was making an entrance as the men debouched onto the plain. Kaloan had the men rest for a few hours by the river, but there was much grumbling about that. Weren't there farms just there, they argued, waiting to be pillaged? Kaloan had to exert all his powers of persuasion just to make tired men stay put.

As he argued, one of the Atya ran up to him. "Loka, the Sihayan asks to speak to you."

Kaloan looked up at the young man. The lad was round-eyed with awe—Inogai was a Sihayan and yet he treated Kaloan as an equal. Kaloan realized wryly that his stature had actually risen in the eyes of his warriors. He felt a pang of separation, of a gulf growing slowly between himself and the others. The mountain peoples cherished a rough equality amongst themselves, so different from the ranks and hierarchies that characterized Zan society.

Well, he consoled himself, it wouldn't matter in the end. And perhaps he would be remembered in song and story. He missed his family terribly, but for the first time, he did not regret having a family of his own, for he would be leaving them without a father. Oddly cheered, he strolled back to the river to where Inogai squatted under a tree, chewing pensively on jerky.

"Good news," the latter said, standing as Kaloan strode up. An Ilokan warrior, armed with the ax and shield of his people, and decorated in bright yellow and blue body paint, stood at his side, grinning dark-eyed at Kaloan. "This messenger says that Chukulundu has been invaded by two of the domains to its north. This means that the Witch-King has no troops to spare for Kaigi."

Kaloan grunted, nodded and smiled at the Ilokan, offering him some deer jerky. "Without men to spare, he will not come out and fight. That was the one thing I feared." His warriors could beat any Zan man to man, but they would be butchered by trained soldiers backed by crossbows and engines of war in an open fight among the fields and farms of the Kun flatlands.

"He is certain we have no way to break those walls and our troops will melt away once they see them. Why risk good men he will need to fight the real enemy?"

The two men smiled at each other in understanding.

* * * * *

The march across the plain to Kaigi went exactly as Kaloan had feared: badly. The men were tired and keyed up at the same time, making them hard to manage. Kaloan had planned to lead them along the river, away from the farms and along a reliably paved road, but increasingly the little army spread out as the men raided nearby farms, burning houses and stripping orchards, paying no attention to Kaloan's entreaties or Inogai's warnings.

Worse, as the pillars of smoke rose above the plains, the local gentry sent out their private armies to contest the burning of nearby farms. Kaloan knew that nervous invaders deep in the mountains were one thing, but desperate men and women in defense of their homes were quite another. The little army destroyed the small groups of militia it encountered, but each one meant a few more dead, and more men chased out of the army. Fighting local bravos was too much like work, and they had come for the loot.

At midday they were halfway to their destination. Kaloan called a halt. The heat was on and the men took refuge in an orange grove along the river, some napping, some stripping to swim. Kaloan thanked the nameless gods for the local militia: their harassment had stopped the men from forming small groups to raid nearby farms or even from leaving the army in twos and threes. There were reports of monsters too, and distant screams, as of men in agony, told of attacks on bravo groups and farmers by the Witch-King's otherworldly pets.

Despite it all, Kaloan, like any old campaigner, managed to find the time to set his back to a tree and take a nap. In a moment he was asleep . . .

He was awakened by the frantic, terrified barking of dogs and shouts of men. Inogai was standing over him. "Kaloan! We need you!"

Kaloan vaulted to his feet and snatched up his sword. He ran to the sound of the noise and in a moment was pushing his way through a crowd of men and madly barking dogs. They had formed a rough semi-circle in front of one of the Witch-King's creatures.

The beast was a hideous thing to see under the bright sun of midday: a creature black as a moonless night, a six-sided body with a toothy maw on each side and a hide that seemed made of quivering worms. It stood on six wide legs that ended in flat feet studded with tiny grasping hooks. At its feet lay several dead Sasayats. It towered over the men, yet neither side moved. The creature's legs oozed purplish fluid from countless sword cuts, and its body was pierced with many spears. It yowled a high-pitched screech from each of its six mouths.

Inogai pelted up beside him. "That thing has to be killed now!" he hissed. "The men are wavering! If they break we lose everything. You're the war leader!"

Kaloan nodded absently, his mind working. He strode forward, sword held up with both hands, wary, legs flexed and ready for action. His men fell back, to give him room.

The creature shuddered and a long tendril shot out of the opening facing Kaloan, driving for his chest. So that's how it had killed his men! He glimpsed a sharp point shooting toward him, and shoved it aside with his mind, dodging, then chopped it in half with his sword. The monster spun and another tendril fired at him. Kaloan could feel the mood among the men swing as he cut that one in half, grins breaking out along the line.

"Loka! Loka!" came the shouts, a chant. "Loka! Loka!"

"Hold!" he shouted as men began to rush forward to help him. He wanted to remove all of its weapons before he let them kill it, to spare his men's lives. He shifted his feet, clutching his sword, slippery with sweat and ichor from the monster. Another face, another half tendril lying on the ground. He circled to his right and sure enough, it switched to that side and he slashed away another one of its weapons. The air broke with a screech as it pivoted. He kept circling and took out the last two of its weapons.

"Loka!" A wild cheer went up, and the men rushed forward as one. In moments the great beast had slumped to the ground, oozing purple. The screeching dwindled to a hiss, and then, to nothing. Even the dogs sniffed it quickly, then turned up their noses at it.

"Loka! Loka!" Hands slapped his back as the men congratulated him and themselves. Inogai took him by the elbow, said quietly. "Let's get the men moving while they are in this mood."

Kaloan nodded and set off, calling the men to follow. The warriors fell in behind him, and they quickly cleared the orange groves and fruit farms. Further on the road turned inland towards Kaigi as the river widened, shifting from a rutted dirt path to carefully laid cobble. The land flattened out to fields of rice and sweet potatoes, and the farms lay closer together.

All was burned.

The mood had shifted. Coming down out of the mountains the warriors had treated the foray as a lark, an adventure, with the promise of women and loot and for some, faraway places. But then the militia had come, and the monsters, and mountain people had died. A great anger permeated the army, and they rolled over the plain, revenging themselves on their hereditary enemies. They burnt their way to Kaigi, clouds of gray smoke rising on every side.

As the sun began to slide past midday they ambled up to a tiny hamlet at a crossroads, Kaigi visible in the distance. Kaloan remembered its name from an old visit: Taichu. Fields of rice ran right up to the bright red brick of the buildings, and the spaces along the house walls were lined with patches of vegetables. A shop tucked in between the houses sold spices from far-away Shevan and animal parts from the jungles of Wueh as medicines. Someone had left longans drying on a piece of white cloth by the side of the road. The little town was deserted.

Kaloan strode into the center of town, stopped. His hair stood up. He was being watched.

A temple to the local god of the land occupied a raised platform where the roads met, overhung by a massive old banyan tree whose branches stretched across the streets to shade all the nearby buildings. Tables and chairs were stacked haphazardly along one side of the temple, waiting for the market to open.

In the banyan tree sat a cat. Anyone might mistake it for an ordinary housecat, so small it was, but Kaloan knew it for a wild leopard cat, a little striped hunting cat that lived in the rice fields next to the farms, taking rats and rabbits, and occasionally, a chicken or two. The Zan farmers hunted and trapped them as vermin, but the mountain people revered them. The cat studied him for a moment, giving him a pitying look, then bent its head and lazily licked a paw, as if to say, *Don't say I didn't warn you!*

A message. For certain. "Stop!" he yelled, waving his arms and running back to the army. "Everyone out of the town! Run!"

The warriors didn't need to be told twice. Anything Kaloan was running from had to be bad. The army spun on its heels and spread across the rice fields like water dashed from a jar.

Kaloan raced out of the village. Behind him he heard a sizzling sound, somewhere between the sound of pork fat frying and a knife scraping across a whetstone. A sharp, acrid smell, frigid and sour, lit the air as though a wind had blown in from Somewhere Else, and then an enormous *boom!* sounded. He winced as a thunderous blast of air scoured the buildings, forming miniature dust devils on the road.

Inogai pounded up to where Kaloan ducked behind a low wall of red bricks, ornamented with fired tiles. Just like the wall in his foster father's courtyard, he remembered. Someone had hung colorful two-piece outfits on the walls to dry, but they were now scattered on the ground at Kaloan's feet. He glanced at them, suddenly recalled to a life when they were worn by the women of his home. He saw his foster mother, scolding him for eating too much while suppressing a grin and sneaking him biscuits. His room, his own private room at the Academy, hung with calligraphy scrolls. There had been a succession of dogs . . .

Tears filled his eyes. He shook his head as Inogai squatted and looked at him questioningly. The pair waited for the smoke and dust to clear.

That life, that family, was long gone. Soon this life would be gone as well. He rubbed his eyes and shot Inogai a sad grin, coming back to the here and now.

In front of him, a giant beast, transparent, the way jellyfish or river shrimp were transparent, had spawned in the town, right next to the temple. Its organs visible for a moment, it formed a shapeless mass that sprawled between the buildings. Then with a sigh it melted and erupted, spewing tongues of clear liquid down the roads.

As a threat, it was a complete dud. The warriors turned to watch the show and started laughing and shouting insults in several languages. The men were still laughing when the dogs ran up to the beast, barking and sniffing, tails wagging, curious.

Then through the smoke came the screams of animals in terrible pain. The dogs howled piteously, yelling, barking, dragging themselves on the ground, their feet melting and smoking where they touched the liquid, then their stomachs when their feet no longer supported them, then death, tongues hanging out and eyes rolling back in their heads. The brave warriors wept and cursed to see their death agonies.

Kaloan realized why the smoke hadn't dissipated. Whatever the beast used for blood was a terrible poison. It was a trap.

The men had been angered before, but now they were absolutely enraged. Their dogs were their hunting partners and brothers—in every language of the mountains there were two words for dogs, one designating a pet, the other a hunting brother. Because of the poison, they could not retrieve the bodies of their brothers. They held a small ceremony in one of the rice fields, then rested.

Then they put the town to the torch.

* * * * * *

They rolled up to the north wall of Kaigi late in the afternoon. Kaloan called a halt well out of bowshot. The men needed food and rest. They were hardened to the trail, and sustained by rage, but Kaloan well knew that if things suddenly went wrong, they would melt.

Walled cities are cities first. That is, they spill out beyond the confines of the wall, curling through the gates to send tentacles of houses and gardens and villas and shops and smitheries across the adjacent plain, much to the chagrin of administrators and military officials. They fill in moats with trash, plant trees in flats intended to be fields of fire, and push holes through the walls. Kaigi was one of the oldest settlements in the land, with its oldest stone-built temple, and was absolutely sprawling. Its walls were little more than lumps of shaped, brick-covered earth pushing above the city, but they were there and there was nothing the warriors could do about them.

Ordinarily.

Facing the town, Kaloan and Inogai stood amidst a little stand of mango trees. The warriors behind them eased on the ground, eyeing the men atop the walls, chewing areka nut for energy and studying the deserted houses outside the city with grim intensity. They were planning a burning.

"Is that the beginnings of a beard I see on your face?" Kaloan asked, teasingly. From somewhere nearby a mule brayed, obviously wanting to be fed. Kaloan's eyes narrowed, thinking.

"Yes. I can hide as a boy, but I must rule as a man," Inogai answered, seriously.

"Ah, so that's why you've been aging yourself."

The other nodded. "We need to move the men up closer."

"Why?"

"Because we need to have as many Zan soldiers on the walls shooting at us as possible, so that when I destroy this wall, they will be killed. I need the men as bait. If we dangle some men there," he pointed, "they will put crossbowmen on the wall."

They are men, not bait, thought Kaloan. He patted his friend on the shoulder. He still thought of Inogai as a young man, as a friend, though he knew what was to come. Strange, he mused, but it seemed that having accepted his fate, he loved this man he hardly knew all the more. The mule brayed again, calling his mind to the problem at hand.

"Never mind the men, let them rest and paint themselves for battle. I know what to do."

He threaded his way through the trees to where the mule stood tied to a tree next to an irrigation ditch, water buckets neatly stacked on the ground next to it. The animal eyed him in the strangely irritated but phlegmatic way of mules, which made him smile. He stripped to his loincloth and his sheath, the slowly dying sun bringing out every line of muscle and every powerful curve of his rugged frame. He rubbed the animal's neck, admiring its rock-hard muscles, then calmed it with his mind and lifted himself onto its back. Inogai, right behind, frowned.

"What are you up to, clever planner?"

"Getting the Zan up on the walls. Follow me," he directed, "and rouse the men. When that wall is full of men you must destroy it and our men must rush in immediately!"

Together he and the mule ambled slowly out through the trees into the open before the walls and stopped. Looking at the city, the mule snorted and shook its head peaceably, sending flies in all directions. The men on walls became alarmed at the sight: shouts, a stirring, and an immediate flash of crossbow bolts, which Kaloan had no trouble misdirecting. He was at peace with himself, serene, knowing what must come, secure in the promise from the nameless gods that he would live to see that moment, that his people would benefit. He pushed aside the crossbow bolts with the simple enjoyment of a Sasayat child practicing against his father's blunt arrows.

It was pure spectacle, irresistible. The man on a mule in the fields before the city, the Zan lining up on the city walls firing madly at him, Inogai hurrying up and down the line, the warriors rising to their feet, cheering: "Loka! Loka! Loka!" There were only a few hundred, but the city shook with their shouts.

The crossbow bolts fell around him like leaves in a typhoon. He felt Inogai lending him support, helping against Zan. Kaloan stopped, the perfect target. It seemed like the top of the wall was a vast smear of red as the Zan crowded against the worn parapets, all trying to kill him. Inogai was there, and something else, another power, trying to interfere, trying to suppress him, and he remembered the boy-not-a-boy's contemptuous remark: *even you are more powerful than any of his priests* and realized it was no more than the truth. He was far more powerful than that other mind he sensed.

What did that mean? He had always taken his powers for granted, never really———.

White blossomed in his mind.

* * * * * *

And so it came to pass that Kaloan returned to Kaigi on the back of a mule.

The wall was gone. Inogai had destroyed it: troops, brick, and earth, all vanished as if they had never existed. A patch of baked ground remained to mark their passing. Beyond it he had taken a swath of the town: a stretch of ground, clean as if no human had ever set foot on it, lined with the rubble of collapsed buildings, shoved its way towards the center of town. The few Zan soldiers left alive staggered out of the rubble only to be cut down by the onrushing mountain warriors. Not an officer was in sight.

The Sasayats ran past Kaloan, painted like figures from a *dama* nightmare, howling and screaming and snatching up burning objects to put the city to the torch. They were a demon army, come to exact revenge for generations of Zan savagery. Seeing them, the rubble of houses and shops vomited people running in every direction, even towards the attackers in their fear and madness. One woman ran at the warriors, waving a doll at them as if it were a weapon, while an old man, his tea ceremony interrupted, threw his cups and pots at the attackers. The warriors killed them all without mercy, swarming over the ruins and spreading out across the city in smaller groups. Screams and shouts and pleas for mercy met their advance.

Sweeping his eyes across the carnage as he entered the city, Kaloan felt only an aching distress. Kaigi had been his home, after all, and this was never the homecoming he had envisioned in his private dreams—long ago given up—of coming back to the family he'd grown up with. The city was littered with wreckage—wrecked buildings, wrecked human beings, the screams of mules, and the chatter of chickens. The stench of burning filled the air. Before him lay the body of a middle-aged woman, both arms ending in stumps. Next to her lay the torso of a young girl. Beyond them hundreds of pigeons, escapees from some pigeon racing enthusiast's dovecote, clustered around the ruins of a dry goods shop, pecking at the dirt. Oblivious to the destruction, two housecats played together on the second floor of a broken house. Suddenly one became enraged and cuffed the other until its face was a bloody wreck.

Kaloan shuddered. He halted the mule, intending to regain control over at least some of his Sasayats, when he heard a cry: "Kaloan!"

"Inogai!"

The latter limped up. Exhaustion creased his face. Kaloan thought he suddenly looked old, perhaps as old as his true years.

"The Sihayan. He is coming."

"I was just about to gather some of the men here. I expect him to come down the main boulevard and turn up there to reach us." He indicated an intersection. "Otherwise he will have to climb over these houses. Very undignified for a Witch-King." He gave a wry chuckle. "I want to post archers in those houses," he said, pointing. He paused from his calculations, studying his friend. "Can you fight him?"

"Yes, I think so. I am tired, but I am the more powerful, and he has drained much of his power in the Summonings and in running the war against the other Sihayans. He hasn't tried to contest our attack yet. Maybe that is a sign that he needs rest." Inogai rubbed his sweat-covered face, wiped his hands on his deerskin vest. He pulled himself up straight. "I will defeat him."

"We came at the right time, then."

"Yes." Inogai drew up to the mule. He looked up at Kaloan, his face bright with wonder. His voice fell as he asked: "How did you know? At Taichu, you warned everyone just before the Summoning. How did you do that? Even I cannot do that."

Kaloan looked at him meaningfully, then looked away. The heat on his face from the burning city was intense. He knew why the nameless gods were keeping him alive.

"The nameless gods talk to you?" Inogai's eyes widened, then narrowed. "That is very useful," he finally said. He rubbed his head, lost in thought. It was clear the news disconcerted him.

"Let me call the men together," Kaloan said, shrugging. He dismounted, and gave the animal a pat on the rump, directing it with his mind to wander back out to the orchard. He began shouting at the men.

* * * * * *

Getting them to stay and fight was much harder than getting them to Kaigi. After a protracted discussion he got a few score Sasayat, Atya, and Ilokan warriors to hide in the rubble of nearby buildings, waiting to ambush the Sihayan and his soldiers, since both groups held individual bravery in high esteem and none wanted to be seen shrinking from battle in front of the others. The Tuga'a fighters, however, were a more practical people. Packs brimming with useful and marketable items, they were of one mind: time to go home.

Inogai stood still next Kaloan, lost in concentration, his mind ranging over the city. "He nears," he finally murmured in Kaloan's ear. "He nears."

The Tuga'a arrayed themselves around Kaloan and Inogai, debating, mountain style, as if they had all afternoon and jugs of rice wine to wet their tongues. Kaloan for once found himself wistfully imagining he could

41

simply give orders like a Zan. Persuasion was more draining than fighting Sihayans, he thought.

One of the Tuga'a shouted at him over the voices, pointing with an arrow held out in his right arm at the presumed direction of the Witch-King: "Loka! You cannot fight the Sihayan! It's madness! Come with us!"

Kaloan laughed, threw out his arms, and pointed with a tilt of his head. "Where is the city wall?"

"Madness!"

"If the Sihayan is not killed, how will you leave the city? And having left it, how will you return to the mountains? The local militias are out. You left the countryside on fire, remember?"

They all started jabbering and gesticulating at him, faces set in anger and worry. Then Inogai intervened.

He stretched out his hand, palm up, and sent a beam of pure white, slim as a fine calligraphy brush, into the gathering dusk. A wrecked temple stood among the ruins of the city not far from the group, its rear abutting the main boulevard of the city, the walls of its courtyard draped with shattered bricks and broken timber from nearby houses. Figurines of gods and magical creatures adorned its eaves and roof supports.

One by one, Inogai shaved them off the building. He closed his palm, swept his eyes meaningfully around the circle of men.

"I will stop the Sihayan," he said. "Just keep his men off me." The Tuga'a fell into an uneasy silence. The message was clear—that streak of white death could just as well have been directed at them.

Kaloan quickly stepped in. "Brother," he said to one of the louder speakers, "if you could set your people on the upper floors of those houses there, I would be very grateful. I need archers to cover that roadway there."

"Yes, War Leader," he replied. He motioned at his compatriots and they started clambering through the piles of broken bricks, scraps of wood, and chunks of rice husk plaster and levering themselves into position. He heard their loud grunting as they ascended, wondered at their energy and strong concentration. He had done little, yet felt drained.

That sound again, heard with other senses, split the growing night: a knife scraping across bone. A smell filled the air, rank and sulfurous. His head exploded: Power. By will alone he kept himself from doubling over in pain. A beam of light rose high into the sky behind the rubble: the Witch-King.

The rubble in front of them blew apart, broken walls and shattered houses collapsing as shards of brick and tile rocketed out towards the mountain warriors, ripping the flesh of the waiting Sasayat. Tuga'a fighter tumbled off their perches, enshrouded in dust and smoke. A giant foot, and another, and another, stomping and crushing the rubble, seeking the lives of the men who hid there: feet gray and coated with scales sharp as obsidian. Above them Kaloan saw the creatures, heads the size of a house, heavy with massive, gleaming black teeth, and knew they had lost: the Sihayan had outdone himself. There were two of the monsters. Two. They would never be able to stop them.

The sun was dying in the west and the Sasayat looked upon the coming darkness and broke. The rubble emptied of its hidden men, first running backwards, staring in disbelief, then spinning to vanish into the night, throwing down their weapons. "Come back!" Kaloan yelled. His sword leapt from its sheath in automatic but pointless defiance.

But there were men there: the Tuga'a. Covered with dust, running with blood, they rose from the wreckage, ghostly and terrifying. They raised their bows and fired arrow after arrow. Their bolts clanked harmlessly off the scales of the giant monsters, but beyond those slowly moving legs were men like themselves: a scraggly rank of swordsmen dressed in black and yellow urged on by the shadowy figure in a simple red robe beyond them: the Witch-King himself.

Kaloan strode forward. He shook his head against the enormous pressure on his mind marking the silent, bitter struggle between the Witch-King and Inogai. Skittering to one side as an enormous leg came down in front of him, kicking up dust and spitting out pieces of rubble, he tapped it gently with his sword, testing, then shoved the point in underneath a scale. From far above came a hiss, then the creature swung its leg round toward him with unearthly slowness. Kaloan lept back . . .

Suddenly a voice in his head. Time stopped and the giant legs, the bowmen, the attackers, all receded into darkness.

Hello, my son.

Then Inogai. *Hello, father.*

Astonishment. *And what have we here? Another Sihiyan. And one so powerful! How is it I know aught of you?*

Kaloan flung up his shell and banished them both, nearly getting stepped on in his distraction. Beams of light criss-crossed the space, each one blocked by its intended target. The swordsmen hesitated, wary of those giant feet and Inogai's power, and the Tuga'a attacked. They fired one last volley of arrows, then took out their swords, aiming for the Witch-King, scrambling over the broken buildings, screaming in battle-fury. The last of his retinue backed toward the Witch-King himself, swords extended outward. The ground in front of them was littered with bodies, not all of which held arrows, and Kaloan understood where the Witch-King had obtained the energy for this last summoning.

And the Atya charged. Humiliated by the Tuga'a standing like heroes in front of the Witch-King and his monsters, they crept back and reformed. Screaming their war cry *Ki-ya! Ki-ya!* they flung themselves across the space, war axes raised, threading between the monsters. Kaloan watched their dogs running behind, barking madly at the enemy, at the monsters, barking for the sheer joy of it.

More beams of light. Kaloan watched in awe as Inogai, standing in front of the great beasts, swept a beam across their legs. He had finally worn down the Witch-King, Kaloan realized, and now had resources to help his people. Partially blocked by the Witch-King's own power, Inogai's beam of pure white nevertheless slashed through their legs like a knife through a dry leaf. A groan that was almost a scream rent the night air, then with a massive thump the monsters fell forward, their giant rear legs kicking uselessly at the rubble. One fell across the city wall with a massive crash, then rolled off the wall and out of the city as Inogai put another beam through its head. Absurdly Kaloan thought of the repair bill Inogai would face. The other fell across the temple complex to Kaloan's left, crushing it to powder. Men scattered in every direction. Yelps and screams of pain signaled the end of those too slow to escape. The Witch-King advanced, urging on his soldiers who grappled with the mountain warriors.

Kaloan glimpsed the terrible face of the monster, now stilled as Inogai finished off the other monster with a beam between those horrible teeth. His other hand was outflung, warding off some attack by the Witch-King. The buzzing in Kaloan's head was almost too painful to withstand, breaking through his shell. He felt himself falling, and reached out. Suddenly, behind him came the cynical voice of an old man and a strong arm across his shoulder.

The Son of Loglon, come at last.

"Well, War Leader, when I said we'd be your right and left hand, eh? I didn't think you'd let them get cut off." He tugged Kaloan forward, a grin lighting his face. His sons stood at his side. "Lead us, Son of Egea. Your people are behind you."

Kaloan turned to glance back, Loglon's strong arm falling from his shoulders. At his rear the Sasayats were creeping forward, swords out, in ones and twos, watching him. A terrible pride nearly burst his heart: they had stayed with him, these men, his men, his people, to see it through to the end. He must lead them, even to his own death. *But I was never meant to get out of this alive*, he said to himself, eyes widening in realization. Perversely, the thought heartened him: the nameless gods would not fail him. He raised his sword and sang out the Atya war cry: *Ki-ya! Ki-ya!*, and clambered up the rubble. Behind him he heard the pounding of sandaled feet and voices rising: *Loka! Loka! Loka!*

He strode across the rubble, heard the Witch-King give orders in Zan. One of his swordsman rushed him. Around him a desperate fight raged across the ruins, a swirl of death: here an Atya warrior bounded onto the leg of the dead monster and stove in the helmet of a Zan swordsman locked in combat with a pair of Tuga'a, there a Tuga'a screamed as a Zan spitted his belly, then drew his sword out the man's side, dragging out his guts. Knots of men formed across the rubble, fighting bitterly in twos and threes. Individually the Zan warriors were better, but there were many more of the mountain people, and with the Sasayat jumping into the fray, the Zan were far outnumbered. The clanging of swords and the screams of the dying cut the night air, lit with beams of white.

Inogai had come. Like one of the nameless gods he strode across the rubble and mounted a low wall, then found a pile of broken bricks to stand on. It seemed to Kaloan that he had grown in size, become immense, a star of white, as he and the Witch-King strove in their esoteric combat.

Kaloan sensed the warrior's sword come down, and once more he automatically shoved aside a blade with his mind. The man grunted in surprise, eyes widening behind his helmet. Suddenly Kaloan felt the pressure on his mind intensify. These were no ordinary swordsman! The swordsman expertly switched to Kaloan's left and he was barely able to fend off the new attack, even with his power. The man was actively blocking his power as he searched for a weak spot in Kaloan's defenses, trying to smash him with the buckler on his left arm as the sword came back around. He was strong, maybe too strong. Unsure for the first time in his life, Kaloan beat off another swing, took a hesitant step backward, and saw the man switch to a low blow at his knee, then suddenly slump forward. A knife blossomed in his back. Kaloan looked up into the grinning face of one of his Sasayats. "*Ki-ya!*" the man yelled, bright-eyed, then spun into the melee and was gone.

Kaloan followed, battle madness at last taking him. His sword danced through the center of the Zan line, weaving a pattern of death as the Witch-King's retinue shriveled before him, their blood spattering the ground at his feet. They fought with their minds, but he was Kaloan in the fullness of his power now, worth any ten of them. Exultant, the mountain warriors pushed them back, chanting *Ki-ya! Ki-ya!* and *Loka! Loka!*

He looked up to see Inogai standing atop his mound of bricks, bathed in white, sending beam after beam crashing down on the Witch-King, who staggered under their blows. In front of him the last swordsman of the Witch-King's retinue went down under a hail of Atya axes.

"Now, Son of Egea! Now!" he heard Inogai shout. "Now!"

Kaloan covered the distance to the Witch-King in two quick strides. He saw the man face him, glimpsed a shockingly ordinary face, flat-nosed and narrow-eyed, with a thin slit of a mouth, no more than middle-aged. Power flared around him as Kaloan's sword came up, but Inogai was there, helping him, suppressing the Witch-King's last desperate attempt to stop him, holding up Kaloan. The buzzing in his head became a roar, and then a scream, and then his sword came down and it was over.

A head rolled into a pile of rubble, and a body clad in scarlet slumped to the earth, a body like any other.

For a moment everyone stood, looking dumbly at the body, scarcely believing they had won. A few black mountain dogs slunk forward, sniffing tentatively, muscles tensed and ready to bolt. Inogai spun, staring at Kaloan darkly. His hands came up and his face furrowed in concentration. His mouth opened in a scream of denial. His hands . . .

Kaloan's head exploded.

The power. It flowed through him, a massive illumination, a massive energy, as if he were walking and flying and swimming and dying all at once. It filled him, grew in him, a torrent and then a flood and then a vast ocean of power. He swam there, a fish born to it. His body felt like lead, like fire, like a feather. Never had he imagined so much power. And the memories! Scenes flickered across his mind, images of Shevan, Zannai, Omungu, and other places, deserts that covered a continent, and another continent all of ice, and places so far away they had no names in any language he knew, places where strange people had skins as pale and pink as the inside of a cockle-shell, and the women had hair of spun gold.

He stood in the battlefield and above it, and elsewhere. He saw a unit of Zan swordsman rushing down the main boulevard of the city. He saw farmers returning to their homes in the early evening. He saw the orchards outside the city smoking where his men had set them afire. He saw behind him Inogai suddenly rushing toward him, arms extended, beams of white light erupting from his hands, zeroing in on Kaloan.

Time ceased to move. Space shrunk to the inside of his mind. Who was this Other in him?

A voice. *My son. Egea never told me.* A long sigh of regret, loss. *Father?*

We don't have much time. Already Inogai has realized you are my eldest.

Can I . . . ?

Let me teach you.

He drew himself up. What had Inogai said of his people? *They are focused only on the here and now.* That is where he must be, Sasayat that he was. He turned his attention to the world in front of him, where the here-and-now was Inogai careering off a pile of broken bricks with hands spewing white.

Like this, your power joined to mine. He felt the other mind guide him. His hands rose, fingers spread. He read Inogai's face and his heart, the mix of shock, anger, and fear. He absorbed Inogai's beams effortlessly into his own vast, onrushing power, the way a river swallows a rain-drop, with only a flicker on its surface.

So this is the betrayal the nameless gods warned me about.

Laughter. *Who is betrayed? It is all a matter of perspective. Patience. Now like this. My, but you are strong, my true-son.* Pride. *And beloved of the nameless gods. Who are you? So little time . . .*

Time continued to creep along, feeling like forever. He curled his fingers into a fist, and beams leapt from them. Around him he sensed the mountain warriors cringing, sensed their fear and their confusion, their minds stuck in the here-and-now, rejecting their new knowledge of Kaloan whom they had loved and who was now a stranger. Worse, a hated stranger. Well, they would understand later, he told himself.

Inogai met his eyes and in them Kaloan saw the despair of a man who had achieved his greatest dream only to have it charred to ashes in front of him. Kaloan's hands burst with power.

Be merciful. He is also my son.

Kaloan turned his hand and a great beam of white cut through Inogai's chest, punching a gaping half-circle of flesh out of his right side, taking his right arm with it. A beam of white sailed harmlessly off into the darkness above Kaigi. His eyes lit for a moment, then glazed. His body fell to the earth next to the Witch-King's.

Kaloan felt the deep sadness of the Other in his mind. *I did not realize how powerful he had become, how he hungered, how he hated me.* Then, a happier tone: *My, your memories! If only I had more time.*

The echo of running feet made everyone look up. A troop of Zan swordsman in battle march turned off the main boulevard and onto the side street into the rubble, drawing to a halt at the cry of their officer when they saw the carnage splashed across the ruins of Kaigi. There were several score of them, clad in the uniform of the Witch-King's personal guard. They were the best the Zan had to offer, and they were obviously fresh. Their hands went to their swords.

Nameless gods! Kaloan thought, groaning inwardly. *Not more! I am so tired. Can I take so many? Can we take so many?* Inside his mind he felt the ghostly smile of Sharrin, Witch-King of Chukulundu, his father, like a caress, like a benediction. Laughter, and then . . . nothing.

He was gone.

The swordsman saw him, surrounded by the Tuga'a, the Atya, and the Sasayats, who had moved protectively around him despite their fear, the wounded and the dying limping to his side, bleeding, swallowing their pain, for they were men born and raised to battle. Minds with other senses probed him. He rebuffed them effortlessly. The officer held up a hand, took a few strides toward Kaloan and the mountain warriors, then went down on one knee in the road. His head bowed low, then looked up at Kaloan's face.

Understanding at last broke across the mind of Kaloan, Son of Egea, Witch-King of Chukulundu.

The Zan officer spoke, averting his eyes respectfully. "Command us, O my King."

Night had fallen, no barrier to the powers of the Witch-King. Kaloan reached in to his father's memories to find the techniques, then reached out with his rapidly expanding mind, gathering the priests—*his* priests—at the temple, calling the warriors back from their sack of the city to his side, dispersing his Zan retinue to tend the wounded and comfort the dying. He looked to where his father and half-brother, the family he had found and lost, lay next to each other in the ruins of Kaigi, the city where his other family had sent him into his long exile a lifetime ago. Behind him the warriors—*his* warriors—shattered the night with his name, weapons raised in the air: Loka! Loka! *Ki-ya! Ki-ya!*

He had come full circle. He was King of the Zan and War Leader of the mountain peoples, and all the domains were his to unite with the blessings of the nameless gods. His mind leapt ahead to the coming campaigns, rummaging through his father's memories for his troop dispositions and supply situation, and suddenly he understood what the leopard had said, how he would be sacrificed: it would be many years before he would return to the mountains, and by then his mother would be gone.

And he would be King. Alone.

THE END

The Love of the Sea

Lin Carter

*In the quiet of a seaside cove Tara of the Twilight finds love—
and a struggle for survival!*

FOR TWO DAYS and one night the frail craft had borne the girl Tara across
the waters of the Inner Sea in the very teeth of the great storm. And for
two days and one night the yelling winds and the hungry waves had barely
given her a moment's respite. By now she was shaking with exhaustion,
as if all the vigor of her young body had been drained to the dregs by the
ordeal.

When the little craft hit the reef and upended, hurling her into the
wind-swept waters, Tara had sunk like a stone. Still new to this world of
Twilight, she had never mastered the skill of swimming. The pure instinct
for survival took over, however: limbs flailed, kicked; lips clamped shut
against the salt water. She rose to the surface, where heavy surf lugged her
upon the shore and left her limp and weary to the bone.

But the retreating surf sucked greedily about her legs and would draw
her back down into the wet maw of the thundering waves. With the last
bit of her strength, the War Maid dragged herself up the slope of wet
sand until she was beyond the reach of the tides. Here a small stream of
fresh water fed into the Inner Sea and from it she drank, rested briefly,
then staggered to her feet and went lurching up into the trees and bushes
to seek a haven from the whips of the wind and the lash of the rain.

She found an opening in the rocky hills and sought entry, discovering
a high-roofed grotto where a pool of fresh, clear water rose from the
bowels of the world to feed, doubtless, the very stream from whose
bountiful breast she had sated her thirst. And therein she found a stranger,
a young naked boy, half in and half out of the pool, gasping like one half
drowned. Her Starhonne vows drove her to the poolside, to drag the weak
boy to dry earth. And then she stopped and stared with widening eyes.

He could only be a Merling, the boy in the pool. Tara had heard of them, the warm-blooded, amphibian semihumans who dwelt beneath the waves, but had never seen one before. He was both like and unlike the men and boys she had seen here in Twilight: perhaps her own age, but huskier and taller than she, his wet hide slick and cold to the touch, pale and slicker than human skin, and tougher, perhaps to hold in body warmth against the cold embraces of deep water.

As she dragged the gasping, half-conscious sea-boy out of the pool, other differences came to her notice. His breast was smooth, devoid of nipples, and his lean belly had no navel indented therein. Evidently, the Merlings bore their offspring live and did not breast-feed them. Also, his genitals seemed withdrawn into the abdominal cavity, for only a fatty slit was to be seen between his strong thighs.

His lips were thick and rubbery, and his mouth was wide, disclosing sharp white pointed teeth. His hair was long and sleek, almost like fur, and darkly green. There were gill slits in his throat. He had a body odor that was distinctly, but not unpleasantly, fishy.

He opened deep green eyes and regarded her blearily, and with puzzlement. "I thought your drowning," she explained. He grinned weakly.

"No, it is the water here; it is fresh, and will be the death of me, for I am bred to the salt sea, and this tasteless land-water will kill me in time . . ."

He fell into a waking doze; Tara, exhausted, wrapped herself about him, tried to warm him with her own warmth, and fell into a doze herself. And woke therefrom some time later, to find him suckling at her firm, young breasts.

The grip of those full, wide lips was strong . . . and thrilling. As he suckled, he explored her warm rondures of breast with cold hands. The women of his race were breastless, and this difference between them fascinated him. She relaxed in his embrace, and let him suckle while her shy hand explored his loins, and found his male organ now extruded. It was both longer and slimmer than those she had heretofore seen, and since it seemed to relieve his torment to be fondled, she fisted it with her strong little hand and brought him relief and rest.

And that was the first day.

While the boy Merling—his name was Aille—was too weak to go down the slope to rejoin the salt sea from which the storm had slung him hither, he was also too heavy for the slender girl to drag or carry. When Lambence came, thin and weak and watery through thick, damp mists, she foraged from the cave, finding ripe fruits and nuts and berries for herself, and fresh fish flung high on shore, with which Aille assuaged his own hunger.

It was unpleasant to see him tear and gnaw at the raw fish with those strong, pointed teeth, but it was the way of Merlings and therefore natural. When he had devoured the fish she had fetched hither, he fell into a doze and seemed stronger than before. Tara knew the lad could not live long out of salt water, and cudgeled her wits to think of a means of getting him down the long, tree-clad slope and into the embrace of the mothering sea.

When he awoke, he reached for her again, since it seemed to soothe him in his torment, she gave herself willingly into his embrace and let him kiss and suck and nuzzle at her breasts, Then she guided his mouth down between her succulent thighs: his tongue was long and rough as a cat's and she derived much pleasure therefrom.

But when he strove feebly to mount her, Tara resisted, mindful of her virgin's vow. This time she comforted him with her own mouth and drew the salty seed from him.

This strange half-love between the War Maid and the dying sea-boy would not last long, she knew, for soon death would claim him. But while he lived, she served his needs and he served hers. Fruits and nuts and berries could not sustain his strength, so thrice daily she went down to the tidal pools in the shallows to see what fish had been stranded by the tides for him to feed upon.

"You are the only land-woman I have ever seen," he confessed shyly. "Your hair is of a hue unknown to us, who dwell in our coral grottos in the deeps, and your luscious breasts are a delight to me. How strange, to live high on the dry land, never knowing the love of the sea that cradles you and rocks you, cool and sweet and comforting!"

She fed him her perfect breast again, and pleasured him with her moist hand until he tensed, gasped, cried out, and bathed his belly with his salty seed.

"Soon I must die," he said sleepily into the warm curve of her shoulder, "never again to see the sea-girls lifted above the waves, combing their long hair with combs of ivory, singing their mournful song . . . never to mount the sportive dolphins, to race among the coral crags, where the sea-bottom lies encumbered with the spars of ships, the bones of drowned sailors, and the great heaps of inestimable gems . . ."

She felt sad for him, but could think of no way to succor Aille, save with the comforts of the flesh.

The next Lambence, however, when Tara descended to the shore to find the fish to feed him, she discovered her own little boat. The waves had tossed it high upon the shore, where tree-roots had snagged and held it fast against the suck of the receding surf. The sharp-fanged reefs had not injured it.

Tara dragged it high up the slope, using the little stream as her road. There at the mouth of the cave, where the stream began, flowing from the pool in the grotto, she beached her craft and told the Merling of her plan. Whether it might work or fail, it was at least worth the trying.

It took the combined strength of both of them to get the sea-boy into the bottom of the craft. Then Tara guided the little boat into the bed of the stream, and let the flowing current float both boat and boy towards the salt sea he craved.

At times the prow or keel became wedged in the shallows, caught between rocks. Then Tara must push and shove and lever the boat free. At length they reached the beach, and the War Maid guided the little boat onto the breast of the heaving waters.

The great storm had long since subsided, its wrath somehow appeased. When she had guided the boat deep enough onto the bosom of the sea, Tara overturned it, letting Aille sink like a stone and return to his element.

Then she swam back to shore as best she might, and found a place to sit on shore rocks slimed with seaweed. She rested, panting for breath, waiting to see if the salt water would revive her young sea-lover, or whether he was too far gone for that.

A time later, he broke water, whipping back slick wet mane with a toss of his head, eyes sparkling, laughing with renewed vigor.

"Land-woman, you have saved a son of the sea!" he called to her, shouldering through the soapy foam. She smiled and waved.

"And the bountiful mother of my kind, the sea, repays all favors!" he cried, tossing her a rounded thing which she caught in one fist and cradled.

It was a pearl of a cat's skull, round and moony, glimmering and shimmering with cold fires. She stared at it entranced: there were princes here in Twilight that had lesser a treasure than this.

With a joyous shout and one last wave of his hand, the Merling sank into the surging foam and was gone forever from view. Leaving Tara with a treasure beyond price, and the memory of a brief love that would not soon be forgotten.

She rose and made her way through the shallows to the slope of the beach. Where the wild wind and wilder waves had carried her, the Starhonne could not say. But all the wide world of Twilight lay before her, and she was young and strong.

She set forth through the woods into another day.

THE END

Thongor on Callisto

Robert M. Price

i. An Absent Friend and a Royal Visitor

THE ROYAL BANQUET hall was well-lit by bracketed torches. Moving shadows danced fantastically as a parade of even more fantastic dignitaries entered the venue. The Sarkoja Jampin, all seven feet of her statuesque physique, queen of the Jegga Horde of Blue Nomads of Western Lemuria, passed into the hall with her retinue. All of them bore savage finery including colorful feather-cloaks, gold-gilded bones both animal and human, flaming gems the size of fruits, and face-and body paints of rare shades. Queen Sumia took in the dream-like procession with a sense of awe, occasionally sparing a glance in the direction of her husband, Mahathongoya, Thongor the Mighty, Emperor of the West. Jampin was quite the sight, a sapphire-skinned beauty whose face and form blinded any observer to whatever clothing she wore, and there was not much of it. Sumia dreaded to see undue interest in her royal husband's golden eyes, but if he felt any lust beginning to stir within him, there was no outward sign of it.

As the Rmoahal titaness took her seat beside Thongor and Sumia, Thongor whispered to his queen, "No Shangoth? I fear some great trouble has pre-empted our old friend."

Sumia nodded and replied, "Doubtless we shall know in a moment, my love."

In accord with ancient custom, all ate in silence, waiting for the feast of boupher flesh, kroter steaks, and lizard hawk filets in fancy sauces to be finished and cleared away (all of which would be given to the cooks and servers), before sarn wine and Valkarthan mead flowed and loosened tongues for conversation.

An hour later, when the rest of the guests had retired to bed, Thongor turned to the matter at hand. Unaccustomed to idle chat, he got right to the point: "My lady, we rejoice in your presence and the honor it does us, but we miss our comrade, Chieftain Shangoth. Is aught amiss? Have you come seeking our aid? If so, you know we shall provide it, no matter the cost!" As he uttered these words, the wrinkles forming like storm clouds above his beetling brows punctuated them, as did Sumia's firm but gentle grasping of her sister-queen's steel-muscled forearm.

A lone tear traced the blue woman's cheek. "I would tell you if I knew. It is what I do *not* know that troubles me, my friend. My beloved Shangoth found himself intrigued by a report from a traveler that the ruins of an ancient city of my people, long reclaimed by thick jungle, had been at last discovered. At once we were inspired to wonder if this might be the legended home of our ancestors, sacred Gorthal, from which in ancient days our foreparents scattered to assume their nomadic existence. Knowing what the recovery of the place would mean to our people, he commanded a large-scale excavation, perhaps with a view to restoring its former glory, making it the center of pilgrimage it once was. No pleading could dampen his zeal!"

Thongor interrupted: "Why try to dissuade him? It seems a worthy quest!"

The visiting queen was ready with an answer: "Legends tell that some great danger dwelt in the place, and that our ancient ancestors fled to escape it. Perhaps that danger still lurks! Shangoth insisted on inspecting the site once the detritus had been cleared away. Once the laborers finished, he set off by himself—and he has not returned after a month! I know not whether he did encounter some eldritch evil there or mayhap some more mundane danger along the way."

Thongor was momentarily silent, considering the matter, great hands steepled.

"We must not enter into this thing blind. If we knew more about that which haunts those ruins, we might gain a real advantage."

"Yes, your Majesty, but that secret is lost to both history and legend!"

Sumia interjected: "Perhaps not, my sister! My cousin, Prince Dru, is something of an antiquarian, though he does his best to hide the fact behind his foppish pose. Let us summon him and inquire of him. In truth, I thought to see him here tonight." Withal, she pulled a hanging strip of cloth to summon a messenger.

"Find Prince Dru and tell him his betters require his presence."

With a bow and a grin, the page hastened to obey.

Presently, a slim, perfumed, but comically disheveled figure rushed stumblingly into the hall. His usually coiffed hair was in disarray, and even now he strove to wipe away traces of cosmetics from cheeks and lips. Then he noticed the eye-filling sight of the blue queen Jampin, and his bloodshot eyes widened.

"I see you've been quite busy, cousin!"

"Yes, yes. Quite busy indeed! Ever vigilant to keep up with my duties!"

Thongor could not suppress a belly laugh. "I can imagine! But we have need of your services, though not the same ones, I'll warrant!"

Sumia, who apparently saw no humor in the situation, claimed Dru's attention. "You have, I know, acquired great knowledge from the scrolls and codices stored away in the archives deep beneath the palace. I have need of some of that knowledge."

All levity had been banished from the great chamber, and from the Prince's countenance. He took a seat as he listened closely while the others brought him up to speed. There grew upon his features an intangible sense of anticipation as if he became more and more convinced he knew what was coming next.

An atmosphere of ominous antiquity had descended upon the dining hall, abetted by certain conspicuous absences. The walls, though constructed of heavy stone and adorned here and there with outcroppings of gold, were denuded of the extensive tapestries that once lined them. They dated back to when Patanga served as the capitol of the Flame Druids of the demon-god Yamath, in whose honor each arras depicted graphic scenes of horrific torture and human sacrifice. Similarly, the walls held bare niches for hideously obscene idols. Thongor, upon assuming the throne, had all these abominations taken down and destroyed but had never caused them to be replaced with more wholesome artworks. But tonight, menacing ghosts of the past seemed to have returned. Perhaps they were listening as Prince Dru began his bizarre recitation.

ii. A Resurrected Myth

The hour was late, and the teller of the tale unlikely, but he knew what his audience desired to hear. So the Prince closed his eyes to clear his besotted head. He sought to draw forth long-neglected information from the cobwebbed archive of his memory as the others waited patiently.

At last he spoke, his gaze directed to no listener in particular. His tone was dreamy, as if he had passed into a trance.

"Long ago, before even Phondath the Firstborn of our kind, before Sharajsha, in the days of the Dragon Kings, there appeared on earth visitors from a far empire, from a world they called Yaddith. They were not like us, nor even like the Dragons. They were more like great insects with many-jointed limbs, with faceted eyes and buzzing speech. They had come to establish colonies on our world. To this end they pressed into service the mighty Rmoahal giants to build their city in what is now the northernmost tip of Lemuria, though its coastlines were not the same as we now see them. At the center of their city they built a great, bottomless well.

"But their endeavor was finally halted by the Dragon Kings who ruled primordial Lemuria. A war between these mighty peoples ensued, but the sorcery of the Dragons prevailed. For all their knowledge, the insect race knew nothing of the Dark Arts. Still, the Dragon Kings could not destroy their foes. Instead, they agreed to a cessation of hostilities. The accord provided that the Dragon Kings would not challenge their rivals' outpost on a world they called *Thanator*, from whence they journeyed to our world. The Reptile Kings even agreed to use their magic to create the illusion of a barren waste of a planet to camouflage Thanator, in order to discourage any other races from attempting to settle on the planet.

"The insect invaders departed, taking their Rmoahal slaves with them. The well was actually a portal between worlds. It was the means by which they had arrived on earth, and now they used it to return to far-off Thanator. The city and the central well were left idle. The Dragons had refrained from destroying them in case they should one day want to invade Yaddith or its colonies. The Dragon Kings, of course, were eventually driven out by Phondath the Firstborn. On Thanator, the Yaddith aliens degenerated in the wake of some disaster, reducing them to a condition of primitive savagery."

Silent during this recital, absorbing every word, Queen Jampin now asked, "O Prince, how much of this is myth, and how much true history?" At this, Prince Dru merely shrugged; how could he know?

Thongor ventured an opinion: "It has not the ring of legend. Strange as the story is, it strikes me as not fanciful *enough*. It is true that we live in a time and a place of marvels, each more amazing than the one before it, as all here have occasion to know. But, given all we have seen and endured, what part of this tale outmatches our own past adventures?"

"I fear you are right, mighty Thongor. But what has this story, whether legend or true history, to do with my mate's disappearance?"

"I know not, though I have my suspicions. And in the morning I will fly an airboat to this city, this Gorthal. Any of you are welcome to join me. Lady Jampin, can you direct us?"

iii. The Well Between the Worlds

When dawn broke, the rising sun's rays touching the naturally silver-hued Urlium hull of the airboat turned it to brilliant gold. Thongor and his companions Sumia, Jampin, and Prince Dru, whose hangover did nothing to dampen his courage or his lust for adventure, were aboard. As they flew swiftly over the unbroken sea of jungle palms and ferns, nothing stood out. Jampin more than once assured them they were still on track.

At length they spied a great clearing ahead and prepared for descent. As they did so, they marveled at the spectacle of what seemed a miniature model of an ancient, foreign city, or, better, a vast and sprawling castle, all one great structure. Before the encroachment of the tropical forest, the city Gorthal must have been surrounded on all sides by open plains, as attested by both common sense and the remnants of fortified city walls. But now the enemy the walls stood against was the jungle itself, lately driven back by the Rmoahal workmen. It was as if history had resumed its interrupted course, as if the same blue-skinned titans had picked up where they had left off ages before, first building the city, then stripping away its shroud.

Once the airboat settled on terra firma, the city assumed its actual dimensions, or so it appeared to the visitors who now found themselves dwarfed by the labyrinthine walls, buildings, and streets, which were surprisingly narrow, as if the intended inhabitants were themselves of modest stature. Thongor, Sumia, Jampin, and Dru agreed to split up to search as many of the empty buildings as each one could, yelling Shangoth's name. It echoed like a battle cry down the winding alleys but brought forth no reply.

From the air they had seen that the city of Gorthal centered about a well mouth that was flush with the surrounding pavement. The rim of the thing could now, close up, be seen to be made of a single mass of some lambent, almost colorless crystal. Surrounding the well was a circle of statues, some in a standing position, other sitting cross-legged. Prince Dru's close examination revealed that the sitting figures were humanoid, while the standing effigies were anything but, looking more like great insects. Not only that, but the latter were the older, the former being recent replacements, probably attesting a drastic change in population.

But in all this, there was no sign of the missing Shangoth.

Prince Dru applied his surprising erudition (long hidden for fear that the possession of great knowledge might taint one's repute as a man of action and a dashing lover) to their investigation.

"These carvings," he announced, "do seem to confirm part of what I learned from the old scrolls. Did you see how these figures resemble ants or beetles walking upright? And they seem to be bearing weapons or perhaps tools."

"Gorm's privates!" swore Thongor, instantly regretting the thoughtless oath. "I like not the look of this."

"Nor I," echoed the others as if in chorus.

Sumia asked, "Can Shangoth have been taken prisoner by such creatures?"

"Doubtful," muttered Thongor, slowly moving his gaze in the direction of the well. "But I am beginning to think I know what *did* happen to him. Look at the well!" For just now a broad beam of pulsing, opalescent light projected upward from below. Thongor sprinted for the well mouth, plunging, sword drawn, into the vacuity framed by the still smooth, pearl-like stone rim of the pit. Then the beam abruptly stopped.

In stunned amazement, Prince Dru and the two queens stood frozen for a moment, then bolted to the well and tried to penetrate its depths. All they could see was a roiling cloud of eerie luminescence. Whether a mist or merely shifting lights, they could not tell. But . . . there *was something* becoming visible . . .

"Get *back!*" yelled Dru, colliding with the two women in order to push them to a safe distance—just before Sarkozan, the sword of Thongor, shot out of the well mouth, as if fired like an arrow by some giant bowman from the unseen recesses below!

Sumia picked up the weapon without hesitation. Looking at her companions, she said, "I believe our king has found his friend . . . or soon will."

iv. Thongor on Thanator

At first, as he picked himself up off the ground, Thongor wondered if he had perhaps overshot the well mouth, for he found himself still surrounded by lush jungle growth. But something was amiss. The dense foliage was *red.* Equally alarming was the fact that his great sword was gone! But he had retained his leather kilt and boots. He knew he had not released his grip on Sarkozan, but it had not made the trip with him, though, thankfully, his clothing had. He dimly realized that metals could not be transported by the strange beam, though living matter, or that which had once *been* alive, could. Hence the cured leather garments he wore, he *still* wore. But these would be of little use if the need arose to defend himself—as it almost always did.

His first instinct was to locate something he might be able to use as a weapon. He knew not what perils he might encounter—or when. But it was likely to be sooner rather than later, for he could already hear echoes of animal roaring. He made a quick survey of the area and realized he might well face mortal danger at any moment: the place was a bone yard, littered with sun-bleached remnants of skeletons from which the meat had been stripped by some great predator. The beasts whose flesh it (or *they*) had devoured had themselves been huge. Thongor could not identify them as any known Lemurian species. Where *was* he?

A sudden cacophony alerted him to some nearby battle between alien monsters, or between man and monster. There was still the matter of a makeshift weapon. Without one, any attempt to investigate the violent carnage would be suicide. Looking about and below him, he spotted a long bone, one end of which had been sharpened to a point by the fangs of a hungry devourer. This he grabbed up and paced as swiftly but silently as he could. Following the noise, the Valkarthan entered a clearing. The mossy carpet underfoot somewhat muffled the roaring of a monstrous behemoth, a thing much like a Lemurian dragon-cat, fifteen feet in length, covered in scale armor and lacerating the air with a tail lined with a row of deadly blades. So quickly did the huge human form dart and dodge, landing a blow when he could, that Thongor could not get a fix on his appearance. He could, however, tell that the human combatant had blue skin, just like his Nomad allies of Lemuria. Was he native to this world, or perhaps a descendant of the Rmoahal slaves the insectoids had long ago brought with them from primal Lemuria? As Thongor stood poised on the balls of his feet, looking for a viable opening to join the fight, to assist the bleeding, weakening form of his fellow human, he saw the desperate face.

It was *Shangoth!*

He, too, had been employing a bone as a rudimentary weapon, whether as a club or a dagger, but it was brittle and broken till only a stump remained.

Fearing that a shouted greeting might distract his old friend, Thongor chose instead to take the direct approach. He would require more momentum than a running start would provide, so he chose to climb the obligingly knotted black trunk of one of the clustered trees. The menacing creature obviously possessed few if any vulnerable points, but there was one place Thongor was fairly sure of, as long as he could get a good shot at it. An arrow would have been a better weapon, but he didn't know if they had been invented on this strange world.

He could not afford the time to take careful aim; Shangoth's endurance was slipping away fast. So the Valkarthan let instinct take over and, once the lizard-cat raised its tail again, Thongor pitched the sharpened bone. It found its mark and shot up the monster's rectum. It howled shrilly and stiffened like a board as life departed like rats from a sinking ship. Thongor, laughing, dropped from the tree limb onto the spongy ground, crouching beside the great blue form and cradling his huge domed head.

"Th-*Thongor*? I had hoped . . . but . . . ."

"Be silent, my brother. We will return to Lemuria as soon as you have some strength back. We are still near the well . . . ."

Shangoth whispered, "But the *Zeta Beam* . . . is it still . . . ?"

v. Prisoners of the Ant-Hill

Thongor was eager for more information, and he got it, though not in the way he expected. For before he could frame his question, and before Shangoth could answer it, a crowd of interlopers appeared, as if from nowhere. They were the living counterparts of the strange bug creatures represented in both carvings and statuary in the excavated city. Could they have pursued Thongor through the cosmic portal? No, there had been no sign of current habitation there. They now surrounded Thongor and Shangoth. The latter had passed out from his loss of blood. Thongor watched in awed silence as one of the creatures exuded some sticky substance and proceeded to apply it to the blue giant's wounds, which rapidly sealed over. Incredibly, Shangoth regained consciousness and was able to stand up, albeit somewhat unsteadily.

The Valkarthan's palm actually tingled from its lack of a sword. These odd creatures were numerous, but they were slight of build, taller than a man but chitinous like an insect. They bore a natural armor, no doubt an exo-skeleton. It might not be too difficult to defeat one or several, but most carried weapons as strange as themselves. They resembled whips, but, instead of hide lashes they trailed what looked like flexible metal strips, deadly sharp along one side. Thongor knew it would be foolish to engage them now. He would have to wait for better odds and further knowledge of his foes. And, he reminded himself, it was the scaly beast that had attacked Shangoth, not them. So he raised his hands in momentary surrender and looked over to his friend who had done the same. The insectoids began to form a cordon around the pair and began to move. Despite himself, Thongor was completely fascinated.

No great distance away lay, not a well but rather a natural-looking opening in the ground and into this aperture the party descended. Of course, the insect-men had swarmed from this tunnel and so appeared as if from thin air. The captors began communicating amongst themselves in a torrent of clicks and whistles. Thongor had never heard the like of it—and yet he seemed to understand what he was hearing! Much of it was still nonsense to him because many things said must have referred to names, objects, or ideas alien to him.

Seeing his comrade's puzzlement, which Thongor did not even think of trying to hide, Shangoth let slip a grin and began to enlighten him.

"As you see, they have not the equipment to speak as we do. But we can understand them nonetheless because of a limited telepathic capability. When we are near them, our minds can pick up some of what they say to one another, or even to us." The notion of mind-reading was by no means unknown to Thongor. He knew that some wizards and oracles possessed the ability, and he had even occasionally witnessed their exercise of it.

"Tell me this, Shangoth. Who *are* these beings? *What* are they? And I care not if they understand me, since such questions seem innocent enough."

"You are right. As for them, Thongor, they call themselves the *Yaddithoon*, or *Yathoon* for short, which I gather comes from the name of their original home. The thing we fought, they call a *Yathrib*, but I think its kind is natural to this planet. By the way, they call this world *Thanator*. You will shortly see their night sky illuminated by a set of *four moons*, perhaps more, as it varies. In fact, Thanator is itself no more than a moon, circling an unthinkably vast globe which you will also see for yourself. As for me, I think of it as the Eye of Gorm."

Thongor struggled to keep up with this barrage of baffling facts.

"But how did we get here? And what is that well? And that light! Is that what you called the . . . uh . . ."

"The Zeta Beam. It's called the Zeta Beam. It provides passage between many worlds.

"And does it strike at regular intervals? I'd much like to get out of here!"

"I agree! But I do not know. It seems the Yathoon do not know either, not that I have been able to tell, anyway. These fellows are one of the rotating shifts posted there in case any new 'guests' should arrive. They can always use more slaves!"

"So they intend to enslave us, do they?"

At this, one of the Yathoon turned his expressionless head and commented, "We have enslaved you already!"

vi. Among the Slaves

For the next few weeks, Thongor and Shangoth bided their time. They did as they were told, which was mainly to join the other captives, descendants of the original Rmoahal slaves. These men and women had inherited very low expectations from life. And those expectations had been fully met. The women prepared the scarce and rudimentary food, mainly tasteless vegetables and occasional fruit, not exactly conducive to building strength and endurance, which one might have thought desirable traits for slaves—unless one feared an uprising. Accordingly, the men were put to work tending to the livestock which provided meat for the insectoid Yathoon. Those Rmoahals with a bit more flesh on their bones (though all were scrawny next to Shangoth) were sacrificed to the arena for the entertainment of their captors. Thongor had been present at one of the gladiatorial matches. It was plain the Yathoon masters had nothing to fear from these weaklings. It was obviously more of a burlesque than anything else. Thongor found the grotesque chittering, which passed for the laughter of the crowd, blood-chilling. And he wondered why they allowed him to witness the farcical display. Surely they did not plan to force him into the games, since it could only result in the wholesale slaughter of their pathetic "champions." Soon he would find out.

The exiled Lemurian king often wondered what had caused the decadence of the arthropod civilization on Thanator. Prince Dru had spoken of some awful catastrophe setting them back culturally and scientifically, but he knew not the nature of it. But what Dru had not known, Shangoth did. One afternoon, the two men's work details coincided, due to a scheduling error, since the Yathoon were usually careful about limiting contact between them. Thongor was musing over this historical mystery when Shangoth, hearing his thoughts, turned to him in surprise.

"My brother, I thought you knew! It was the double dealing of the Dragon Kings! They had made peace with the Yathoon but did not destroy the well connecting the two worlds. Their scheme was to bide their time and then use the Zeta Beam to invade Thanator! In this foul plan they more than succeeded. What benefit they sought or gained, I know not. Neither records nor campfire tales tell of that. It may be that the Dragons sought to establish their own outpost to which they might repair in case they themselves were one day defeated, as of course did finally happen. Only they were for some reason unable to reach the well between worlds."

His friend commented, "I will have much to think about till I enter the arena tomorrow."

"You? *You* will fight tomorrow?"

"Yes, Shangoth. Will you attend the debacle?"

"I should say so! For I, too, am slated to fight there!"

Thongor spoke, mainly to himself: "By the Nineteen Immortals, things are becoming clear! Our captors have watched our labors in order to assess our strengths. They feared what they saw, and now they seek to be rid of us, each at the hands of the other! Come, Shangoth, we have but little time till the morrow."

Shangoth smiled, surmising the obvious.

In the wee hours, lamps lit up the cavernous slave pens as Shangoth spoke boomingly to the assemblage. There were no longer very many of them. His countrymen listened with puzzlement to the newcomer, understanding most of what he said, despite the fact that centuries of isolation had witnessed the evolution of their dialects along disparate paths. More than likely it was the overarching telepathic field that smoothed out the communication. This meant the Yathoon might be listening in, but perhaps not, since they believed their grasp on their slave population was unshakeable. But it hardly mattered since the actions planned by Thongor and Shangoth would commence at once, if at all.

vii. Blue Vengeance!

Thongor listened to Shangoth's stirring speech to his kindred, urging them to overrun their captors, something they had never even thought to try! It was a fine speech, a call to freedom. Shangoth outlined how the mass of them should overrun the lackadaisical guards and make for the armory. Equipped with the Yathoon whip-swords, they should have a fighting chance. Thongor admired Shangoth's courage, as he always had, but now he was not so sure about that of these latter-day Rmoahal captives. Their willingness to follow Shangoth seemed more like habitual passivity than the fire to rebel. Well, dawn was coming, and he would soon find out one way or the other.

It was over before it started. Shangoth, backed up by Thongor, led his pitiable troops to the weapons storage and succeeded in overwhelming the sentries there, but then the blue-skins stood there trying to figure out how to wield the whip-swords. They had seen the Yathoon making effective use of them all their lives, but somehow that did not help. They managed to inflict ample wounds on themselves and each other. Shangoth felt like taking out his frustration on the confused weaklings with one of

64

the weapons, but Thongor tried to calm him down.

A large force of Yathoon, larger than Thongor had yet seen, suddenly appeared, alerted by the ruckus, or perhaps by their telepathy. Their mere presence was enough to cow the slaves into mute submission. Nor were they punished, only escorted back to their pens.

And for only the second time, one of the Yathoon addressed Thongor personally. The gist, which was all Thongor understood, or needed to, was: "Come along, Lemurian. And bring your blue ox of a friend. It is time for the games to begin." Thongor looked at Shangoth quizzically, and both followed their arthropod escorts.

The arena was not much to speak of. When Thongor had first seen it he could suppress a laugh only with great difficulty. It was like the time he was obliged to attend a wedding ceremony among the Patangan nobility, just the sort of chore he most hated. Some fool had allowed the bride's untalented sister to sing a celebratory hymn, and when she groaned out the piece, Thongor found himself in a death struggle with an inner demon of exploding hilarity. For Sumia's sake, if not his own, he managed to wrestle his merry foe into submission.

But things were more serious now. He reckoned his prospects of winning against Shangoth as about even. But it was winning the match, not losing it, that he feared. He could not live with himself if he killed his blood brother and comrade. But neither did he relish the idea of getting killed.

It was to be bare-knuckled combat, to the death. As he and Shangoth began a mutual pantomime, neither delivering any blow calculated to do any real damage, Thongor suddenly felt a peculiar steeling of his resolve. A jolting flush of blood lust galvanized him! From the look of him, Shangoth was evidently experiencing the same thing. Each redoubled his efforts, fighting in earnest, seeking bloodshed, hurling deadly blows. The combatants were being reduced to mere puppets.

But amid the clouds of red haze being projected into his brain, something like a penetrating ray of light struck Thongor's consciousness. It distracted him momentarily, hampering his instinctive attempt to dodge a fearsome blow. The Valkarthan all at once realized that the telepathy must work both ways! Otherwise, telepathic communication would be impossible. So Thongor retreated a few paces, shook his black-maned head, then concentrated, directing his thoughts toward Shangoth. The two of them stood side by side, together projecting onto the Yathoon spectators a wave of fear and the illusion of an attacking force surrounding the arena. What form the spectral attackers took in the minds of the panicking insectoids, Thongor could not guess and did not care.

But all at once, his astonishment overtopped theirs!

For at that very moment an actual assault force appeared! Climbing and leaping over the low walls of the arena was a small legion of Rmoahal amazons, Queen Jampin and the bodyguards who had accompanied her into Thongor's royal court. Sumia, lithe and muscular despite her diminutive proportions compared to these women of the Jegga Horde, was there, as was her cousin, Prince Drew. They had grown tired of waiting, returned to Patanga for reinforcements, and then back to the ruins of Gorthal to wait till the unearthly light should erupt again. Once on Thanator, they looked around for materials to fashion rudimentary weapons. Having seen the well eject the sword Sarkozan, Sumia knew it would be a vain effort to arm themselves on their own side of the well. But now, a wide smile emblazoned her pretty face as she beheld Thongor and tossed him a home-made flint axe. A few of the Yathoon fell before the assault while most cast away their whip-swords and fled. Seeing this, Jampin laughed and embraced her delighted husband with a rib-crushing hug.

* * * * *

Thongor and the Rmoahals did finally return to Lemuria via the Zeta Beam, bringing the freed slaves with them. But there had been no way to know when the beam might erupt again. So several months passed while they waited. The small group set about constructing a tiny settlement. More than once they derived great amusement from the fact that the miniscule village counted no less than four royal rulers! For a while, on the earthly side of the well, a cordon of Thongor's and Shangoth's troops stood guard until it became clear that none of the aliens who dwelt on the other side would appear. They were packing up to leave when the Zeta Beam returned and, with it, Thongor and company. The guards promptly turned into a welcoming committee. The former slaves decided to stay and rebuild ancient Gorthal, just as their ancestors had erected it in the first place. There they and their children would live in freedom and peace, under the protection of the Jegga Horde. As for the well between the worlds, none dared either to enter it or to destroy it. Perhaps one day another hero would have use for it.

THE END

Manticora

Glynn Owen Barrass

THE PAIR WALKED quickly through the rain, across grassy earth rapidly turning to mud. Their goal was the forest surrounding the Karthian Hills, a safe harbour from the weather if not much else. Not known for anything pleasant, it was the haven of goblins, manticores and worse, if the legends were true. Ansell had never met a manticore, and was in no mood for one now. She had her sword unsheathed, just in case.

Her companion Tamara strode beside her, head hooded against the rain. The girl, a fire mage of great power, had become a true friend. This companionship still felt strange to Ansell. She had once adventured in a group of three, a swarthy man and a ghoul from the underworld. Both had died horribly, cruelly. Since then, Ansell had travelled alone, until Tamara, the raven-haired, pale-skinned girl, entered her life.

The twilight sky was a doomish shade of purple above deep black storm clouds. Everything was blurred by the torrent, Ansell moving by instinct more than anything else.

Shelter. Good in theory, Ansell mused as they neared the wall of trees. She half-expected some primeval mutation to leap out from the wood's spurious protection.

What the hell does a manticore look like anyway? "Ow!" Ansell said, nearly slipping in the growing mud. She felt Tamara's steadying hand on her arm.

"I'm okay. Thanks." She looked to Tamara, saw a face pale and spectral beneath the hood.

Ansell's left boot was leaking, each damp and squishy step making it worse. The rain had drenched her cloak, entered her leather armour to soak the undergarments beneath. It chilled her to the bone, the icy wetness, plastered her hair to her scalp while making her head and ears numb.

Manticore, she mused, shifting her thoughts away from her drenched condition. She recalled seeing a picture somewhere, depicting a lion with an elderly man's face, huge bat wings.

Damned thing will have trouble flying in this weather, she thought, and laughed as they took their final steps into the forest.

The oaks appeared to lean forward as they entered, the boughs clutching hungrily for their water-sodden forms.

Desperation to escape the downpour drove Ansell on regardless. Of Tamara's thoughts she had no idea, didn't know if the girl knew the rumours surrounding the place.

It was a strange transition, leaving the wilderness for the woods. A sudden, sinister darkness enveloped them like the deeps of an abyss.

A flash of lightning accompanied by a low thunderous roar illuminated the trees. Twisted brown trunks were briefly revealed, rain-slashed by the tumult.

Ansell blinked, stepped forward with her hand raised to avoid walking into a tree.

Tamara cursed loudly, though the storm drowned out her profanities somewhat.

It seemed a veritable tempest had engulfed the land beyond the forest. The skies, as another roar and slash of liquid light proved, were tearing the world asunder.

"Rain's thinning out here," Ansell yelled, striding forward.

"Light. We need light," Tamara shouted back.

What would I do without you? Ansell thought fondly. The pair had just travelled from Ulthar, their ultimate goal the port city of Hlanith. A journey across the Cerenarian Sea would follow, then to Celephais for Tamara to continue her wizard training. A quicker, more direct route would have taken them past the Enchanted Wood, but Ansell was avoiding that area. Her last business there had left a man half-dead and gained the enmity of a few hundred Zoogs.

The end of the journey would be the end of their association, for now: something Ansell didn't look forward to.

A glow of light interrupted her train of thought. Unlike the harsh lightning, this was a warm, hearty radiance. Ansell looked round, saw Tamara's hands clasped around a globe of orange fire.

She paused, waited for the witch-girl to catch up, then patted her water-soaked shoulder.

The canopy of trees was doing its work: the leaves and boughs turning the tumult into a gentle shower.

Tamara halted, took the flame one-handed and pulled her hood back with the other. The soaked fabric peeled away reluctantly. Her purple cloak was absolutely soddened with water. Brown leather straps, tight across her shoulders, held a pack bearing her belongings. Ansell wore a similar pack, though hers was heavy with weapons. She watched raindrops trickle down Tamara's face.

Ansell experienced a sudden, unexpected melancholy. It would be a sad day, parting with this young friend.

"Come on," she said abruptly, turned and headed forward.

They walked in silence, trudged really, across the mulched forest floor.

Ansell led the way by instinct and the assumption that keeping the hills to the left would eventually lead them from the woods. Tamara's light was a great help. The forest felt endless however, a monotonous obstacle of bent trees, grabbing branches. The invisible sky grumbled at their escape.

Tamara's light flickered out. Ansell halted, a sudden weight in her gut. She turned, expecting to see the witch-girl gone.

A gasp of relief escaped her lips. Tamara was there still, facing west. She turned to Ansell. "Sorry, I lost concentration. But look. Lights!"

Tamara grinned enthusiastically, began heading west.

"Wait." Ansell's voice was weak. She was befuddled, disorientated. *What lights? What could they mean?*

Her next thought was danger. Hurrying after Tamara, she gripped her sword tightly.

As the trees thinned out, Ansell noticed a glimmer of light between them.

"Hey, hold on," she said to Tamara's back, but her words went unheeded.

A few moments later, she caught up with her. The forest had parted, revealing an open, grassy glade.

Near the centre of the clearing stood a two-storied cottage. Constructed from logs, its tall, sloped tile roof extended over a low balcony. There was a door there, flanked by two bright windows. Beyond the roof Ansell spied the nebulous shapes of the Karthian foothills.

She wanted to wait, scope out this unexpected find, but as always, Tamara rushed forward without a care. Far too naïve in the ways of the world, the witch-girl darted across the glade.

Ansell hissed, then pursued her, suffering a renewed blast of rain for her trouble. Her sword flashed in reflected lightning; the sky roared at the rediscovery of its tiny prey.

Only in the open a few moments, it was still enough to re-soak her. She blinked away water, following Tamara onto the cottage's balcony, glad of the shelter if not the source.

Ansell noted a stack of moss-covered logs to her right. There was a large, ancient-looking woodaxe laid on the boards near them. Around the side of each window, bundles of yellow star-shaped flowers hung.

"Agrimony," Tamara said, "Used to deter hostile magic, dark spirits."

A wreath of blackberry was nailed to the door.

The witch-girl raised her hand to knock.

Ansell felt the brief, irrational urge to pause her hand, but too late, Tamara knocked, and the deed was done.

She noted her sword was still unsheathed, gripped very tightly, so replaced it into the scabbard. It would be unseemly to call on someone bearing a weapon. Ansell wasn't a robber. Not currently, anyway.

A commotion issued beyond the door; the noise of bolts being pulled.

The pair shared an uneasy glance. Tamara stepped back and Ansell moved closer to her.

The door opened a few inches to reveal an elderly, deeply wrinkled face. The woman wore a whitish bonnet greying with age. She examined Ansell from head to toe, and her eyes narrowed.

"You——"

"We request shelter from the storm," Ansell interrupted. "The young lass and I."

The door opened a little wider.

The old woman wore a dark brown bodice, matching skirt, the white sleeve of her blouse rolled up to reveal a thin, frail arm.

Behind her was a brightly lit room. Movements inside spoke of another occupant.

The old woman's eyes widened at the sight of Tamara.

"Ah," she gasped. "You're a mage! Come in dears, both of you, out of the horrid weather."

She had seen Tamara's amulet, Ansell guessed. The old woman, her cracked face beaming now, opened the door.

Ansell felt a little confused.

Travelling mages were often treated with suspicion, fear in the lands she traversed. There were always exceptions, however.

The room beyond the door was spacious. Light issued from candles stood upon a half-dozen worktops and corner tables. The source of the sounds, a hulking bear of a man, approached them as they entered.

Ansell paused and Tamara followed suit. A few heads taller than Ansell, the man was round-faced, ruddy-cheeked with a head of balding white hair. He wore a long, red leather tunic, brown boots and black britches. He also had large, powerful-looking hands, was muscular despite his age. Someone not to be underestimated, if this quant cottage proved to be the den of villains.

She had the distinct impression he scrutinized her with similar thoughts. *Wise fellow*, she thought and stepped forward.

"Thank you, sir, ma'am. I'm guiding this young lady, Tamara, to Hlanith. My name is Ansell."

The man smiled, an honest, amiable expression. They shook hands, his huge around hers.

"Come in, miss," he said, his voice surprisingly gentle in comparison to his bulk.

"Yes gosh. My word, yes," the old woman added, leading Tamara's dripping form towards a roaring fire.

Ansell smiled, nodded at the man, then headed towards the fireplace.

"Here," the old woman said, noting Ansell's approach.

A Buopoth head hung mounted above the cobblestone fireplace, and there were animal furs on the wooden floor. *So hunters then? Probably.*

Two chairs flanked the fireplace, most likely the couple's seats before their arrival. *Or, they were waiting for us*, a voice of suspicion muttered.

The fire's heat hit Ansell, strong, bracing, and quite welcome. The old woman rushed forward, nervous and bird-like in her motions, giving Ansell unnecessary help into her seat.

"My name's Marta, by the way, dear, and my husband over there is Thom."

She pulled a rag from her skirt, reached between Ansell and Tamara to retrieve a blackened iron kettle from a hook beneath the mantel.

"I'll make you two a cup of tea!"

Ansell watched Marta head past the table behind Tamara. Its surface was dotted with candles, idols of whatever gods these folks worshipped.

A sudden wind, rushing down the chimney, made the fire flicker. It sent a chill down Ansell's spine.

She looked at Tamara, found the girl glancing round the room, the ceiling mostly.

Ansell cricked her neck, stretched her shoulders, and proceeded to remove her left boot.

"Amaranth . . . burdock," Tamara said in a whisper. "They're afraid of something."

Halfway to removing her right boot, Ansell looked up. The witch-girl was staring at her.

"Did you encounter anyone out there, my dears?" Marta asked, puttering about at a corner with her back to the room.

"Hush, Marta. No-one else need be involved," Thom said with a sternness in his tone.

Marta turned; Ansell saw tears in her eyes. "Aldo and Gifford. Our boys." She sent her husband a defiant look. "They went seeking treasure . . . gone three days now."

Ansell raised her head, let her boot drop to the floor. "Treasure?"

* * * * *

Ansell felt warm sunlight on her face, smelled a sweet fragrance on her pillow. The latter was another herbal ward against evil, no doubt. She stretched her arms from the blanket, accidently nudging her companion as she did. Tamara moaned in her sleep.

The room held two beds, but through habit, Ansell and Tamara had slept together. Habit, and protection. Anyone attempting to abscond with Tamara would have her to deal with. A deadly mistake.

She opened her eyes, turned to face the window. The storm was gone, the sky above the forest a clear, heavenly blue. Ansell removed Tamara's arm from her chest, eliciting another groan.

I think she could sleep through anything. Ansell sat up, placed her bare feet on floorboards warmed by sunlight. Dressed in long johns, her belongings lay piled on the floor at the foot of the bed. As always, she had slept with a knife under her pillow.

She turned, examined Tamara's pallid face. The girl's eyes were moving beneath her lids. Ansell wondered what she dreamt of, whether she travelled a world less harsh than theirs.

"Hope springs," she said, stood, and strode towards the window. The sun, high on the horizon, made her blink and fight a sneeze.

Bunches of flowers flanked the window, the yellow kind she had seen outside last night. The glass had four panes, the inner frame forming a target against the green forest beyond.

It appeared so calm without, like the storm had been naught but a disturbing dream. So was this the dream within the dream? *No, I'd be richer,* Ansell mused. She examined the area beyond the forest, the Karthian Hills rising to the horizon. It was a beautiful sight for jaded eyes.

A nearer hill, an island in a sea of luscious green, was different from the rest. It held ruins, a cylindrical tower and the fractured remnants of walls. According to Thom, those ruins had existed for time immemorial, long before his grandfather built this cottage. They had a dark reputation, were supposedly the haven of witches and ghouls. Ansell had encountered both. Neither was as dangerous as a man with evil intent. Or woman, for that matter.

Her gaze remained on the ruins. The tower was where the ghost light sometimes shone. So Marta claimed, anyway. It appeared on cursed nights when the moon rode high in the heavens. And on those nights, a path to treasure was revealed. Supposedly. Aldo and Gifford had thought so. Young fools. The pair had gone there and promptly disappeared.

Ansell stepped nearer to the window, placed her hands on panes cold despite the sunlight. She could barely take her eyes off that crumbled edifice. Treasure. Gold, rubies . . . perhaps nothing but battered silver in the grave of some long dead knight.

Perhaps a lich, haunting the ruins, had swallowed the sons' souls for their trespass.

If it was haunted at night, well . . . she would just have to go by day.

"Uhn. A real bed. Can you believe it?" Tamara's voice was a sleepy purr.

Ansell pulled her palms from the window, felt suction-like resistance as she did.

"We set off after breakfast," she said as she turned.

Tamara, squinted, dragged the blanket over her face and issued a muffled groan.

* * * * *

A hearty meal of porridge and sweet biscuits awaited them downstairs. A tearful farewell from Marta, and a firm handshake from Thom followed, the pair seeing them out as they headed towards the ruins.

The oldsters assumed they were going to find their sons. So Ansell had promised the night before. It wasn't a complete lie.

"On a scale of one to ten, ten being the highest, how sincere are you in finding Aldo and Gifford?"

She looked to Tamara, found her staring at the ground with a grin on her face.

"Dolt!" she replied, and thought, *You know me far too well, girl.* "I think, my smart-mouthed friend, they either went up there and got eaten, or found the treasure, ran off, and are currently whoring and drinking in some less than reputable port city."

They were nearing the forest now. The tree leaves were spotted with beads of moisture that resembled tiny jewels.

Jewels, I want jewels.

The grass was damp, but not muddy. Treetops concealed the hill Ansell had observed from the attic window.

"And if *we* find the treasure?" Tamara asked.

Her companion paused at the forest's outskirts. Ansell turned to find her saying a blessing over her amulet.

"We run off, find an unreputable port city, and spend it getting drunk. Not much whoring, probably."

Tamara tucked her amulet beneath her cloak, grinned at Ansell and stepped forward. Moments after, they were surrounded by trees.

The place was far less intimidating during daytime. The forest floor was mulchy under their feet. Bold branches reached for them incessantly, but gentle light filtered from the boughs above. The smell was gorgeous: the fresh odour of soil and greenery that always followed a rainstorm.

"Think we'll find them, though?" Tamara asked. Walking to Ansell's left, she lagged behind a little.

Ansell considered this a moment. "My girl, I hope not really."

"Explain?"

"It's really quite simple. If they're still up there, then something bad happened."

"Fools rush in," Tamara replied.

A short while later, quicker than Ansell expected, the forest opened out onto a clearing.

The hill was tall, steep-sided, the ruins above bleached white in the sunlight.

"Here we are, then," Ansell said and headed for the hill's lower slopes. Foliage, wild bushes and small trees, surrounded the base. She entered the greenery and mounted the hill. Tamara made noisy passage through the bushes behind her.

It proved an easy climb, mostly. At some points she had to grip wet branches that flicked droplets of water at her face.

"Damn. My boots are going to get soaked again." Ansell slapped the branches angrily as she continued her ascent.

Tamara laughed. "Perhaps you can purchase new ones with all the treasure we find?"

Ansell snarled, then smirked. Her young companion was developing a sense of humour much like her own.

The shrubbery parted, putting Ansell near the top of the hill. The immediate area was dotted with scattered masonry.

She turned, waited for her companion. Tamara appeared, head bowed, with stray leaves in her hair. Ansell offered her hand, which the witch-girl accepted. She pulled her up a little before continuing to the summit.

Built upon a level plateau, the ruin's weathered, uneven walls were spotted with lichen. Trees had taken root within its boundaries, growing from walls and floors. The tower, which had battlements around its apex, cast a long shadow across the ruins. To Ansell's left, a stone gateway led into an overgrown courtyard.

"Seems nice," Tamara said, and headed towards the courtyard. She used the gateway, whereas Ansell took a direct route across the crumbling walls.

"Wouldn't like to be here at night, though," Ansell replied, stepping off the wall. It felt chilly in the tower's shadow. She shivered, and not from the cold.

The courtyard's flagstones were cracked and uneven, choked with nettles and other wild plants. Puddles of water lurked between the stones, tiny oceans surrounded by shores of stone and muck.

Ansell kicked through the wet growths towards Tamara. The witch-girl was bent down, hands on her knees as she examined the floor.

"Footprints in the dirt here," she said, glancing at Ansell.

Ansell halted. The flagstones Tamara scrutinized were coated in dirt. She saw footprints there, some overlapping. All appeared to head one way: deeper into the ruins.

Tamara stood, turned to face the trail. There, the skeleton of a doorway led to an area thick with foliage. It was very dark there.

Ansell shivered again, composed herself and raised a hand to her chin. "They went that way, and so shall we."

She pulled her sword from its scabbard and walked forward. Tamara was quick by her side. As she entered the doorway, Ansell thrashed the sword to clear a path.

A shroud of shadows enveloped them. The air's moist chill dissolved Ansell's remaining good spirits.

"I'll make some light," Tamara said, then whispered an incantation.

Ansell gave up on slashing the bushes and just pushed forward. A few moments later, she encountered a space between the foliage. Although the floor here was clear of weeds, it was still a mess. Flagstones had been removed, revealing a hole beneath an ancient-looking wooden trapdoor. It further revealed a stairway leading underground.

An orange glow appeared, illuminating the top of the steps.

"Great," Tamara said. "Another dungeon crawl."

Ansell stepped round the hole, placed her free hand atop the vertically hinged trapdoor. The damp wood crumbled a little from her touch.

Her companion came forward, crouched before the entrance to stare into the depths. She lowered her left hand, using the light to peek deeper within.

"Halloo!"

Echoes answered her; a sound of wind so weak it was barely discernible.

Tamara looked to Ansell. "Steps, probably some old cellar. You think?"

"Let me go first," Ansell replied, and walking around the hole looked down.

She sniffed the air, found it damp and musty, but not terrible, not charnel like she expected. This was no den of beasts, undead or otherwise.

They shared an acknowledging nod, then Ansell started her ascent.

There were fewer steps than she anticipated. They were a little slippery from the storm. "Watch out down here. Stairs are wet," she warned Tamara. The floor turned level after around a dozen steps or so.

The witch-girl, appearing to Ansell's left, proceeded to aim her light around. The illumination revealed a large, square-shaped vault hewn from black stone. Water trickled down the walls, meeting small puddles on a floor of uneven, hexagonal tiles.

Of the sons, there was no sign.

Ansell cleared her throat; an echo returned the sound to her. The noise issued from a doorway ahead. It led to darkness, the sounds of dripping water, more echoes as she stepped tentatively towards it.

"Damn!" Ansell paused, looked down. She had stepped in a puddle, already felt water inside her shoe. Her anger urged her to turn back, depart this dismal underground vault. Instead she continued forward.

"Let me look inside first." Tamara crept forward, getting between Ansell and the doorway.

"Oh dear," she continued, "You'll want to see this."

As Ansell stepped on, Tamara raised the orb to her lips, whispered to it like a lover making a private promise.

The orb escaped her hand, floated through the doorway ahead of Ansell. She saw another orb appear in Tamara's palm.

Ansell paused just beyond the threshold. This vaulted room was the twin of the one behind them. Here however, a crumpled body lay to the left of a stygian doorway.

Tamara's orb hovered near the ceiling, illuminating the vault with stark light. Ansell strode towards the body. It belonged to a young man, sprawled out with his back against the rime-encrusted wall. A mop of blonde, curly hair surrounded a face as pale as her companion's, though his pallor didn't appear natural. He wore a dark brown tunic, britches of a lighter shade. His feet were bare and dirty.

Ansell knelt when she reached him, heard footsteps behind and the splash of a puddle.

She raised her free hand to her mouth, clenched her teeth around gloved fingers. The leather tasted sour as she pulled her hand free.

"Is he dead?" Tamara knelt beside her.

Ansell looked up, saw curiosity on the witch-girl's face. Returning her attention to the body, she lowered her bare hand to feel the man's neck. It felt cold to the touch, but there was a pulse.

"Alive!" she replied and, tucking the glove under her arm, sent a smile Tamara's way.

This was one of the errant sons found. Perhaps the parents would offer a reward. *Doubtful . . . what did they even own but—*

"Look at his skin," Tamara said, disrupting her train of thought.

"What about it?" she replied.

Tamara indicated the man's face.

At first, Ansell didn't see it. Then, leaning closer, she did. Webs of thin blue veins patterned the man's neck, disappearing into sunken cheeks.

Oh hell, and I touched him. She shuffled back, searched the floor for a puddle. Ansell found one, its surface shining brightly from the ceiling globe. She dipped her fingers in, swished them around before standing up.

Tamara was still crouched, examining the man's face intently.

Ansell shook her hand in anger, said, "Get away from him; he could be contagious."

Tamara stared at her innocently. "I've not seen anything like it . . . Poison perhaps?"

"Let's just go a little further then get out of here."

Ansell pulled the glove back onto her hand and headed to the next doorway. *Treasure be damned, and damn the weather that brought us to this.*

"I wonder if it's Gifford or Aldo?"

She ignored Tamara. *I just wonder what did that to him.*

The following doorway led to another vault. This was a little larger, higher of ceiling than the previous two. Also, and this intrigued her greatly, beyond a final doorway steps ascended to daylight.

"Well, this is unexpected," she said, more to herself than her companion.

"I'll douse my flame," Tamara said from behind. They continued towards the stairs together.

"Oh wait. There's something carved there." Tamara raised her hand to the doorway's lintel. The orb-light revealed chiselled words.

Lasciate Ogne Speranza Voi Ch'intrate

Ansell recognized the letters, but not the language.

Her companion stepped closer, mouthed the words on the lintel. Tamara shook her head. "I don't know what they mean."

"This doesn't feel right," Ansell said, but mounted the steps regardless. The orb flickered out behind her.

She had the irrational feeling they had been turned around, that going topside would return them to the ruins. Upon reaching the steps' upper termination, Ansell found herself gratefully wrong. The uneasiness remained, however.

The sun shone brightly within a clear blue sky. But the sun was too high, Ansell noted; they hadn't been underground *that* long.

"Shiny," Tamara said, and Ansell felt a tap on her forearm.

Something was wrong with the sunlight, the wrongness extending to the blue sky, the green, rolling meadows. Ansell couldn't pin it down. Nor could she explain, after turning her head, how the steps below were connected to the vaults beneath the hill. They hadn't walked far enough for the Karthian Hills to just disappear like that. This was a totally different topography.

"This is . . . weird," Tamara whispered.

She nodded, scanned their surroundings. A stream flowed to the west, disappearing at the horizon. Its babbling waters were a golden hue, beautiful yet unnatural. Despite the scene's beauty, there was nothing innocent about this place, Ansell thought.

"This land."

"It seems bewitched," Tamara added.

Ansell turned, looked at Tamara.

She was staring east. A thick, sprawling forest covered the land there. A snaking cloud flowed up from between the treetops. *Chimney? House? Perhaps some answers*, she thought, and sheathed her sword.

They walked towards the woods in silence, across emerald grass that bore no hint of last night's storm. Ansell looked south, where, in a normal, orderly world, the forest and Karthian Hills would be. This place, however, this land of the unknown, was far from normal.

There was another mental alarm, the distinct feeling she was repeating the events from last night, an undeniable sensation of *déjà vu*.

"They say folk visit other realms when they sleep," Tamara said, breaking the silence. The trees loomed closer, the trunks and leaves bearing the subtle wrongness that defined this place. "And some say our lands are but a dream for someone else's nocturnal slumber."

A dream, were this such, would be nice.

They entered the trees, continued towards the smoke. *A house? A funeral pyre? A manticore smoking a pipe?* Anything was possible.

More silence, more trudging through undergrowth dryer than it should be, and then they reached a clearing.

Tamara gasped. Ansell hissed through her teeth.

Near the clearing's centre stood a cottage. The attic roof shone in the sunlight; a gentle, wispy smoke flowed from the chimney.

It was the twin of Marta and Thom's cottage.

"We haven't . . ."

"No." Ansell knew what Tamara was about to say. This couldn't be the same cottage.

They remained still, lurkers on the threshold of this eerie doppelganger world.

A quietude lay upon the scene. Hills stood beyond the house, but there were no ruins. Of this, for a reason Ansell couldn't quite place, she was glad.

Then, in a sky clear a moment earlier, a cloud appeared. It turned the clearing dark, cold.

Ansell shivered, watched as shadows drenched the cottage, turned the windows black.

"I. I . . ."

Tamara didn't need to continue, Ansell sensed it too. If evil could emit an invisible aura, it felt like this.

The cottage door opened.

Ansell felt the warning in her gut. "C'mon," she said, putting her back to the clearing.

"Oh no… Don't look back!" Tamara said. Her voice was high, frantic, more terrified than Ansell had ever heard it. "My gods, their faces."

They made their escape between clawing boughs, jumped across fallen branches. Tamara panted; Ansell perspired. By the time they reached the fields beyond, they were holding hands.

Then the sun turned black, a hollow hole in an insidious sky. A wind picked up around their feet, assailing them from all directions, wailing like the damned.

Despite the sun's transformation, the light remained bright. The stream continued flowing with gentle, golden currents.

"The sun!" Tamara yelled over the wind.

"Don't look. Don't look at anything." Ansell's reply was half lost as the howling wind nearly knocked her from her feet.

Her eye caught movement, impossible movement from the sun. Something crawled from that circular void, unbearably dark and massive.

This cursed place. It didn't want to let them go.

They reached the steps to the ruins. As Ansell nudged Tamara forward, the wind blew frantically at her hair. Its unwanted touch felt warm, had a charnel smell about it. When the witch-girl entered the darkness, Ansell dashed after her, not wanting to be alone, not wanting Tamara to be alone in this hellish doppelganger world.

Tamara was at the foot of the steps, getting her breath. Ansell grabbed her hand. They went forward together, through near total darkness.

She skidded to a halt halfway through the vaults.

"Where . . ."

Ansell squinted towards the corner where the man had lain. Tamara released her hand, and a few moments later they had light.

The room was empty.

"Gone," Tamara said.

"Gone," Ansell repeated.

"I don't. Um." Tamara cleared her throat. "I don't think that was their son. Not anymore."

Ansell turned, found her companion's eyes wide, her lower lip trembling in fear.

Their gazes locked and they said in unison: "The parents!"

Tamara left her orb floating behind them as they continued their escape.

A mad dash up the steps followed, then they reached daylight, charged through bushes and between broken walls. Soon after, they were stumbling down the hill.

If Aldo or Gifford, or whoever, had left the ruins, there was only one place she imagined him going. A confusing, frightful thought, it invoked a dogging foreboding as they made their frantic return to the cottage.

The forest was still, quiet but for the noise of their progress. The trees here at least didn't attack them.

At the clearing they paused for breath.

The cottage, its rear anyway, stood as they had left it. A trickle of smoke, rising from the chimney, entered a partially cloudy sky.

"Let's . . ." Ansell took a deep breath. "Let's go." She was perspiring under her armour, the pack she had carried throughout their journey a dead weight on her back.

She pulled her sword from its scabbard, dashing around the cottage with Tamara in swift pursuit.

Everything appeared so normal, so innocent. She would feel a fool if they arrived and nothing had changed. A fool but a relieved one.

Ansell leapt over the steps, ran to the door and paused on the threshold. "My gods."

Numbed to her core, she stepped back.

Ansell heard Tamara mount the steps behind her.

The words Ansell found left her lips weakly.

"Tamara, make a flame, the most powerful you can." She looked right, saw the axe from last night. "I'm going to need that."

* * * * *

They left the farmhouse aflame, neither of them looking back. The mewling screams of what she had tried to kill were awful enough, screams that would haunt her for many nights to come. She didn't need to see it still moving, attempting to escape.

Her companion had done a fine job, immolating bodies dead and half dead, engulfing them in magical, cleansing fire.

Aldo or Gifford, the abomination had changed quite radically since their first encounter. She had found his inhuman form doing blasphemous things to his parents.

They at least, had died easily, what remained of them. Aldo or Gifford had taken many cuts of the axe, giggling and howling and too stubborn to die.

Soon they would depart the forest, continue on to Hlanith. Ansell promised herself they wouldn't pause but for the briefest rest. And if the rain returned, well, they would just have to get wet.

Tamara was subdued, quiet as they headed through the forest. Some things weren't suitable for eyes as innocent as hers, or for that matter, Ansell's own, somewhat jaded gaze.

END

Dark Continent

Wayne Judge

1. The World's Weirdest Criminal

A BOLT OF lightning stabbed angrily from the wine dark skies over Manhattan, blasting the tar-covered planks under the feet of Ascott Keane! In a shower of sparks the distinguished criminologist staggered backwards. He was blinded from the strike and numb with a bitter metallic taste in his mouth combined with the stench of burning hair assaulting his nostrils. He tottered at the rain-soaked, wind-swept edge of the roof he stood on. It was a thirty-story drop to the street below, but Ascott Keane had a very special tool to help keep his footing: righteous determination.

Shaking the spots from his eyes, he pulled a solid gold crucifix from his coat pocket and held it towards his enemy. Another flash of light arced across the sky, revealing his target: a man garbed entirely in crimson, a devil-horned cowl covering his face and a cape that billowed behind him like curtains fluttering from a castle window in a horror movie. Behind the garish figure was a woman, pretty, young, and very much in need of clothing. She was strapped into a bizarre piece of machinery with a strange cup-like device over her mouth. From what Ascott was able to discern, the torturous gizmo amplified the girl's screams through some sort of conduit and focused them out the other end into a devastating sonic blast. The terrified girl was merely the weapons ammunition. The spent corpse of the sonic cannon's previous battery lay at the feet of the horned fiend who smiled as he turned the device towards Keane.

"We are too equally matched in the art of black magic, my friend, but I stand supreme when combining magic with science! *Ha-Ha-Haaaa!!*"

The cannon hummed to life as the villain pushed a button, causing a small blade to slowly and shallowly cut the girl, eliciting screams of pain. Ascott's eyes grew wide in anticipation of the blast he had no way to avoid from his current precarious position. With a blinding flash of light accompanied by a tremendous crash it was all over!

Keane opened one eye carefully, surprised to find himself still alive. He took in the scene with grim realization. The terrible weapon had somehow attracted a lightning bolt when it powered up, and it struck the machine, blowing it to kingdom come. Where the device had stood a moment before was now a huge, smoldering hole in the roof of the building. There was nothing left. The poor girl was most assuredly dead, but now at least she would be spared further torture by her captor. Descending the fire escape ladder to a balcony below, Ascott Keane could only hope and pray that his arch-nemesis Doctor Satan had been destroyed as well.

The enormous charred hole in the roof had naturally drawn the occult investigator's eye, but had he looked up he just might have caught a glimpse of crimson fabric fluttering from the water tower atop the same building. It was there that the blast had thrown the evil Doctor Satan. Bruised and stunned as he was, the cold rain helped bring the master criminal to his senses. He watched from his perch as his old foe disappeared down the ladder from the roof.

The mild burns and injuries he had received in the explosion did not sting nearly as much as the fact that he had been once again defeated in his plans by Ascott Keane! The two were both diligent students of sorcery and evenly matched in the skills of mystic combat. The outlandishly costumed Doctor Satan possessed the additional advantage of an intellect unsurpassed in scientific genius, but Keane possessed an uncanny skill of perception and deduction that seemed to even the field on that front as well. If he wanted to defeat his implacable foe, Doctor Satan realized he would have to learn something new.

The blast of a ship's horn sounded from the bay, a freighter bringing in exotic goods from Africa. The criminal smiled as a thought occurred to him: perhaps, he thought, a study in more primitive magic would give his unholy arsenal the edge it needed.

2: The Lord of the Jungle

Ominous drums reverberated through the deep Congo jungle. A mournful sound that told all who understood them one thing: the Cult of the Red Snake was about to claim another victim! Banished into the deadliest and most forbidding part of the jungle by the witchdoctors of more peaceful tribes, the worshippers of Ba-Shza, the undead red serpent, had kept to themselves for many years. So much so that they were believed to have vanished. In recent months, though, many hunters who ventured too far out never came back, and more and more the sounds of dark drums were heard under the light of the moon.

Tembu George sat stone-still upon his perch among the sturdy branches of the treetops. The mighty chieftain of the Masai Warriors listened to those wicked drums and scanned the shadows below for signs of movement. He had tracked a strange woman deep into the forbidden kraal, a woman who was last seen with Tho-Ga, one of Tembu George's men. Tho-Ga was missing, and his chieftain feared the worst when the drums began to pound in the night.

Stealthy as a jungle cat, the muscled Masai tracked the woman from the branches above to a clearing ringed with torches. There on an altar of human skulls lay the bound form of poor Tho-Ga, a river of crimson life flowing from the gaping cavity carved into his chest! In a tall, painted wooden mask an evil witchdoctor danced in a chaotic and macabre circle around the victim. In one hand he held a curved obsidian dagger, slick with fresh blood, and in the other the severed heart of Tho-Ga. All around the madly dancing priest Tembu George counted a dozen naked warriors, armed only with cudgels, which they raised with a cheer towards the scene of fantastic depravity.

Eyes narrowed and blood hot with rage, the mighty chieftain notched a poisoned arrow into his bow. The poison was a gift to him from N'Geeso, the diminutive yet fierce leader of the pygmies. The tar-like substance was instantly lethal with no known antidote. Tembu George would avenge his fallen tribesman!

Pulling the shaft back and selecting the witchdoctor as his first target, he readied his shot. The copper ornamental circlet on his arm glinted in the moonlight. A sudden needle-like prick in the side of his neck caused his vision to blur and his arrow went wild! Reflexively his right hand slapped at the pin-pricked area to find a tiny dart. Arms and legs stiffening and mind reeling, he saw parallel to him in the branches the very girl he had followed! With a wicked smile she lowered her blowgun even as he fell from the canopy to the waiting arms of the evil tribe below.

It seemed like only a moment later when intense heat stirred Tembu George from the blackness of unconsciousness. Or was it the screams? He could not be sure if he had been out for mere minutes or hours, but he awoke to find himself in a dire situation indeed! Truth be told, the chieftain was surprised to be waking up at all, but awake he was and what a sight he beheld. Trussed and tied to a sturdy pole, he was suspended over blistering hot coals like a rabbit on a spit! The worshippers of the Red Snake were *cooking* him! Why then did they seem to be in a panic? Straining his head to look towards a blur of commotion, he smiled despite his situation. For what he saw now was his salvation.

A bronze-skinned, golden-haired giant of a man garbed only in a leopard skin loin cloth was savagely dispatching the voodoo cult with the ferocity of a lion! His eyes were gray, narrow slits and his mouth an animalistic snarl as his dagger claimed the life of one warrior, while at the same time his vise-like fingers choked the breath from another! Several lay dead at his feet already including the masked priest whose head now seemed to be facing the wrong way.

This was Ki-Gor, the White Lord of the Jungle: sworn brother to Tembu George and protector of the primeval world wherein the two lived. He had been born Richard Kilgoure and as a small boy had come to the jungle with his father, a missionary. Through mishap the young boy had been orphaned in the deadly jungle and grew to manhood learning the ways of the beasts. Ki-Gor knew little of the outside world and, though a brutal and savage fighter, he had learned much of kindness and civility from his wife Helene.

Helene Vaughn had herself come to the jungle by accident, crashing her private plane while seeking adventure. Rescued by Ki-Gor, she fell in love with him, and while he taught her the ways of the jungle, she taught him the ways of civilized man.

As the last man fell beneath the blade of the Jungle Lord, he ran to the aide of his friend. With tremendous strength he lifted the spit from its setting and cut the bonds from Tembu George's blistered and shuddering form.

"It's all right now my brother! The Cult of Ba-Shza is destroyed. It's a good thing I followed your trail when N'Geeso told me what you set out to do." Tembu George smiled at the bronze-thewed champion with whom he had shared countless exploits.

"Once again, my white brother . . . I owe you my life. I saw . . . two men run. Run into the trees . . ."

Ki-Gor waved a hand at Tembu George in admonishment. "You are poisoned and the heat has made you very sick. Do not speak, my friend, save your strength. Besides, what can only two worshippers of the Red Snake do? Especially with their master dead."

Carefully helping his friend to his feet and bearing the brunt of his weight, Ki-Gor smiled reassuringly and took to the trail home. The jungle had been saved from evil once again.

3: A Most Unusual Safari

Machetes cut away the growth to reveal a trail through the jungle vines which constantly sought to reclaim the man-made paths. Two hired men acted as scouts and guides closely followed by what at first might appear to be a semi-shaven ape dressed in khaki bush clothing. Closer inspection, however, would reveal it to be a very ugly and brutish man with distinctly simian features. Behind this ape-like man was a litter borne on the shoulders of four more native men. The litter supported a covered compartment similar to the ones used by royalty as they parade through the streets in the desert kingdoms. The passenger within the small compartment was obscured from view by thin screens used to keep out insects. His silhouette, however, seemed to reveal a man deep in contemplation.

The monkey-man was no stranger to cruelty. The whip he held in his right hand was quick to lash out and sting the backs of the guides if they slowed before their master gave the order to rest. As they toiled onwards, a hack with a machete dropped several broad leaves to reveal a startling totem: a carved pole that resembled a pillar of skulls with a red serpent coiled around it. The snake seemed skeletal at its tail, but closer towards its head it was depicted as strong, fierce, and whole.

"Stop!" came the commanding voice from within the covered sedan. The bearers lowered the litter to allow an eerie and imposing figure to emerge. As crimson boots approached the dread totem the hired natives averted their eyes from the devilishly caped and costumed Doctor Satan. He ran a gloved hand over the totem and smiled.

"The symbol of Ba-Shza, the undead serpent! British explorers ran afoul of the worshippers of this deity some fifty years ago and wrote of the fantastic things they witnessed! That is why we have journeyed to Africa. This is the power I seek Girse! We are close!"

Girse was the simple name of the brutish simianesque slave and henchman of the nefarious villain. He now eyed his master as perplexed as ever.

"Boss, couldn't you just learn this stuff from a book? You said those British guys wrote about it. This place ain't fit for man nor beast!" He swatted away an enormous insect and mopped the sweat from his glistening brow as he protested.

Doctor Satan shot an annoyed look at the thug. "They did not understand what they saw, just as you would not, fool! I must wrest the secrets of this most ancient black magic from their witchdoctor himself. This totem alone . . . ." The sentence was left hanging unfinished as the demonically garbed criminal and his entire party turned with a start towards an incredible sound! It was unlike anything the two strangers to the dark jungle had ever heard. It was clear, strong and fearsome, like a primeval rally of some sort. Doctor Satan noticed the natives' terrified expression and heard the word they whispered upon hearing the bestial call.

"*Ki-Gor! Ki-Gor!*" They muttered in a combination of fear and respect.

Their cloaked employer took one of his litter carriers by the chin with a firm grasp and peered deep into his eyes.

"***Testamanos Secri.***" His voice echoed strangely with the incantation.

The native's eyes glazed over. He was completely in the thrall of Doctor Satan's mesmerizing power, a spell to force answers from him.

"What is this *Ki-Gor?* Why do you fear it?"

The native slipped from his inquisitor's grasp and slumped to the ground unconscious. His weak mind could not handle the invasive spell. A disgusted Doctor Satan motioned for one of the guides to take his place.

"Leave him for this . . . *Ki-Gor*, then. Be it man or beast, it concerns me not." With a sneer, the evil mastermind boarded his sedan and gave the command to move on.

4: Resurrection of the Red Serpent

Once, centuries ago, the Cult of Ba-Shza had numbered in the hundreds. Now only three remained. Shunned, hunted, at the last their number was almost wiped out by the white Jungle Lord, but they vowed to rebuild. The worship of the undead serpent was, if nothing else, about resurrection. The two surviving male cultists painted their faces in ceremonial white mud and swore revenge with a blood oath against the Jungle Lord. They would rebuild at any cost and revenge was the first order of business.

The third surviving cultist was the very girl whom Tembu George had followed. Quite nearly to his own doom. This was Gataka, the high priest's daughter. She would be considered beautiful by any standard regardless of race, and she used her charms to lure new sacrifices to the altar of the snake god. She knew from her dealings with Tho-Ga, the Masai she last bewitched, a good deal about Ki-Gor. She planned to use this knowledge to aid her cult brothers in bloody vengeance!

With ceremonial fires lit, the two men danced in a circle and muttered prayers in a language long dead. Gataka shook her father's bone rattle and with dread intent cast a handful of a fine red powder into the flames. Swaying to the rhythm of an unheard song, the three called upon the undead snake god for counsel. They beseeched the terrible Ba-Shza to grace them with its presence! This was the Dark Continent, a place of mystery and ancient secrets never blemished by the hand of civilization. Here the old ways throve still; here to beseech a spirit to come forth was a part of daily ritual. The juju of the hidden tribes was strong. With a pulsating hiss. the face of an enormous red serpent appeared wraith-like over the flames and in an unearthly voice it spoke!

"sssSSeek you one who wearsssssSS my colorssSS! He will aide you . . . he will be powerful . . . yessSS! We know thissSS one . . . He isssSS named of a dark god from another land. SssSSeek him out for he issSS near!"

The three fell to their knees with eyes averted. The great and terrible undead serpent Ba-Shza had commanded, and so shall they obey. The image having vanished as suddenly as it had appeared, the last worshippers of the red snake readied themselves for a guest. Gataka would seek out an outlander in red and he would help them to rebuild their evil order.

It turned out that the girl would not have to look far, for, even as the terrible trio had performed the summoning ceremony, Doctor Satan had sensed the taint of magic in the air. With his acute mystical senses he directed his group towards the source as a ship might be guided by a lighthouse. As if summoned himself into the secret clearing of the snake worshippers, the devil-garbed villain stepped from the vines into view. Like a dread spectre from a forgotten jungle tomb the demonic doctor stood half-masked by the darkness. Just out of sight and behind strode Grif with pistol at the ready.

The three native cultists were startled at the figure and instantly knew that this was the one their horrible god had spoken of. In supplication they fell to their knees. Doctor Satan gestured for his henchman to holster his gun and with a wicked smile regarded the two men and the beautiful young woman.

"This will do nicely . . . . Yes."

5: Secrets of the Dead

Lying on a mat of soft reeds and ferns within his tree house, soothed by the comforting rush of the great waterfall, Ki-Gor opened his left eye and peered down towards his feet with an annoyed look. There sat the grizzled old Pygmy chief N'Geeso, wearing little more than a doeskin loin cloth and a troubled expression.

"Ohh big brother! I did not wish to wake you!" offered the diminutive warrior as he noticed the Jungle Lord's perturbed look. Ki-Gor sat up and stretched his bronzed and muscled arms while stifling a yawn.

"So it was your goal just to stare at me as I slept, then, little one?" he retorted sarcastically. Noticing the completely confused look on his old friend's face, the Jungle Lord laughed. "What is it, little brother? Do the speaking drums of the territory guards warn of danger?"

N'Geeso sat on the floor next to his friend and shook his head. "The drums spoke of strangers in the jungle four moons ago, about the same time your mate befriended that . . . woman." There was a note of dislike in the Pygmy's voice that did not go unheard by Ki-Gor.

"Helene has few women friends. Though Tampani is a stranger to our kraal, she seems kind and Helene enjoys her company. I see no threat from that slip of a girl."

N'Geeso gazed out of the open door towards the crashing and majestic waterfall.

"Something about her is not right. I would keep my eye on her. That is all."

The bronze champion smiled at his protective friend. "I will tell Helene to be careful. Where have they gone?"

"Towards the jub jub grove, big brother. The sacred spot of our ancestors."

Without another word Ki-Gor slid down a vine ladder from the deck of his fantastic tree house to the ground below. Grazing at the edge of the nearby water was Marmo, the great elephant. Patting the gentle giant on his flank caused the creature to bend down, allowing the Jungle Lord to climb up onto his back. Using his knees to guide the pachyderm, Ki-Gor steered Marmo off towards the sacred jub jub grove to see what his mate was up to with her new friend. As the elephant strode along it suddenly stopped. Walking towards it on the trail was a white-skinned beauty. Her hair cascaded down to her shoulders like an autumn sunset. Pouty lips and sensuous curves were just barely covered by the scant leopard-skin bikini that clung to the young woman's body like a second skin.

"Ki-Gor!" the stunning beauty called out with a smile. This was Helene Vaughn, the wife of the mighty Jungle Lord. Sliding down off the back of Marmo, Ki-Gor landed gracefully as a cat in front of his woman. With a fond embrace the two lovers began to stroll back home together hand in hand.

"What were you and Tampani doing in the sacred grove?" asked Ki-Gor casually.

"She was teaching me to read bones. To tell fortunes. She's very good!"

The hair on the back of the bronze warrior's neck stood up and he stopped in his tracks. "Magic? The magic of the tribes is not meant for playing. I don't want you to do this anymore!"

Helene smirked with a hand on her hip. "Oh come now! It's just like reading a palm. Surely the mighty Ki-Gor isn't afraid of a little thing like that!"

Ki-Gor's face grew hot with anger. "It is not a joke! It requires a great deal of respect for the ancient ways." Staring up at the elephant that strolled alongside, he continued under his breath: "Women can be so foolish!"

The remark dropped the spitfire redhead's jaw. "Foolish? . . . *Foolish!?* Ohhhhhhh! Sometimes you're still a pig-headed barbarian, Ki-Gor!" she snapped while cuffing him on the side of his arm. Stomping away down the trail towards the tree house, she mumbled angrily. With a sigh, the Jungle Lord could do nothing but watch her fume away. Marmo's trunk brushed the side of his head as he watched his mate disappear in the distance. Patting the elephant's trunk, Ki-Gor decided he probably should not go home right away. Instead he would give Helene a chance to cool off while he checked on Tembu George who was still healing from his injuries. He had not gone ten steps, however, when a cry startled him from his thoughts. It was Helene! With the speed of Shezra the leopard, Ki-Gor bolted towards the sound. As he burst upon the scene with deadly knife in hand, what he saw stopped him dead in his tracks.

Helene seemed unharmed but had backed against a tree in horror. The object of amazement was the shambling and half-decayed form of Tho-Ga, the dead Masai! He, *it*, moaned unintelligibly and plodded clumsily towards the jungle maiden with a slow, strange gait. The hole in his chest where his heart had been removed was still gaping and insects crawled about within. The smell of rot and decay clung heavy in Ki-Gor's nostrils as he stared, momentarily dumbfounded, at the gaunt, putrid form that he had once called friend.

"Tho-Ga? What deviltry is this?"

At the sound of its name the walking corpse turned to face the Jungle Lord. Its eyes gave off a sparkling red glow. Helene, keeping her back against the tree, scooted around the other side and ran behind her husband.

"Oh Ki-Gor, it's *ter*rible! Tho-Ga is dead! W-what is *that* thing?!"

There was no chance to answer as, with a skeletal grimace, the zombie lunged at the bronze-skinned giant. Ki-Gor twisted lithely out of the lumbering thing's path and sank his knife into the creature's side as it raked by. It was as if he had stabbed a water skin as a foul-smelling liquid spurted from the wound! The stench was death itself, and Helene found herself vomiting almost instantly.

The thing turned for a second attack, and Ki-Gor stood ready, steel-hard muscles flexed with the anticipation of the kill, but a thought damned on the Jungle Lord: *How do I kill a dead man?*

He awaited the next attack while mulling this over—until a familiar battle cry arose. Suddenly dozens of tiny arrows and blow darts sprouted from the undead thing, it staggered back with their staccato impact. N'Geeso and his Pygmy warriors had arrived! Doubtless they had heard Helene's terrified cry and came running.

A gnarled hanging vine caught the attention of Ki-Gor. It was just over the shambling mockery of a man. He leapt into the trees as easily as a chimpanzee and, tearing the vine from its place, he quickly looped one end into a noose and dropped it around Tho-Ga's neck from overhead. Grasping his makeshift snare, he dropped from the trees, hooking the vine over a sturdy branch. His intention was to hang the terrible thing. If this tactic did not kill it, at least it could do no harm suspended in the air. The results of his action were not what he had hoped for, however.

As his weight tightened the snare, jerking its burden upwards, the head of the once-proud Masai warrior was torn from its shoulders with a sickening POP! As the decapitated form slumped to the jungle floor like a discarded ragdoll a sibilant hiss could be clearly heard.

Landing from his jump, Ki-Gor turned in time to witness a tendril of luminescent, crimson vapor writhe out of the rotted neck of the zombie like a snake and disappear with the fading of the serpentine noise!

N'Geeso pointed wide-eyed towards the apparition. "Ba-Shza! Ba-Shza!" The Pygmy warriors muttered amongst themselves in fearful tones as the Jungle Lord saw to his wife who was regaining her senses. Ki-Gor held her in his strong arms causing her to feel instantly safe and in a stern tone he spoke.

"Dark Magic. Nothing good ever comes of it."

Helene buried her face in the chest of her savage husband and, though she did not say it aloud, she agreed wholeheartedly. She realized in that moment that blacks in civilized lands were falsely accused of superstitious fears when actually they retained ancestral memories of genuine horrors in their dark homeland.

Her silent reflection was interrupted by a harsh noise from the trees: the baleful *caw* of a large, black bird. It took flight into the jungle as Ki-Gor stared at the unfamiliar fowl.

"A bad omen, big brother," remarked the Pygmy chieftain. "A bad omen indeed."

6: Noble Blood

"Fascinating!" exclaimed Doctor Satan as he stared deeply into the eyes of the large crow perched on his gloved left hand. "So this *Ki-Gor* is a man. Doubtless some half-crazed deserter from an expedition or something, taken in by local natives." He smiled as he let the bird take flight into the trees again and returned to his task. Sitting on a crude chair, he dutifully inscribed notes and sketches as he watched the two male members of the nearly extinct cult perform various rites of their order. If nothing else, he had gained the knowledge of how to reanimate the dead. He laughed to himself at the thought of unleashing a horde of the undead on the streets of Manhattan.

This was child's play, however. Through discussions and mind-reading he had learned of a spell which would keep him safe from all but the most severe harm. A spell that would make him nigh invulnerable! The altar was constructed and ready, but the key element of the ceremony was missing: the sacrifice to Ba-Shza of a woman of noble blood. Slapping the book closed, Doctor Satan waved a hand at the two men to stop and frowned as he stared at the altar of skulls.

"Where am I supposed to find a woman of noble blood in the middle of the jungle?" he mused aloud.

Gataka moved close and took his arm in hers. "The mate of Ki-Gor is from your land and a wealthy family. Tho-Ga told me of her when I seduced him. If anyone were to be considered nobility here, surely it would be the wife of a man regarded as the Lord of the Jungle?"

"Perhaps . . ." He smiled at the evil girl. Though she had spoken in her native tongue, the master mystic had cast a spell which allowed him to understand the natives and they him.

"Bring me your friend, then, *'Tampani.'* It can't hurt to try!"

The girl laughed along with the crimson cowled villain. The revenge she craved against the Jungle Lord was soon to come! If the nefarious Doctor Satan had the slightest inkling that his estimation of Ki-Gor was far indeed from the true nature of the man, he might have thought twice. As it was, he set his machinations in motion without a trace of concern.

That night the drums beat loud and strong within the clearing where the Pygmy tribe of N'Geeso held council. A powerful evil threatened the jungle, and there was much to discuss. Ki-Gor sat strong and proud in the council circle. He had proved the greatest champion and protector of the kraal time and again, and naturally now, in the face of this strange attack on his mate, the natives looked to the Lord of the Jungle for hope. By his side sat N'Geeso, old yet fierce. Next to him an empty spot marked the position Tembu George would have taken had he not been bedridden, recovering from nearly being cooked alive. The gruff little chieftain held up his right hand authoritatively and commanded the drums to stop.

"The red serpent mist has been seen. The mark of Ba-Shza! They cause the dead to rise against the living and no one is safe until we can stop them!"

The gathered natives, both Pygmies and representatives from other nearby peaceful tribes murmured amongst themselves in worried tones. All grew silent as the bronzed form of Ki-Gor stood, his heroic frame almost glowing with power as the flickering lights of the council fire reflected from his iron-sculpted muscles.

"Two of the snake-worshippers escaped my wrath. I did not finish the job, and I see now that it was a mistake. Evil thirsts for revenge just as the righteous craves vengeance! Brave warriors, will you hunt with Ki-Gor this night to bring this dark force to justice?"

Spears and knives in hand, several young warriors who looked up to Ki-Gor raised their arms and shouted a call of solidarity to the cause. Little did they realize that a pair of unkind eyes watched from the shadows of the nearby trees. From his hiding place Girse watched the Jungle Lord rallying the spirits of the natives. With him was one of the hired guides his master had employed when they first landed in Africa. The native's name was Roko. The monkey-like thug turned towards Roko with an impatient look.

"Well? What's nature boy saying in that jibber jabber language?"

Roko was no stranger to murder and thievery, but even so he had developed a marked distaste for the ugly man and his flamboyantly dressed wizard of a master. He replied with a tone of disgust to Girse's uncultured remark. "The Jungle Lord is gathering men to hunt us down. He intends to kill us."

"Well now, we can't have *that*, can we?" replied Girse with a smirk.

From his belt he removed a crystalline cylindrical tube about one foot in length and three inches in diameter. At one end it was open like a gun barrel; on the other it was fitted into a sort of sleeve-like handle studded with a single button. It was in fact a fiendish device invented by Doctor Satan himself, which focused and discharged electrical blasts. The villain had referred to it on occasion as a "lightning tube." Girse aimed the weapon squarely at the bronze giant who stood gesturing to the assembled tribes as he spoke.

"Time to demoralize the troops with the power of god!"

At the very moment the henchman's thumb began to press the bizarre weapon's activation device Ki-Gor squatted down to grasp a gourd cup of bitter beer offered him by one of the seated Pygmies. With a flash of light from the tree line and a loud crackle of sparks, a bolt of deadly electricity shot through the air where the Jungle Lord's heart had been but a second before! Missing its intended target, it instead struck the crude iron spearhead of a seated warrior and arced down the shaft into his unwitting form. With a scream the man convulsed violently and then lay still, dead and smoldering on the cold ground.

The natives stared in shocked silence for a lingering second, and then panic set in. Bodies ran in every direction as a second bolt flashed out, dropping a young Wasuli who just happened to run in front of Ki-Gor!

Herding his old friend towards the safety of his hut, the bronze champion realized that both lightning strikes had been intended for him! The smell of ozone was strongest in the direction of the trees that ringed the back of the Pygmy kraal, and now his keen gray eyes discerned definite movement. Enough so that, as a third bolt lashed out, he was able to avoid it with an agile diving roll that tumbled him head over heels and back to his feet as nimbly as any acrobat.

Roko was yanking furtively on the sleeve of Girse who was cursing at his poor marksmanship.

"He has spotted us! We must flee!"

The simian-like thug did not take kindly to being treated like the trained ape he resembled and turned to strike the native with the still-smoking lightning tube.

"Hands off, you idiot! You ruined my shot!"

Meanwhile back at the tree house home of Ki-Gor, Helene leaned over the rail of the deck porch towards the faint sounds of commotion coming from the not too distant Pygmy village.

"It sounds like men are being men, my friend!" called a lilting voice from the ground below. Looking down, the jungle maiden spied the smiling, pretty face of her new friend, Tampani.

"Probably drinking bitter beer and telling outrageous stories," she laughed. Helene was glad to see a friendly face. Especially after the events of earlier that day. Ki-Gor had bid her to stay in the treehouse and draw up the ladders so that she would stay safe while he was away for council. Bored beyond belief, she hurriedly lowered the ladder for her friend to ascend, little realizing that her recent acquaintance was in fact Gataka the daughter of the slain leader of the snake cult!

"O Tampani, am I glad to see *you*! Come on up and keep me company." Gataka smiled slyly.

"My sister, come down instead. I have brought you something, but it is by the water, and I don't think I could carry it up the ladder."

Helene had no reason at all not to trust her friend. They had become good companions almost immediately and so she gave no thought to hastily sliding down the vine rope ladder to the ground below.

"A present? That's very kind! Whatever could it be?"

"Here is a sample, my dear sister," said the native girl, holding up a handful of a strange sparkling black powder. Helene stared at the substance with a confused expression. Gataka blew the powder into her face with a cruel laugh.

"Wh-what have you . . . done . . . ." The redhead's voice trailed off as her vision went black and she fell to the ground unconscious. The evil false friend snapped her fingers, and, seemingly from nowhere, two more of Doctor Satan's hired men emerged from the shadows and bore the slumbering girl off into the dark jungle.

At that very moment Girse was struggling with Roko who had determined he had had quite enough of the ugly man's belittling ways. As the two struggled over possession of the electrical weapon, Girse noticed the strength suddenly drain from his opponent even as his eyes grew wide with fear at something behind the thug's right shoulder. With a sudden realization, Girse also ceased his fighting and looked blankly at his insolent hired hand.

"The jungle guy's right behind me, isn't he?"

Roko nodded slowly in the affirmative and swallowed hard. "Damn it. Guess I hafta do this the hard way," sighed the cold-blooded thug. Wheeling around, he swung the crystalline tube like a club, only to have his wrist grasped in the surprisingly Gorilla-like grasp of Ki-Gor. Bones popped and cracked in the crushing grip, sending Grif immediately to his knees in excruciating pain.

"AAHGH! Son of a . . . !!" With his free hand he reached across his body awkwardly for the pistol in its holster. Roko was no help as he was too busy running away as fast as his legs could carry him. Ki-Gor's keen eyes saw the movement of the villain's free hand and knew all too well what lurked in the holster it groped for. Crushing even harder on Girse's captured hand and eliciting a loud curse from the monkey-man he then planted his tough, bare foot firmly into the scoundrel's stomach with a snapping force. The impact folded Girse in half, knocking the wind from him and causing his eyes to bulge from their sockets. The Jungle Lord yanked the pistol free and flung it away.

"Who are you, ugly little man? Why did you try to kill me?"

Girse was surprised to hear perfect English come from the savage's lips. He was also stubbornly embarrassed at being so easily manhandled by the bronze-skinned man.

"Let me go or you'll never see that woman of yours again, ape-man" was his growled response.

Ki-Gor let go of the broken hand, which dropped the electrical weapon with a thud. He replaced his hold with both hands, lifting the smug henchman to peer into his cold gray eyes. What Girse saw in those burning orbs sent fear into him like an icy dagger. Behind the thin veil of man was an animal, a vicious primordial animal.

"Where is Helene?! I will not ask twice."

7: *Mystic Might Vs. Primal Fury*

The red drums pounded and sickly sweet smoke filled the air. In tall, oval wooden masks the two remaining members of the Cult of Ba-Shza danced wildly about the blood-slicked altar hidden deep in the jungle. It was comprised of bleached human skulls topped with a red stone. If the stone was truly red or stained with blood it was impossible to tell. Atop its surface lay the beautiful form of Helene Vaughn. Daughter and heiress to the Vaughn fortunes in the western world and here beloved wife of Ki-Gor, Lord of the Jungle! In ancestry and title a woman of noble blood and the perfect sacrifice for Doctor Satan's ritual.

By the terrible altar around which the men danced stood the crimson-cowled and cloaked master of evil himself and by his side the lovely and deceptive Gataka.

"Hear me undying serpent! Hear my plea and accept my offering!"

As he spoke thus Gataka handed him an obsidian-bladed dagger. Taking the sacrificial instrument he cast a last, lurid look over the alluring body of the unconscious girl before him. The drumbeat rose to a fevered pitch and the dancing men whirled faster and faster in a mad bacchanale of flailing limbs accompanied by wild leaps and twirls!

"The blood of this sacrifice to quench your thirst! Harm to the innocent so that I may be unharmed in your power! Accept my sacrifice Ba-Shza!"

Doctor Satan raised the ancient blade high with both hands grasping the hilt. Like a blood-red scorpion poised over his prey, he tensed to bring home the killing blow!

Suddenly, with a startling shock, the bestial lion's call of Ki-Gor erupted through the clearing! The drums stopped, the dancers turned towards the familiar and feared sound, and Gataka shrank away, afraid of the wrath of the Jungle Lord to whom the call belonged.

A blur flew from the darkened treetops and crashed to the ground beside the gruesome altar of skulls. It was the battered and broken form of Girse. He was still alive but, from the looks of him when he awoke, he might well have wished he were not. Satan glared with disgust at his henchman as he left off his strike, the ceremony ruined by the interruption.

"Useless fool!" he snapped at the unmoving thug that lay battered on the ground.

The next form to drop from the trees was Ki-Gor. Even before he had hit the ground his bow had sent two arrows into the mask-wearing snake worshippers with lethal accuracy. Landing with the grace of a jungle cat, his next shaft was released with uncanny speed towards the devil-garbed villain who stood over his wife. But at a gesture of annoyance from the costumed diabolist, the arrow careened away into the trees, much to the astonishment of Ki-Gor. Doctor Satan laughed at the surprise on the bronze warrior's face.

"You dare challenge me? A naked savage with arrows and knives against my power? FOOL!"

The caped fiend pushed his hand towards Ki-Gor with fingers outstretched and, though a distance of several feet lay between them, the Jungle Lord felt as though he had been pushed with tremendous might! He shot backwards with whiplash force into the jungle stopping only when his back struck the trunk of a Banya tree. The wind as well as his bow and arrows were knocked from him, and he gasped for air on hands and knees in the dark.

Gataka emerged from the shadows once more. Amazed at the power of her new master.

"Even the mighty Ki-Gor falls before you! You are truly powerful!"

"Bah!" replied Doctor Satan in a dismissive tone. "That mere mortal was hardly a challenge, much less a threat."

To his surprise, however, the golden haired warrior had regained his senses and with amazing speed rushed from the dense vegetation towards him once more, teeth bared like an animal and bloodlust in his eyes!

Doctor Satan made a practiced, intricate gesture with his hands.

"Manos Impedos!"

Eldritch chains and shackles visible only to the victim of the spell and its caster appeared on Ki-Gor's wrists and ankles. His movement was slowed to a crawl like an ant caught in molasses. Satan laughed.

"You do have spirit, my savage friend! But my magic gives me power over the will of most any man. I will allow you to die knowing that there really was little you could do to save your woman. You are, after all, only a man."

Doctor Satan readied a final spell to dispatch the struggling jungle hero. As he looked into his would-be foe's eyes he hesitated, what fire of will!

Chained by the ghostly shackles, Ki-Gor strained his steel muscles in agony against their hold. He heard the mocking laughter of the strangely garbed outlander. He saw the chuckling form of the girl he knew as Tampani. He saw the helpless form of his mate upon the altar, and he knew there was nothing he could do against the strange powers this evil man wielded. So with no hope and no recourse, he let go of his humanity.

There was no Richard Kilgour anymore, there was no trace of civility or humanity, no Lord of the Jungle. There was only Ki-Gor the savage. A beast which survived because it could conquer all other beasts within the primordial world in which it had been orphaned. If Helene had been awake to see her husband, she would scarcely have recognized the snarling animal that growled at the startled villain even as he broke free of his mystical bonds!

"Th-that's im*pos*sible!" cried Doctor Satan. He had not even time to think as Ki-Gor was upon him. Like a lion that must kill or be killed, Ki-Gor rained down a volley of vicious blows that sent the refined but evil mystic sprawling to the ground spitting blood and broken teeth. He could feel that two of his ribs had been broken by the surprise ferocity of the jungle man.

Standing over his foe with spittle flying from his mouth, Ki-Gor reared back his head and unleashed his fearsome cry once more. Gataka fled with heart pounding into the jungle as fast as she could.

Cold gray eyes locked onto Doctor Satan, and a gleaming knife leapt from its scabbard into the hand of its master. Satan with painful breaths scampered backwards up to his feet and concentrated on the fallen obsidian dagger that lay near the altar. Doctor Satan was a man of mystical and scientific genius, but he also possessed the mental ability of telekinesis, the power to move objects with his mind. Focusing on the ritual knife, he caused it to shoot from the ground towards the savage hero. It was a sudden attack, but even so the agility of Ki-Gor saved him from a lethal blow. As he twisted aside, the dagger pierced him in his left shoulder, blood quickly dying the black blade. It began to glow.

Ki-Gor yanked the dagger from his shoulder and threw it to the ground. The pain of the strike snapped his mind back from his bestial reversion and as humanity resurfaced he turned once more to Doctor Satan, only to find him surprisingly quiescent. Having his jaw broken by the savage, rapid-fire assault of the Jungle Lord, the absurdly costumed criminal found himself unable to properly utter the verbal incantations required for his attack spells. So enervated with pain was he that he could not even marshal his mental powers. And worse yet, the dagger had drawn blood. The *mystic* dagger. Satan realized his fatal error far too late. The blade shimmered and gave off a steadily increasing red glow. A sibilant voice echoed through the jungle night, seemingly from everywhere at once.

"Ba-sssSShza demandssss a price for hiss sssummoning mortal! No blood of a noble woman? Then I take YOU who wielded the black blade!"

Unearthly luminescent crimson tendrils slithered from every shadow in the area. Like ghostly snakes they coiled about the cloaked form of Doctor Satan, hissing and biting! More and more wrapped themselves about his form and, with a pleading last look towards Ki-Gor, he ran into the jungle with the horrible spectral snakes following. They paid no mind at all to the Jungle Lord as Ki-Gor lovingly lifted Helene from the altar and caught a low vine with an effortless leap. As he sped away from the nightmarish scene, he tried desperately to forget the feral beast he had momentarily become. Helene would thankfully remember nothing of her misadventure when next she awoke. Ki-Gor was almost certain the bizarre red-garbed sorcerer had met his end, yet he had learned from his past mistakes. He would search for him come the dawn lest yet another defeated enemy come back for revenge.

As the Jungle Lord swung from vine to vine back to friends and a warm fire, Gataka found herself out of breath and panting in an unfamiliar part of the jungle. She was unsure of the ability of her new master to defeat the savagery of Ki-Gor. She would journey to a different land and bide her time until she could rebuild Ba-Shza's followers once more. Until then she would do what she always had, use her powers of seduction to survive. The sounds of revelry drew her ear from nearby.

"Good," she thought smugly. "My womanly charms will gain me trust and shelter."

Stepping into a small, mud-walled village, she spied several strong male warriors dancing about a fire in a circle. Smiling coyly, she strolled seductively towards them. The dancing stopped as one of the men noticed her, and as they turned she could see their tribal markings. Her blood went cold.

White paint streaked in patterns mimicking a skeleton covered their black flesh, and they smiled at her with sharp, filed teeth. These were the Du'Ani, a tribe of head-hunting cannibals. As strong hands led her towards an enormous bubbling black kettle she fainted at the thought of her fate. Often the jungle metes out its own unique brand of justice.

THE END

The Garden of Xylom Phom

Glen M. Usher

Snowfall in Dalakh

IT WAS MID-winter in the city of Dalakh, and the elemental spirits were blowing a rare, huge cold front from the great frozen southern landmass to this shimmering jewel of a city in southern Lemuria, clothing its rooftops and shining temple spires now beneath a veritable white mantle. Strangers to such weather, the city's residents cowered inside, while those less fortunate who had no shelter were welcomed in by those temples and the alms houses.

Varla of Valkarth chewed over the remains of her bouphor steak and re-fried sweet corribor roots. It had all been a bit too spicy for her; still it all went down very well when you hit the third flagon or so to wash it all down. Still, none of this bothered the warrior maid overmuch: her blood was that of the high-plateau tribes, well inured against the freezing ice and snows which far exceeded those the city of Dalakh was now enduring.

It was a less-than-busy night in this tavern where she frequently holed up, The Sark of Yezgeg Chun. It was an out-of-the-way watering hole by the wharf on the riverfront of Dalakh, sufficiently obscure to escape the usual patrols carried out by the Watch, whose palms were well-greased with smugglers' gold.

An Errand fit for a Fool

She belched appreciatively as the innkeep's new assistant, Kardus Voy, wiped the table tops with a dirty rag, turfing out all the old plates and flagons. He was some years Varla's junior and the nephew of the innkeep, Sardus Jome.

Her soft belch served to attract his attention. He dropped what he was doing and came over to her. This drew her attention as her senses sprang from her slightly tipsy state. "What is it, Kardus? Are the Watch about to raid? I can make for the back through the scullery. Or the upper landing, of course; last raid, they blocked the scullery . . . hope they haven't wised up and blocked that landing or I'm really . . ."

"No, Varla, nothing like that. I'm just seeking some advice." Varla was taken aback. "Surely not from me? I'm not any good at that, Kardus. Don't ever consider a life of thievery, 'cause your nerves will be torn to shreds. Me, I've a knack for it, born on the high plateau. It's in the blood, you know. I doubt the likes of you would take to that life. Kardus Voy, you're a student. Study hard, enter the employ of the Sark. You might even become head of his parliament or an envoy. Enjoy a life of soft beds and lush, spiced food, also a paunch and gout."

She was slurring just a little at this point and decided maybe she'd imbibed sufficient for one night.

"No, it's about a girl, Tarqina."

Varla frowned and squinted her eyes just a little. "Tarqina, that woman of means that they say is buying up much of the warehousing over by the wharf; it's said she's a wealthy widow? Haha, surely you could do better for yourself than that, Kardus, though they do say she's quite a dish! Maybe you like them older, heh?" She landed a playful slap upon his slender and sinewy hindquarters, to which he laughed in an awkward fashion.

"Well, it's her on whom I've pinned my desires," he said, summoning up a dash of dignity. "Maybe I *have* sought advice in the wrong quarter . . . sorry to have imposed on your drinking time, Varla."

"Come now, Kardus, no need for that. Simpering is a most unbecoming trait. Go ahead, lad, I'm listening. What is your plan to woo this fancy woman of yours?"

"Oh, and what is this?" remarked Varla as she spotted a shiny object just barely visible protruding from his smeared apron. She deftly plucked it away, examining it in the dreary light of the dim oil lamps in the corners of the tavern.

"It's something she gave me, a token of our love. "

Varla's face broke into a sneer. "I truly hate to impart this news to you, Kardus, but this isn't worth a flagon of Boupher piss."

He pulled up one of the crude wooden stools so he could sit as close to Varla as he could and not be overheard by the other patrons, not that there were too many on this night.

"Do you know those lovely and well-tended gardens up on the third rise past the Thieves Cemetery? Just adjacent to the temple of Kadjie? It is there where they grow the black roses of Xylom Phom. Tariqa desires one such rose, and I plan to go there tonight and cut one from the inner tier of that garden."

"That accursed garden and those blooms are a lure for gullible fools, Kardus! You place your life at grave peril. They are laid as bait for the likes of you! That whole quarter is evil, even the Guild of Thieves hold the place in dread! Methinks you're being made a fool of, or this woman is knowingly sending you to your doom."

"This coming from you Varla? I thought you were one of the greatest thieves in Dalakh? I think you lose your edge a bit; mayhap you should lay off the ale?"

Varla's rage now rose to the surface as she reached over and grabbed the youth by his smock and hauled him across to her, her face and his almost touching.

"You young fool, you come to me for advice and throw it back in my face! Why, I'll . . ."

At this there was a sudden *bang*, and a harsh and tremendously loud voice cried out, "Everyone remain where you are, I am Captain Stefak, of the Watch! There has been a robbery this night. The governor of the wharf district's manse has been breached!" Men armed with pikes and swords then began ransacking the tavern, roughly grasping the patrons.

Kardus had turned around to observe the commotion, suddenly realizing Varla had released him. When he turned back around, Varla was nowhere to be seen. As the men tore up the tavern in a vain attempt to find their elusive prey, Kardus chuckled to himself, "Ha, Varla, yes indeed, it seems you *did* have a good night." The jewel he was showing Varla was gone, too. "I, too, have somewhere to be tonight." With that thought, he made towards the scullery to gather some things for the task he had in mind for this very night.

Tariqa

She jumped and scurried, carefully judging all the landing spots as well as her finely-honed skills could manage, rarely misjudging her leap from one building to the next with the sure-footedness of a snow Vandar, the predator cat of the crags and ice-crevices of Valkarth. In due course she found herself veering into the wharf quarter, by the riverside where the barges were loaded for their trip down to the gulf.

Gaining a foothold on a large lotifer tree, now bent over with the weight of the snow, she was soon clambering in among its higher branches, overlooking what had been one of the many warehouse buildings of the district, but which had now been altered quite extensively. Its high, crude stone and mortar wall now contained within it what appeared to be a huge garden within a glass structure, lit with strange crystalline devices on high posts. Varla had never seen the like of them before: devices which stored and emitted captured sunlight.

About the course of the long, elliptical wall encircling this strange garden encased in the glass dome were strange mirror-like refraction devices located at carefully measured intervals, but now it seemed their effectiveness was shutting down as snow began covering them and the lighting grew steadily dimmer.

In a rare misstep, she slipped off the rim of the wall onto the snow-laden tree branches below her. Varla landed awkwardly, dislodging some snow and debris which almost landed on the head of a guardsman patrolling below her.

"Who dares creep about up there?!" He screamed into the blackness above him, raising his long pike in threatening fashion up towards the unseen foe. With all the commotion, another guardsman soon appeared from out of the pitch darkness, clad similarly to the other although more slender of frame. "What the hell was *that*, Krosis?"

"Someone is up there, lurking in the dark amid the snow! Part of the guttering almost brained me, look . . ." The second man grinned, "In order to be brained would require a brain to start with, Krosis! The roofs and gutters all across the city are collapsing under the snow this night. This city wasn't built for such rare snowfall as this." Krosis smirked at this man whom he disliked tremendously. "Shows what *you* know, Grinko, you scrawny-rumped bigmouth! One day I'll show you. Near twenty years I've served, and I know but one thief who is so fleet of foot upon the rooftops, that she-hellion Varla."

He pointed to the scar across his chin, "It was her that gave me this a while ago, one in the torso, too, lucky for me she missed my vitals. She got clean away! The surgeon was able to fix me up. If I ever lay my hands on that wench again, I'll wring her scrawny neck, make no mistake." Grinko replied, "Krosis, how much have you been drinking on the sly? You're jumping at shadows! Now keep your mouth shut or Lady Tarqina will have us up there patrolling the rooftops looking to follow your imaginary hellion."

Varla listened to all of this out of sight up on her perch.

She crept further along, carefully keeping to the wall's center and maintaining silence as she surreptitiously crept onwards.

The glass structure within the wall contained what appeared to be a vast jungle of greenery, tall-stemmed flowering plants of indeterminate color given the dim light, but they occupied almost the whole interior of the dome. A great many pots of seedlings of the same plant were scattered about all over the place.

Two figures carried on a conversation below her at one of the entrances to the glass structure, Varla was now within earshot and listened in. The two were unaware of their eavesdropper up above, in among the rapidly falling and settling snows.

One of them was a woman, doubtless the woman of whom Kardus had spoken: she looked tall and lithe, her black mane of hair marked out by a noticeable white streak betraying her age belying her otherwise flawless form. She was attired as one would expect among the aristocratic and wealthy mercantile classes of the city: in expensive silks, sturdy leathern boots, and an expensive fur-lined cloak to keep the unearthly chill at bay.

By her side was a stooped character, a man of thinned and greying hair, attired in a white apron and smock with bandy legs. This was her apothecary, the vile Dornang. With manifest urgency, he hissed, "I must have those cuttings from Xylom Phom's garden! It is essential if I am to cultivate this genus, this type."

The woman replied, "The men I sent to get those cuttings never returned. They are a cowardly and superstitious bunch, and the rest now refuse to go. So this very night I have sent another who shall have better fortune procuring these cuttings. And should *he* fail, well, there shall always be another young stripling right for the task."

"My dear Lady Tariqa, why do we not merely gather a force of men, storm that garden, put this Xylom Phom and his man to the sword? We could then take all the cuttings and plants we need and be done with it."

"Have you taken leave of your senses, Dornang? Xylom Phom wields power and influence with the Sark! Our heads would surmount the chopping block! Such crudeness is not my style, well, not *usually* in any event. No, much simpler to send some poor beguiled dupes to carry out this task, leaving no trail leading back to us." A smile crossed her evil yet beautiful face. Consider also the added bonus: you say these devil blooms require much blood, whether that of beast or man? Well, either way, soon they shall dine in opulence and plenty."

Dornang smirked. "Ah, your feminine wiles, Lady Tariqa! Potent magic indeed!"

* * * * *

"What is the trouble out there, Grinko? The noise and commotion disturb me! Is it that big bufoon Krosis again?"

"It is merely nothing, Lady Tariqa, just him jumping at shadows again. I suspect he's been on the grog again; he acts like this from time to time."

At this Varla, silently spying, stiffened: surely this could not be the "girl" Kardus was set upon? Beautiful, yes, but she could be his mother!

"Take me out there now, Grinko!" snapped Tariqa.

It was there they came upon the bulky Krosis, still peering up into the darkness from whence the disturbance had come.

Tariqa dug in the pile of snow and debris that the nocturnal intruder had dislodged from the roof. Something gleamed there, and she retrieved it.

"The worthless carbuncle I gave to that young fool Kardus Vol yesterday . . . how did some thief come upon it?" Her face twisted in a fit of rage.

"My plans are compromised. Grinko, get some men together. This night we shall pay a little visit to the Garden of Xylom Phom and see who turns up!"

* * * * *

Varla made her way with all the haste her supple and lithe form could muster, leaping from building to building like she would have done amongst the rocky crags and crevices of her Valkarth homeland far to the north. She knew very well the dread tales which surrounded the Garden of Xylom Phom, the stories circulating within the ranks of the Thieves Guild. The very place that their members shunned with superstitious dread, the place where the guileless youth Kardus must now be going to his doom, duped by the wanton Tariqa. By the frosted beard of Father Gorm, this she could never allow!

Ere long she reached the quarter of religious cults. The shimmering spires of the temples hove into to view. Then she spotted it, the Garden of Xylom Phom, situated adjacent to the Thieves' Cemetery. The snow which lay thickly all around for some reason did not settle in this bleak and evil place. Doubtless it was some wizard's spell that could control the climate and the weather in such a domain as this.

Her sharp eyes scanned everywhere for some sign of the youth but found none. The garden was very verdant for this time of year. Without a deep blanket of snow obscuring its design, it could be seen that the garden was arranged in many tiers.

Then Varla spotted him, the youth Kardus, in among the beautifully tailored and yet strangely vile array of the necromancer's beloved blooms. At that very moment the idiot youth was using a blunted knife which he had appropriated from the scullery to snip one of the accursed blooms. As he cut at the stems of the wizard's evil flowers, they began emitting some noxious fumes. The youth began to falter and to stagger. Kardus managed to place the cut flowers into a small bag. He then turned around and headed up to the pathway and the gate which led out from this evil place, but he was staggering like a drunkard.

Varla looked on as the lad collapsed upon the shingles of the footpath. She climbed down from her position in the high tree, keen to render aid to the impaired youth. But before she could do anything, two figures emerged from the shadows, one a tall, skeletal man with a shaven head, the other his small and stooped companion. Vrla had not seen them approach.

Very approached the figure of the fallen youth. The short man let out a horrid cackle. "There's another one for the lovely blooms to suck dry."

A faint recognition blazed in Varla's eyes as she realised who these men were, this was indeed the necromancer Xylom Phom and the infernal gardener Pengryn. "Move him over to the flower beds," snapped the tall figure to the dwarf. "The lovelies will dine well tonight."

Varla approached the two men under the cover of the shadows of the poorly lit garden. All of a sudden, tendrils and limbs began to writhe and to quiver as the infernal plants wrapped themselves around the stricken youth. Their colour rapidly changed as they ingested the steaming blood of the youth, and the two men looked on with knee-slapping amusement at his predicament.

Varla, on the other hand, could bear it no longer, she broke cover and went directly at the two men. Her razor-sharp sword flew from its sheath, and the hideous head of the wizard was separated from its trunk and landed face-down into the flower beds. Feeding frenzy ensued as the carnivorous flowers drank deep of the steaming blood.

The hunchback turned and screamed but an instant later was transfixed by her sword. He let out a sigh and fell backwards into the wriggling mass of blooms. Recognizing these mindless things as her real enemy, the Valkarthan swordsmistress turned to hacking furiously at the writhing blossoms, freeing the youth and dragging him clear of them.

Kardus groaned from the large amount of the narcotic he had ingested as Varla shook him and tried to massage some life into his limbs.

Just when it seemed that things were looking up, more figures appeared from behind the wall by the gate of the garden. These figures Varla recognised: at their head stood the tall, beautiful Tariqa, her face twisted in an evil smirk. She was accompanied by four armed men. All easy targets—except that her sword lay out of her reach where she had been hacking at the flowers.

She stood up to face her enemies, perhaps to make for her sword a short distance away, but before she could do anything she felt a vice-like grip around her middle and the life being squeezed from her. In mere moments, the world went entirely black for Varla.

Some time later, she knew not how long, Varla began to stir. Her senses began to revive, albeit with a vague throbbing. She opened her eyes and at once surmised where she was, back at the warehouses by the wharf, flat on the ground, now covered in the snowy mantel.

Various figures looked down at her, faces she recognised, foremost among them the woman Tariqa. "Ha, I see you begin to stir, Varla!" She looked her up and down, and Varla rose to a seated position, finding her arms and feet bound when she tried to move. One of those who stood next to Tarqina was the big burly one whom she had meet some six months before, the one she had given as a memento a facial scar when she had escaped his vice-like grip.

"Korvis here has an old score to settle with you. Just now he damn nearly crushed all life from you, Varla. Lucky for you, I interceded on your behalf. After all, you shall soon find we have an actual use for you and the youth, Kardus. You have actually all played useful parts. You see, I coveted those evil blooms sired by the necromancer Xylom Phom, determined to them grow within my own greenhouses. As you see, they possess great narcotic properties and foster an addiction. I now have all the cuttings I require to sire my own supply. My expert apothecarist Dornang shall distil their properties."

"So *that*'s why you have been buying up warehouses and properties hereabouts?" came Varla's reply.

"Quite true! Of course, the ongoing cultivation will require a steady supply of human blood in order the nourish the seedlings to maturity. Animal blood seems not entirely adequate, especially seeing as we've been having some rather inclement weather recently."

She got up close to Varla's face. "I offer you a bargain, Varla. I've knowledge of you and your exploits as a thief in these parts, the only woman to my knowledge ever to have done so. I likewise cut my swathe as a woman in this hard world of the mercantile, and I thrive! You could join me! You have intelligence and guile and you'd make for a welcome change from these idiots I'm surrounded with, day in and day out! I'll cut you in for a percentage. She paused, "Caravans and barges carrying the distilled narcotic will make us all rich, the very length and breadth of . . . "

The men behind her all began to shuffle and move about nervously at her rant; it was Grinko who then raised his voice. "Lady Tariqa, you're offering *her* a cut? I thought you and *I* were . . ."

She turned with a venomous look at the guardsman. "You thought *what?* Fool! *You*'ll be the one with a cut, your tongue cut from your mouth! Never deign to interrupt me again!"

Varla stood still for a moment and drank in all of this, then smiled before proffering her reply. "Tariqa, what of this youth here, whom you exploited and used as a mere pawn?" Tariqa raised her hand.

"Within the mercantile world, one must do what is necessary to stave off the competitors. The youth Kardus was useful, even a good lover, though I would suppose a little young for me."

Varla smirked at this golden opportunity. "Well, I would suppose it no small endeavour for you to find one your own age; I believe tomb desecration and robbery have recently been outlawed in these parts."

The calm demeanor upon Tariqa's face turned to rage, as if by magic. Her face twisted, and she lashed out with an open palm, landing a slap across Varla's face. It landed with such force that it split Varla's lip open, drawing blood. Varla was helpless either to defend or attack due to her bound hands. Tariqa then drew her slim dagger from her hosiery belt, waving it in Varla's face. "You'll pay for *that*, you uncouth slattern!"

The great oaf Krosis stepped forward, "Lady Tariqa, why kill the wench? She might yet be persuaded . . ." But Tariqa only screamed and lashed out with the dagger, slashing across Krosis' forehead, just below his helmet. Her lieutenant staggered backwards, holding his bleeding forehead in a state of stunned disbelief.

"Don't you *dare* tell me my business, you lummox! Ha, now you shall have a matching pair of scars, one this slattern gave you, another from your lady Tariqa!"

With this, several of the other guardsmen roughly shoved Varla to the ground, next to Kardus, who now began to show signs of stirring as the narcotic effect of the blooms wore off. For the moment, some distraction commanded Tariqa's attention, while Varla lay upon the cold ground of the warehouse. Next to her the youth stirred, and she heard him whisper, "Varla, be still while I loosen your bonds. I still have the knife I used to cut the stems of the devil's blooms." Their captors were deep in worried conversation, paying little heed to what was going on.

"Very well, Kardus; they seem distracted, and there are but a few of them. Circle around in the darkness, and we can take them. One of them looks to be injured anyway. Keep to the shadows behind the urns and pots. I'll signal when I need you, so don't get yourself killed! Oh, and keep clear of those wretched plants!"

The Brawl

She snuck along the area by the wall where she hoped she was out of sight. She found her sword along with some other discarded items carelessly unattended. She padded silently to where her foes remained in blissful unawareness. Flipping her sword blade, she came up behind one of the guardsmen serving as an outlier sentry. Varla smacked him hard at the back of the skull, whereupon he collapsed with a groan, senseless upon the stone floor. In a moment, she fell among her enemies, hissing like the hellion she was known for being. She grasped the scrawny neck of the apothecary Dornang, holding her razor-edged longsword to his neck. "Now *I* hold the advantage, Tariqa!" she hissed. "Without your scrawny druggist, you'll never cultivate your devil blooms or produce your potions!"

Grinko, Tariqa's henchman, stood at an opportune angle, and from his gordel he produced a secreted throwing knife. Varla's keen Valkarthan senses came to her aid in the nick of time as she turned, and, instead of killing her, the blade embedded itself in her shoulder. As she turned, streaming blood, the loathsome Dornang sprang free from her grasp.

Clumsy Krosis who had been sitting among some pallets and ceramic pots nursing his wound with a dirty cloth, now sprang into awareness. The two remaining guardsmen grabbed Varla, now wounded and not able to do much. Tariqa barked an order: "You two, bring the bitch over here to the blossoms. Let's give her a little demonstration, shall we?" They dragged Varla over to where Tariqa stood. Forcefully, Tariqa plucked the embedded knife from Varla's shoulder. She flinched but did not emit the scream that Tariqa expected. The goons held her over the blooms, and Varla's blood now dripped freely as the devilish blooms writhed and slithered in eager anticipation at the tasty ichor now proffered them.

The pale green of the foliage and blooms were now changing from a sickly grey, then to red, then to a dark ruddy hue as they imbibed deeply of the ichor. Tariqa savoured the sight, greatly satisfied with her handiwork. "Good, good. Now throw her in among them."

At that moment there came a great crack as bits of pottery flew in all directions. Tariqa groaned and slumped to the floor. Behind her stood Kardus, holding the remains one of the pots.

"You were entirely right, Varla: she's not my type at all. I think I'd be better off mating with a slorg!"

With surprising speed, Krosis emerged from the shadows hoisting his long pike, and Kardus was overtaken by a sudden dread of what now befall him. But instead, Krosis lunged and impaled one of the guardsmen who was holding Varla fast. Krosis's blow carried the fellow into the writhing mass of flowers, now excited to an orgasmic frenzy of waving tendrils and stems.

Krosis swiftly laid hold of the other guard who was too taken aback to move. Getting him in a bear grip, pinioning his arms, Krosis increased the pressure until there was a sickening crack, and the man slumped to the floor.

The scrawny apothecary leaped upon the back of the youth, Kardus Voy. "Stop! You'll ruin everything, all my hard work, you damned meddler! I warned Lady Tariqa about you!" His high-pitched hysteria was comical. Kardus shrugged and cast the loathsome creature from him, right in among the writhing mass of blooms. The old man's screech, but this was cut short almost instantaneously.

A short while later, Varla, Krosis, and the youth Kardus Voy were all seated on warehouse crates. The two men closed the mechanism which opened the vast skylight above the devilish garden of blooms, while Varla nursed her shoulder. As for young Kardus, he did his best to stem the blood flow from Krosis' headwound.

"What you did back there was most appreciated, Krosis, bearing in mind what I did to you some months back."

Krosis shrugged his meaty shoulders. "I cannot abide unfairness. That's why I spared you. You'd best get yourself to a surgeon, preferably one who won't turn you over to the Watch for a reward. As it happened, I know one such."

"Don't concern yourself on my account, my friend. I shall be just fine. Those of my race have great powers of healing and resilience, or so a sorcerer from Saar once told me. Here, take this." She tossed him a bag of gold coins that she'd been keeping in her belt. They were embossed with the emblem of the governor whose manse had been ransacked this very night. "Mayhap it shall make amends for what I did to you, keep you in ale for a bit. But what of Tariqa?"

"Varla, she's gone. I just went to check on her. I was afraid I might have killed her, but she was unconscious but breathing fine. I returned in a few minutes to check her again, and she was gone."

"Did the plants get her?" Kardus pondered.

"No, they seem dormant for now. They've had their fill, and I pulled her out of their path. I wanted to see her face justice. Grinko is also unaccounted for, but I think we should be gone.

Kardus opined, "Mayhap we should have finished her off whilst the chance to do so was ours. I'd way sooner those hell-blooms had consumed her!"

"Not sure that would have worked Kardus," replied Varla. "I think there's a form of comradeship between blood-suckers. I don't think we should waste time trying to hunt her; let's just be gone from here before she brings the Watch down on our heads." With that the three crept off into the night, into the rapidly thickening snowfall which now threatened to overwhelm the city of Dalakh. But from the enveloping darkness, eyes observed them, eyes which burned with loathing and vengeance.

THE END

The Tomb of the Titan

Robert M. Price

i. Entombed in a Book

SIMON SAT IN his rented garret above the bustling cobbled street outside. Most foot traffic had subsided with the departure of Helios from the skies above the old Philistia, now part of Samaria. Only the dawn of darkness signaled the less reputable dwellers in the ancient town of Gitta that it was their turn to tread the winding lanes, engaged in dubious commerce. Indeed it was from one of these, a dealer in exhumed antiquities, that Simon had at last obtained a crumbling copy of the long-lost and long-sought *Book of Jashar*, whose tattered and stained pages he now gingerly turned. It was a kind of alternate version of the Hebrew Scriptures which gave a rather different version of familiar biblical stories. The book was so rare because the religious authorities were urgent to suppress its heresies. Simon was curious what it might have to relate of his ancient countryman Goliath.

His slow-burning candle illuminated his face as much as the pages he pored over, his broad cheekbones and clenched brows, his squinting eyes and reflective raven locks. He found the passage he sought without too much difficulty. To his surprise, he discovered that the titan Goliath was not slain by young David, as is always told, but was rather put out of commission by the magical arts of an Israelite sorcerer named Elhanan, who caused him to be entombed alive. Or at least so said the ancient scribe.

After this there was again war with the Philistines at Gob; then Sibbecai the Hushathite slew Saph, who was one of the descendants of the giants. And there was again war at Gath, where there was a man of great stature, who had six fingers on each hand, and six toes on each foot, twenty-four in number; and he also was descended from the giants. And Elhanan the son of Jaarcorcgim, the Bethlehemite, caused Goliath the Gittite, the shaft of whose spear was like a weaver's beam, to fall into a deep slumber so that he could no longer wield his sword against the men of Israel. And no man knows where he lies even to this day.

Simon's eyes rose from the page as an inspiration struck him. He recognized that the text's profession of ignorance was a device to keep a dangerous secret. It must have been thought that directions to the tomb were too perilous for the casual delver, worse still for the purposeful interloper. But Simon surmised that the most logical solution lay in plain sight, though the passage sought to hide it in a cloud of false mystery: the tomb must lie somewhere in Gitta, though likely unmarked, the name suppressed in favor of the "official" version of events.

The Magus was intrigued by the possibility that the tomb might contain funerary tokens of use to him, given that Goliath was reputed to have been one of the Nephilim: what fantastic weaponry might lie there unused? And, himself both swordsman and sorcerer, he might be the ideal, or only, one able to use them.

He laid the book aside and donned his black cloak, making sure his gladius was secure around his loins. Complete concealment was not possible given the powerful lamplight provided by the full moon. Before long he had reached his objective, a deserted burying ground. There were no other visitors present as far as he could tell, and not just because of the late hour. Clearly, no one had been interred here for many a year. There might have been a wise owl here or there, mourning the transience of human life, cut short in its futile quest for wisdom. Whispering winds seemed to warn Simon to turn back, but he did not. Wordlessly, he trod the paths of the graveyard, musing that a cemetery like this one was as dead as its inhabitants and by rights should have sunk into the earth along with them. Who was buried in such a forgotten place? Simon carried a lamp, but even placing it close to the headstones still intact told him nothing, as age had completely eroded most of the inscriptions.

His search was bearing no fruit, and he was about to give up and dismiss the whole scheme when he caught sight of a decrepit mausoleum, hardly distinguishable from the mud and detritus that had collected around it, obscuring its outlines. But this he cleared away, only to find no trace of a name, but only a star-shaped sigil. Immediately he knew it for the fabled Elder Sign, the removal of which should set the fumbling forms of darkness free. Simon stood still, pausing to consider: should he dare it?

Suddenly a soft, cracking voice spoke: "Have a care, Simon Magus! Even you may prove no match for what lieth therein!" Simon spun round, all alert, to find the source of these words. Was it his own inner voice, his better judgment rebuking him? But no, now he saw the shadowed form of a bent old man.

"Who are you, grandfather? Surely not the caretaker of this place! For plainly, it has wanted for care for many years, nay, centuries!"

"The care I take is for the fools who upon occasion think to violate the terrible sanctity of the place. For the magic that keeps the tomb's inhabitant dormant frays and grows thin—as do I."

"But I ask again, who are you? And who was it who assigned you this chore?"

"I am called *Elhanan.*" Simon recognized the name.

"So you are descended from him who first imprisoned mighty Goliath in this ground? It is your hereditary task, then?"

"Nay, Simon Magus, I myself am he who banished the Giant of Gath, or, as the men of this time say, Gitta."

Another would have scoffed at this declaration, but Simon lived in a larger world than most, having knowledge of possibilities and realities that the run of mankind sleeps more easily for not knowing.

"Are you he whom Ibn Schacabao calleth *Umar at-Tawil,* the Prolonged of Life"?

"I am not. But he is of my kind."

"And how is it, pray tell, that you know *my* name, old father?"

"I foresee many things, including your coming. I foresaw myself asking your name and you answering, so that now I need not ask."

"But then you saw wrongly, no? Or else you would in fact have asked!"

The old voice emitted a dry chuckle, almost a choking sound. "Why bother, once I knew?"

Simon shook his head to clear it, then asked, "Do you mean to prevent me, then?"

"Nay, for I have seen that you will enter."

"But if I should decide not to enter . . . ?"

"But in fact you will."

Increasingly stymied, Simon replied with an edge to his voice, "But should I? Does misfortune beckon?"

"For *some*one, yes."

"*Arrrgh* . . . . Well, how do I enter? Can I shatter the seal?"

"You need not. Here, I have foreseen that I shall admit you."

Simon thought better of making further inquiries lest he become even more confused.

"Do it then!"

Elhanan stepped, or perhaps drifted, to Simon's side. He bent close to the stone plate bearing the five-pointed star with the flame at its center. He whispered something to it, carefully keeping it from Simon's listening ears. The five arms of the star retracted like the petals of a sleeping flower. The star shrank into a pentagon. When it did, the heavy stone door rumbled and shook, then fell outward, shattering on the ground before the two visitors, who barely managed to step back just in time.

As Simon had suspected, Goliath had been interred with his weapons. His mighty spear was indeed the size and weight of a weaver's beam. His sword and shield were present as well, relics of a lost age of warfare and armament, much earlier than the historical epoch with which the great warrior was associated. But one scarcely noticed any of this; Simon's wide eyes were instantly fixed upon the occupant of the tomb. For Goliath, even clad in his armor, defied all expectation. So outrageously alien was his physical form that it hurt one's eyes just to look upon him. Angles and outlines appeared to shift unstably. Clearly Goliath was a refugee from a different dimension.

He fully matched his legendary estimate of over nine feet in height. His face was goatish. What first might be taken for horn ornaments on his helmet were, on closer inspection, real ram's horns growing out of his misshapen skull. The tree-trunk arms were convincingly human in general shape, but they were mottled and squamous like some extinct reptile. An ungainly abdominal plate had fallen away, its leather straps long since decayed. It had once protected a horrific nest of serpent-like tentacles, now stilled and shrunken. The legs were hooked like those of a dog or a wolf, the foot extending forward fully twenty inches before ending in six toes. The hands, too, possessed six digits each.

Simon was speechless for a long time before he asked Elhanan, "What *is* this thing? Surely this cannot be Goliath of Gath . . . ?"

"But it *is*, my young friend, it is! Would you like to ask him his name? I will wake him up for you . . ."

"I shall take your word for it, O wise Elhanan."

ii. That Is Not Dead Which Can Eternal Lie

The thing on the slab began to stir. Simon noticed and unconsciously clasped the hilt of his sword more tightly.

"I begin to surmise that it was you and not my own curiosity that drew me here, Elhanan. If that is so, tell me what you have in mind. If it is to engage in combat with this creature, I confess I am no match for it. I doubt my weapons would have any effect on it."

"Aye, that is so, young Simon, though you are a mighty man of valor.

But I do in fact have in mind a mission for you. Your considerable skills in the mystic arts will serve us well, I think."

"For what, old man?"

By this time, the one called Goliath was sitting up. Simon's unbelieving eyes remained fixed upon him, though he was speaking to Elhanan. "You must of course tell me more, much more." Goliath had as yet said nothing but, like his fellow Gittite, was content to listen.

"Goliath and I hark back to the dawn age, before the Great Flood. In those days men were long-lived, hundreds or even thousands of years of living, and with scant deterioration, as you can see for yourself."

"Yes, provided you are speaking the truth."

"Yes, given that proviso. You know that Azathoth, whom some call Sabaoth, unleashed Yamm, the Living Sea, to wash away the world he had created. This he did to cleanse the earth of corrupt humanity. And how did they become corrupt? It was the result of the comingling of human stock with the lusting Old Ones. Some now say it was the sinful wiles of mortal women that seduced the innocent gods, others that these deities lusted for the daughters of the human race. But neither was the true cause."

"Then what, Elhanan?"

The old, old man continued: "The cause stands before you now, Simon."

"*Him?* Goliath? I have heard him accused of many crimes, but *this*?"

"Nay, nay. It was *I*. I summoned the Old Ones from beyond the firmament, from Yuggoth, Shaggai, and Yaddith where they dwelt. I took pity upon the frailty of the sons of men, that they fell prey to beasts, diseases, and poison fruits. I believed that the race could be strengthened by an infusion of the divine essence. The Old Ones heeded my call, and thus heaven and earth came together in the flesh. The infamous Nephilim were their offspring. No two were precisely alike. Some resembled Goliath here.

"Fool that I was, I did not foresee that they would use their great powers to dominate the earth and its inhabitants. Hence the volcanic eruption of blood and violence as these Titans battled one another and treated their human inferiors as slaves and cattle. You know their names: Nimrud, Enkidu, Orion, Chedor-Laomer, Gilgamesh, and the rest. The day came when they combined their efforts and strove to build a great tower as a siege engine in an assault on heaven itself. In the end they failed, and most died, all in fact but Goliath, who lived on, as I did, for ages upon ages."

"Quite the revelation, old sir. I'll grant that. But what do you want with *me*? And why bring back that ugly fellow over there?"

Elhanan had obviously expected the question, or one like it.

"As a True Spirit, possessing a spark of the Pleroma of Light, you have knowledge that even I, an ancient of days, lack. I need such knowledge, or one who has it, to complete a design I have cherished for many centuries as men reckon time. As for Goliath, he may prove a helpful ally; having once attempted to invade the heavens, he may be eager to try again, and this time, at your side, he may well succeed!"

This time, it was Goliath who spoke. It was, as expected, an unearthly sound. It was like a reverberating echo without any original voice to make it. "I have a plan of my own! You know what it is!"

Simon shuddered, not at the words themselves, but at the sound of them. He was not even certain he had "heard" them at all but perhaps perceived them in some other way. Elhanan was not surprised, any more than he had been at the fantastic appearance of the giant.

"In truth, Goliath of the weaver's beam, I know right well. That is why I awakened you after a full thousand years of sleep! But be my guest and explain your meaning to your Gittite kinsman."

Simon wished the ungainly being would not look directly at him. His head commenced to ache as soon as the blood-red orbs locked on him.

"My kind are gone. There is nothing for me in this half-world. There is no one for me. And none of it is my doing. I have only hate."

Simon, who sometimes felt this way himself, nodded involuntarily. The hybrid abomination before him was a curse to others but much more to itself, and the Magus could now feel only sympathy for it . . . for *him*.

"Who is it who merits your hate, great Goliath?"

"Those who spawned me and abandoned me to unceasing agony in this pit of pain! Because of my human part I suffer every moment in the human world!"

Simon felt the pieces of a mental jigsaw come together with a seemingly audible *click*. "You were begotten by the Lords of Pain, whose meat and drink is the suffering of all earthly creatures! But being what you are, poor man, their feast is your poison!"

"It is so! I would do anything to end my torment."

"So you wish to *destroy the Lords of Pain themselves!* Goliath, your audacity outmatches even your great strength!" Simon smiled. "How shall we go about it?"

Now it was Elhanan's turn to smile. He motioned Simon to come closer and placed his ringed hands upon the heads of both Simon and Goliath.

He began to intone a chant in the Coptic tongue, and the meaning of it was this:

"I see indescribable depths. How shall I tell you, my sons? How shall I describe the universe? I am Mind, and I see another Mind, the one that moves the soul! I see the one that moves me from pure forgetfulness. You give me power! I see myself! I want to speak! Fear restrains me. I have found the beginning of the power that is above all powers, the one that has no beginning. I see a fountain bubbling with life. I have said, my sons, that I am Mind. I have seen! Language is not able to reveal this. For the entire Ogdoad, my sons, and the souls that are in it, and the angels, sing a hymn in silence. And I, Mind, understand."

iii. Pilgrimage of the Damned

Whether in the body or out of the body, they knew not, but it seemed to Simon and to Goliath that they found themselves mounted on huge winged beasts, known in certain old books as Shantaks. They rode on their backs through the heavens as if they had been flying for a long time, as if suddenly having awakened from sleeping in the saddle. The sensation was nothing new to Simon Magus, since he had many times flown, or seemed to, under the influence of certain rare potions, but the Philistine giant was suffering acute panic.

"What madness is this? We shall surely perish!"

Simon tried to stifle a laugh. "Fear not, mighty champion! It must be a dream. In any case, just hold onto the reins as you would those of your earthly steed! You will not fall."

"Fool! Think you a man of my stature can ride upon a horse? They are no bigger than dogs to me!"

Simon laughed aloud this time. "I see what you mean, my friend! Nonetheless, you need not fear . . . But what are *these*?" Ahead of them appeared a crowd of some three dozen figures, all more or less human in form, but with a menagerie of animal faces, some lions, some rams, others like donkeys, goats, fish, scorpions, serpents, even crabs! With a single voice they seemed to cry out: "We are the thirty-six elementals, the world-rulers of this darkness. Nor shall you twain by any means prevail against us!"

Instinct took over: both Simon and Goliath prodded their mounts forward into the fray and took their swords in hand. The horde of elementals unleashed their own weapons: great clouds, winds, blinding snow, pelting hailstones, searing lightnings. But all these proved ineffective against those who did not fear them. Goliath roared, "With bad weather you think to drive us back?" The swords of both men batted the projectiles aside, deflecting, melting, shattering all as they advanced toward the panicking *stoicheia*. Ordinary humans had no real defenses against stormy nature, but these Shantak riders were not, or no longer, mere mortals. Simon was heard to shout to his battle companion, "We struggle not against flesh and blood but against Principalities and Powers, against the spiritual hosts of wickedness in the heavenly places!"

As the defeated spirits dissipated like a spring rain, Simon cried out, "Look up ahead!" He pointed to a strange sight, a great wall extending across the horizon with no more foundation than a vast cloud bank. And in the middle of it, like the buckle on a belt, stood a huge, fortified Gate. As the two riders approached nearer, a guard appeared from nowhere. To their surprise, the entity bore the shape of a naked woman, wearing exquisite jewels but nothing else. Her flesh glowed green. Brash and smirking, she announced, "Who dares approach my lunar sphere?"

Goliath very nearly confessed his name, but a gesture from Simon put him to silence. "In her mouth, our names would become weapons against us!

"I cannot seem to recall my name, Lady, but I remember your own! Unless I am much mistaken, you are *Onoskelis*!"

In a moment her alluring beauty disappeared, replaced by a great snake with the head of a wolf! But she offered no further resistance, slithering aside as the two riders passed through the Gate, now opening by itself.

Goliath, seeming to have momentarily laid aside his antipathy toward mortal men, shouted over to his comrade, "Most impressive, Simon Magus! How did you do it?"

"By the knowledge that Elhanan lacked. He is as old as Methusaleh and has gathered much wisdom, but he is not a True Spirit as I am by nature. And my training has brought to memory part of the knowledge that is my birthright: the secret names of the Archons. Hearing it, they are bound to let the ascending soul proceed."

"And I?"

"You, my mighty friend, hybrid spawn of the Old Ones, *have no soul*, no more than these great birds we ride." For the first time since awakening, Goliath unleashed a resounding laugh, the sound of which caused Simon as well as the Shantaks to shudder in their flight.

THE TOMB OF THE TITAN

iv. Beyond the Ogdoad

Simon could not but be reminded of his days in the Essene monastery when his wizened mentors revealed to him the secret angelic names—as well as the greatest secret: that the "angels" presiding over the planetary spheres were in truth the Archons, devilish lieutenants of the Old Ones themselves, who dwelt upon worlds unsuspected even by the master astrologers of Persia and Babylon. Simon had learned his lessons well, memorizing the potent names and their correct pronunciation, as only in this way might the ascending soul pass the Guardians of the Gates unmolested. Now that knowledge proved its crucial value. By the use of them Simon and Goliath made rapid progress from one heavenly sphere to another.

What a gallery of the grotesque they encountered! The second Archon on duty was Ephippas, manifest as a pillar of purple mist. Next was Asterioth, having all the limbs of a man, but without a head. Perhaps, Simon snidely speculated, he had lost it to the awful Tribolaios, who sported no less than three of them! After him they passed by Obizuth, a woman's head without any supporting body. The Archon Pterodrakun possessed the face and hands of a man, while all its limbs, except the feet, were those of a dragon, complete with membranous wings on its back. Fearsome Enêpsigos wore a womanly form, but from her shoulders grew two other heads, each side-winged with human hands. Kunopaston was perhaps the most bizarre, having in front the shape of a horse, but the rear part of a fish. As the two riders passed this last one, Goliath noted its similarity to Dagon, the fish-tailed deity of his fellow Philistines. As an afterthought, the giant warrior added, "Samson was one of us. You know, one of the Nephilim."

Simon thought a moment, then said, "I'm guessing the seven locks of his head were tentacles?" Goliath nodded.

"Well, little man, where next? You seem to have all the answers."

"Not by a long shot, I fear. But I *do* have an educated guess in this case. The Pain Lords, who subsist on the sufferings of sentient beings, exist on the planet of Yuggoth, undreamt of by even the greatest star-charters. It is not like the seven known planets through which you and I have just passed but is rather a kind of extension into our universe of an altogether different realm. You have, so to speak, one foot in each cosmos, hence both your power and your torment. Ancient manuscripts refer to this realm as the Ogdoad, the one beyond the seven. I should call it a 'super-cosmos,' in which our own amounts to no more than an atom.

We are now headed into that dimension. There we will confront the very Lords of Pain themselves. What will happen to us then, I cannot say. Great Goliath, you and I are pioneers, trailblazers. I pray we will prove equal to the task."

The Philistine colossus grumbled, "Your ignorance is eloquent, Magus, containing everything but the answer."Simon could not disagree.

* * * * *

At length they beheld a strange and shadowed surface below them. As they descended toward it, they glimpsed citadels of basalt, sluggish rivers of molten pitch, even the occasional volcano spewing forth blackly radiant lava. At first they saw no sign of life, as if anything *could* live amid such a hellscape—but then they were upon them! Winged demons resembling nothing so much as great crabs or lobsters with chitinous exo-skeletons and multi-jointed legs and stalks. None had real heads but only quivering mops of cilia where a head ought to be. Goliath, himself no Adonis, grunted in disgust as he reached for his sword. "These things are worse than the demons who guarded the Gates! Have you no passwords for them, sorcerer?"

But they weren't going to be able to fight their way out of this one. The crustacean host kept their distance just out of range of the invaders' weapons, then unleashed their own: their many legs began to rub up against each other. Their antennae vibrated as well. And this array of buzzing sound waves wove some irresistible hypnotic spell. Whether Simon and Goliath fell oblivious from their saddles or merely shifted in their dream-laden sleep, they never knew. In any case, everything had changed in a single moment. Each found himself alone, or at least thought so.

Simon awoke on a floor of rough-hewn wooden boards. He turned himself over and saw, in shadow, a thatched room's ceiling upheld by wooden rafters. He appeared to have found himself in a sparsely furnished house of some poor farmer or petty craftsman. Once his bleary eyes adjusted to the dimness, he realized he was not alone in the room.

In one corner was a crude chair, cushioned by heaped blankets. More blankets draped a hunched figure, almost swallowing his face. He must have suffered the incurable chill to which the elderly are subject, though he did not visibly shiver. His face looked waxy, indicating some serious skin condition. But, even stranger, his lips did not move to match his feeble speech. Nor did his stiff hands ever move an inch.

"Ah, my friend, you are awake at last, I see! You have journeyed far, perhaps farther than any man ever has. You must indeed be weary. You may go back to sleep soon, if you like. But first, consider a friendly proposition, won't you?"

Still a bit groggy, Simon made the inevitable reply. "Excuse me, sir, but who are you? And how did I come to be here? And where is this place? I do not see my traveling companion. Where is he? And, of course, thank you for your hospitality."

"As for my hospitality, it is nothing at all. Most of the furniture I've had to use for firewood. I wish I could offer you greater comfort. But in fact there is much more that I *can* offer you."

Scanning the empty room, Simon said, "What besides a welcome can you possibly offer, old sir? Have you gold beneath the floorboards?"

"I know you do not desire such things, Simon Magus. Secrets and mysteries are your stock in trade, are they not? And those I may share."

"So I ask again, just who *are* you? *What* are you?"

"I am His Messenger," the robed man said. "And I am sent, in this amenable form, to bestow upon you a great destiny. And great, great knowledge. Simon, would you know, and *see*, the mines on Yuggoth? The Catacombs of Irem, the Whirlpools of Shaggai, the unspeakable spawning of the proto-shoggoths? And most of all, would you gain a taste for the delicious suffering of all creatures? For it is a veritable feast of delights! In our service you may increase that suffering among mortals, magnifying our vitality as well as your own. You shall become the King of Pain! Only worship me and Him who sent me!"

Simon scarcely heard the odd figure's words; his mind was wandering amid chaotic visions of brutality, sadism, the crying of mothers for slain children, the despair of debt slaves, the groaning of the oppressed—and he *savored* it! This, he thought momentarily, was boon enough, even without the promised *gnosis*!

v. Scapegoat with a Thousand Young

Simon let out a terrific scream as he pressed both hands to his seething temples. He half gasped, half shouted, "Get thee behind me, Nyarlathotep!"

The whisperer in darkness made a peculiar buzzing sound, of which Simon must have been subliminally aware before. But this outburst might have been as much of a laugh as this masked creature, as Simon now realized, was capable of. "If you do not trust me, Magus, I think you will heed the voice of your friend. Listen."

Simon knew the seated figure was talking about Goliath, so he looked around the room once more. This time he noticed what he had missed before: on a long table were lined up seven or eight canisters made of some dully gleaming metal (glowing even in this dim light). They were of uniform size, about a cubit high. Each had mounted atop it a set of small, complex devices, one of them in the shape of a tubular horn, flared outward around the mouth. From the nearest came a voice. It sounded like Goliath's as if filtered through a slightly distorting medium.

"You may trust him, Simon. He kept the promise he made to me before he awakened you. You told me I could never ascend to the Pleroma of spirits, not having one inside me. You spoke the truth. But the Lords have granted me the next best thing! I have sloughed off my misshapen body. Only my head and brain rest in this metal cylinder. In this form, their winged minions will carry me through the starry heavens, nay, even to the very throne of Azathoth! Rejoice with me, sword-brother!"

"May it be even as you say, my gigantic friend!" But inwardly, Simon was sure his comrade had been deceived. After all, what about the other canisters on the table? Were they *all* awaiting a sight-seeing tour? It was far more likely that these cylinders contained the heads of victims whose brains, artificially stimulated, were being tortured in unthinkable ways, all for the delectation of the Lords of Pain. Goliath would soon be sharing their awful fate.

"You shall not fool me so easily, devil! Subject me to your torments if you must, but it would be worse for me to become like you, reveling in the agonies of the innocent!"

"A shame indeed! But if that is your wish, you are entitled to it!"

* * * * *

Abruptly, Simon came awake again. A dream within a dream? His ears were assaulted by an ocean of throat-ripping screams, not least his own. He twisted his neck in a frenzy of rude and shocking pain. Not looking around him for anything, he nonetheless noticed the disposition of his pain-flaming body. His head was all he could move; his body was affixed to a great cross of no recognizable substance, neither wood nor metal. It was of no finite dimensions; vertical and horizontal bars looked as if they extended without end.

It was nightmarish: he was not pained by bodily wounds, he had none, but rather by endless waves of awful torment crashing against him from without. It seemed to him that he had been doomed to feel in his own person all the pain of the inhabited worlds. In no time, he knew, he must lapse into the mercy of madness. He knew not how long the ordeal continued, as he had no sense of passing time. He was imprisoned in a frozen eternity of Now filled with shrieking torment. In a split second of lucidity, which only made the agony worse, he cried out:

"Elhanan! Elhanan! Why have you forsaken me?"

And inside his ringing head he heard a still, small voice: "I have not forsaken you, my son. In truth, this is the moment of your victory! The sadistic Lords thought to crush you with the force of universal suffering, little realizing they were cutting off the very supply of that which fueled their existence! In condemning you to the celestial cross, they unwittingly signed their own death warrant. *They are no more.* Mankind will continue to suffer through their own folly, but you have lightened their burden! Well done, thou good and faithful servant!"

* * * * *

The morning sun shining through the window of Simon's rented garret woke him. He did not feel rested and refreshed. He stretched and yawned, trying to recall a dream, or perhaps a nightmare, but it was no use. He washed himself, donned a fresh tunic, and went downstairs to meet whatever challenge might be waiting for him today.

THE END

Black Snow

Pierre V. Comtois

Prologue

Jongular trudged along behind the family cart as they made their way up the shoulder of Mount Monongala. The boy was tired and hungry but his father had insisted that they keep walking, stopping for nothing until they were out of the accursed valley.

With them were his six siblings and thousands of other refugees extending in a line all the way back to the foot of the mountain. In fact, upon a switchback in the trail leading upward to a ridge and imagined safety, he had looked back the way they had come. And there, in the valley that had once been their home with its lush grasses, fruit laden orchards, and fields of wheat, all he could see was barren destruction, an ugly wasteland such as the priests of Ulith had warned was the destination of all who erred in the path of righteousness.

All around the valley, the peaks of the Madmollon Mountain range, which had always seemed to be friendly Guardians of the people, now were truncated, their peaks gone and in their stead, craters belching fire and oily smoke that drifted across the land leaving ash and molten morsels to harry and kill the people.

Those who were left.

For the signs that not all was well in the valley had been there for the wise to heed.

"We must flee . . . now!" bellowed his father two days before.

He had burst into their modest but comfortable farmhouse when the rest of the family was still abed and blissfully unaware of the looming disaster. A disaster that had come upon them like a thief in the night. They had all retired at sunset the night before, as always, with his mother singing the songs of sleep for the youngsters just as she had always done. And Shinya, the youngest, had asked for a drink of water, also as she had always done. And he, Jongular, had fallen asleep thinking of the chores he had to perform upon the morn as he always did.

And then they were all awakened just before dawn by a great booming sound far in the distance. At first no one knew what to think; until their father had thrown the door open so suddenly with his wild admonition.

"What is it, husband?" asked his mother.

"It is the Guardians," declared his father, taking her into his arms. "They have betrayed us. Volunterique has exploded in wrath and even now sends his messengers of death raining down upon us. We must pack up as quickly as we can and flee by the northward road."

Seeing that his father had already drawn the family cart before the door, his mother asked no more questions but began to dress the children.

"Jongular," said his father. "You must be a man today and help as best you can. Dress quickly and crate the chickens."

Jongular had dressed as his father had instructed, but when he stepped from the house, he stopped, mesmerized by the changes wrought in their valley by the glowing nub Volunterique had become. Suddenly, he could see flames licking from what remained of its peak, and another explosion rent the air. Glowing missiles flew in all directions, setting fire to the surrounding wheat fields.

In mere minutes, it seemed, the cart had been loaded high with their belongings and younger children. Wasting no time, his father urged on the family's single ox with a rod of yew and slowly they left their farm and moved in the direction of the northward road.

They had been lucky.

Among the first to sense the danger, his father had managed to join other residents who had chosen to flee before the rest had realized anything was amiss. By the time the family had reached the foothills of Mount Monongala, the other Guardians had also exploded in fiery violence, each followed by gasps and wails of despair from the people. One by one, the Guardians expressed their anger, and the fires from their spewings spread through the whole valley.

Even now, looking back, Jongular could see the village was completely consumed, as were most of the outlying farms. And now he could see the last stragglers, running madly, all their belongings left behind in haste, as a final roar like a mighty beast in the night echoed in the distance. The ground shook beneath his feet and rocks shivered and tumbled down the slopes of Monongala as a great fissure opened up on the floor of the valley. In horror, Jongular saw many of his neighbors swallowed in the yawning pit as it opened wider and wider.

There were screams and shouts of terror, and wringing of hands, and pleadings to the gods for succor from the line of refugees that had evaded that final doom, but his father ignored them and urged his ox with greater fervor, commanding his family to turn away from the frightful sight and concentrate on escaping over the ridge into the hoped-for safety on the other side.

Jongular, a dutiful son, did as he was told.

1. *A Summons in the Night*

"Absolutely not! I forbid it!"

"You forbid?"

"It's not often I insist on my union prerogatives, but this time I insist!"

At which point in the dispute, Mystrel turned on her heel and exited the room.

She and Elak had been in their bedchamber on an upper floor of the dwelling they had confiscated after the wizard Naganos, who had occupied it formerly, disappeared never to return. In leaving, the wizard had also left behind a sizeable treasure upon which Elak and Mystrel had established their domestic arrangements after forming a permanent union. Up till now, that union had been a happy one, one which Elak suspected was still unruffled, with Mystrel putting on an act for his benefit. His lovely spouse, scarce out of her teens, had a playful nature which he normally found refreshing. This time however, she seemed to be carrying the drama too far.

Or was she?

Suddenly concerned that he might have been reading her wrong, Elak hurried from the room and followed Mystrel to the garment chamber where she plied her not-unsatisfactory haberdashery skills.

"Mystrel, you know the country folk in these parts," Elak said after he found her there. "They would not understand your appearing at the spring festival in one of your big city outfits."

"Big city outfits!" said Mystrel, spinning about to face him. "I'll have you know that this is the same gown with which I ensorcelled you when we first met."

"You didn't need any kind of magic to hold my attention," returned Elak, admiring his wife's form among the sheer folds of the gown. Indeed, it was the same one she wore that night almost twelve months before, the one that came with a minor enchantment ensuring that no vitals could be inadvertently exposed. That said, it still revealed enough. Too much, so far as Elak was concerned. "No. Absolutely not! I forbid you to wear that outside of this house!"

Mystrel looked crestfallen. "Oh, pooh!"

Suddenly, Elak was sure it had all been an act. But he was willing to play along.

"No one but me shall ever see you in such a garment," he said, trying not to smile.

"Ever?"

"Ever!"

"You're such a killjoy," said Mystrel, but Elak could tell that his reaction was the one she had been looking for.

"Now why don't you consider wearing this outfit," suggested Elak, pulling a traditional ensemble worn by the local women on festival days.

Mystrel considered it. "Well, I could do something with the bodice if I tightened the laces enough . . ."

"Then that's settled," breathed Elak with a sigh of relief.

Just then, there was a booming knock from the lower level.

"We have visitors," said Elak.

Leaving Mystrel to figure out how to make the traditional dress look as alluring on her as possible without violating her husband's sensibilities, Elak went to the door. There he was met by a man in the livery of the royal court of Poseidonis. Behind him stood a great stallion clearly of a breed from the king's stables.

"To what do I owe the honor of a messenger from King Jovianus?" asked Elak.

"I do not have the privilege of being in the king's confidence, sir," replied the messenger, holding out a folded parchment held together by the king's seal. "If you are Elak of the province of Mondresori, I'm authorized to tender you this message."

"I am he," said Elak, taking the letter. "Remain here. I may need you to take a reply back to the king."

The man nodded and returned to wait by his mount.

Closing the door, Elak broke the seal and read the message. It was a summons by the king sure enough. And although there was nothing seemingly urgent in the request, Elak knew that a message from the king, no matter that he was also a friend, could be nothing less than important.

Still, recalling how he had been instrumental in gaining the throne of Poseidonis for Julianus, Elak knew that any call by the king for himself personally, would be for a service beyond the daily doings of the court or diplomacy with neighboring states.

Without further consideration, Elak threw open the door again and went out to the messenger.

"Inform his highness that I will heed his call and leave for the city in the next day or two," he said. "No written reply will be necessary."

The messenger sketched a respectful salute before throwing himself into the saddle. The spirited animal gave a nicker and a snort, champing at the bit to be off. "Salut!" called the man before horse and rider cantered down the road in the direction of Poseidonis many miles to the south.

Now Elak faced a problem of another kind: what to do about Mystrel?

He had no doubt at all that as soon as she learned of the summons, she would insist on going along and after running through every excuse he could think of, Elak gave up and reconciled himself to her company. Not that he was against it, but he did not know yet the nature of the king's summons. Would it involve danger? The nature of the hazard would loom large in any decision he made whether or not Mystrel would accompany him any farther than the city. In fact, he would prefer that she occupy herself there with shopping than whatever duty he was called upon to perform by the king.

Now, after climbing the stairs to their living quarters, he decided to cut to the chase.

"I've been summoned to the city by the king," he said upon returning to the garment chamber. "I suppose you'll want to come?"

"Silly man! When do we leave?"

"At first light. But please, don't over-pack." And as an afterthought: "And leave that big city gown behind!"

A week later, they entered Poseidonis, the greatest port city in Atlantis. Once inside its imposing walls, Elak found its broad avenues and narrow streets as busy as ever as thousands of its citizenry went about their daily business. The temple district rose as a dividing line between the outer warrens and the homes of the rich that in turn crowded close to the king's palace and its supportive offices of state. On the opposite side of the bustling city were the docks, warehouses, and factories that gave Poseidonis its preeminent position among the cities of Atlantis.

Having timed his entrance to the city for business hours at the palace, Elak headed immediately in that direction. Being a favorite of King Jovianus, and bearing an official summons, he expected no difficulty there.

There was none.

His horses were taken into the custody of royal equestrians, and he and Mystrel were both quickly ushered into the king's private quarters through a rear entrance reserved for personal visits and not for public usage.

"My dear Elak," greeted the king as his guests were bowed into his private office, a cavernous affair lined on every side with cubby holes stuffed with scrolls. "It was so good of you to come on such short notice."

"When the king calls, what choice do I have?" said Elak, smiling.

"Ah, my friend," said the king. "Poseidonis owes you more than it can ever repay for relieving it of a much reviled tyrant. You've already given us more than can be expected from any man."

"Nevertheless, I'm ready to be of service to my adopted homeland."

"Well, then, certainly I am no good host not to have offered to make your lovely wife comfortable," said the king, taking Mystrel's hand and leading her to a heavily cushioned settee. "To tell the truth, when I summoned Elak, I didn't expect him to bring you along. But I'm glad he did! Delighted to make your acquaintance again, my lady."

Mystrel smiled, recalling their first meeting wherein she and Jovianus had pretended a tryst to fool anyone trailing the former senator.

"As I yours," she replied. "You've come up in the world since the days you were a mere politician."

"Don't let the trappings fool you," said Jovianus. "There's more politicking than ever now that I am king."

Elak joined Mystrel on the settee as Jovianus turned to the big logati wood desk that dominated the room. There he poured a golden liquid into three tumblers and, returning to the settee, offered them to his guests.

"Very good," said an appreciative Elak after taking a tentative sip. "Lindoviani wine, isn't it?"

Jovianus nodded. "My only vice."

"But I'm sure you didn't ask me to come all the way from Mondresori simply to imbibe your wine?"

The king cleared his throat. "No, I didn't. In fact, I have a little task I thought you might welcome. I want a clear-eyed opinion of the situation, which would seem routine at a distance, but could nevertheless provide some unforeseen challenges. And I'd prefer someone in charge whose first impulse would not be to tell the king what he wanted to hear, but the unvarnished truth."

"Of course, but what exactly is the nature of this task?"

"A journey. A long journey, I'm afraid."

"Where?"

"To Zhondarf, the most distant province under the rule of Poseidonis."

"That's to the far west, isn't it?"

The king nodded. "It's a long journey as I've said, but we've received disturbing rumors from the region. Fire and earthquakes have driven out its population, or so early reports from refugees arriving in the ports of

Gundimi and Uloodna have stated. No reason has been given for the disaster save that the gods, somehow, have been angered. Furthermore, the governor there, one Jindamus, has been completely absent from the picture. Elak, I need to know exactly what is happening in Zhondarf. For all I know, Fahrer could be invading the province from the north or Sylnatian pirates ravaging the land for slaves. Whatever the case, I need to know what's going on in Zhondarf so that appropriate measures can be taken.

"Now, I have arranged transportation by sea from Poseidonis to Uloodna. I've sent word ahead with the court geographer to meet you there with a pack train fully equipped for an overland journey to Zhondarf. Of course, you'll be in charge of the expedition, but I'll expect you to consider the advice of the geographer who's very knowledgable in his craft. Who knows? Maybe the doings in Zhondarf are not an invasion or the spite of angry gods but simply the vagaries of nature."

"So I am to merely assess the situation and make recommendations to the court?"

"Exactly," said Jovianus.

Elak looked at Mystrel, who smiled knowingly, her eyebrows lifting just enough to suggest an unspoken question.

"Then from all you've told me, I think it might be safe enough to allow Mystrel to come along," said Elak, reading his wife correctly.

The king expressed surprise. "I had looked forward to Mystrel's pleasant company in the palace while you were gone, but if you and she are in agreement, then I have no objections."

"Thank you, Jovianus," said Mystrel, jumping up and throwing her arms about him in a playful embrace. "You're a dear!" And granted him a peck on the cheek.

"Ah, Elak," the king sighed. "You're indeed a lucky man!"

2. *The Journey Begins*

It was just dawn the next morning when Elak and Mystrel and their wagon of belongings were escorted by a small troop of the palace guards to the city's docks. There the fishing fleet was just underway as hundreds of small boats, their gaily colored sails catching the wind, headed for the open sea. Already their nets hung over the gunwales, and sharp eyed lookouts manned the prows. A cloudless sky promised a good catch by day's end, adding to the city's sense of pride as the greatest port in Atlantis.

All about them the harbor was filled with ships of every kind, their crowded masts like a floating forest beneath the city's protective sea wall. Everywhere stevedores, sailors, and roustabouts came and went, hauling freight from new arrivals from every corner of Atlantis or provisions for outgoing merchant vessels that took the city's finished products to lands as far away as Doona and Xotalanc.

"Isn't it thrilling?" said Mystrel, taking in the bustling scene.

"It is impressive," agreed Elak as they were led into the inner harbor where the city's naval fleet lay at anchor, protected by long, curving walls that enclosed the area in a pair of arms that nearly came together forming the only exit to the sea. Strong points were located on the tip of each of the horns, protecting the harbor from forced entry.

The inner harbor itself contained dozens of ships of different size and purpose including biremes and even a pair of triremes, one of which was under sail and just then nosing its way toward the open sea. Warehouses, factories, and barracks lined the long docks, and ships were under construction in the slipways.

Gaining entry to the inner harbor was made easy by their escort, and soon they pulled up before a trim-looking galley whose crew were busy getting ready for imminent departure.

"This is where I leave you," said the captain of the guard. "Bogort is the name of the ship's captain. In fact, here he comes now."

Elak looked and saw a sturdy-looking fellow making his way down the gangplank, still on his sea legs.

"Ahoy there," he called. "Be ye Lord Elak and the Lady Mystrel?"

"We are," acknowledged Elak.

"Then I surmise that wagon holds yer things?"

"They do."

"Avast there!" Bogort called back to the ship. "Some of you boys come and carry these things aboard."

Quickly, a gang of sailors trundled down the gangplank and began hauling their bundles onto the ship and into its hold.

"How soon do you think we'll get to Uloodna, captain?" Elak wanted to know.

"Well, we have an easterly wind today and I don't expect it to ease up for at least a few more days," replied Bogort. "We'll be able to tack against it as we move south, but after we begin the western run to Uloodna, we'll have to use the oars. I figure a week will see us to Uloodna."

Elak judged that good time and nodded.

"And the name of your ship, captain?" Mystrel wanted to know.

"She's the *Wild Blossom,* my lady," said the captain with pride.

"A pretty name for a warship."

"Due to her usual station patrolling the Scented Isles."

"I've heard of that land," replied Mystrel. "You'll have to tell me about them after we're underway."

After verifying with the captain of the guard that their horses would be cared for back at the royal stables, Elak accompanied Mystrel aboard the *Wild Blossom*. There he noticed the rowers chained to their oars were being given their breakfast of gruel and bread.

"They look fit enough," said Elak of the rowers.

Bogort nodded. "Prisoners fresh from the city gaol as ordered by the king. His highness wants you to have a smooth ride and a swift voyage!"

Not long after, with the tide coming in, semaphores at one of the distant strong points signaled all clear, and tugs began to pull the *Wild Blossom* away from the dock. Once there was room, the oars were lowered and the rowing master began a steady tattoo on his drum. Soon, with the air filled with calling gulls as they swooped about the ship and dove into the water to pluck some unlucky fish from the water, the ship glided swiftly through the harbor exit into the open sea.

Once there, the oars were shipped and the sails lowered and made fast. Instantly, they filled with wind and the ship picked up speed. Watching the white foam that gathered around the prow, Elak was satisfied that they would make Uloodna in the week that Bogort had estimated.

By the time the *Wild Blossom* had rounded the Cape of Frnorza and began its westward run, the sails were lowered and the oars took over again. Meanwhile, Elak kept mostly to his cabin, studying maps of the regions north and west of Uloodna where they were to cross. It would be useful to familiarize himself with the area in case of emergency. Goatherds knew of trails not marked on any map and Elak intended to find out about those, too, in case of emergency.

The rest of his time was spent with Mystrel, her long locks streaming in the ocean breeze, as they leaned on the ship's rails and watched the land slip by as they passed.

"I never realized how swiftly the city ends and the countryside begins," noted Mystrel, indicating the cultivated fields and ordered orchards just then in sight.

Elak nodded. "Those in the cities often take farmers for granted. They buy food in the marketplace but give little thought to how it gets there."

Later, the mannered farms and orchards petered out, giving way to endless forests whose towering trees marched inland as far as the eye could see. This was where Poseidonis found the lumber to build its ships as well as the more exotic woods used to furnish the homes of the wealthy which could occasionally be glimpsed in these otherwise empty spaces.

Finally, the week was up and, just as Bogort had predicted, the *Wild Blossom* came into sight of Uloodna port. Elak congratulated the captain on the accuracy of his predictions as the ship maneuvered toward a vacant siding. To do so, it had to avoid a number of large, flat-decked vessels waiting to receive Uloodna port's main export: the marble blocks from its quarries used to build the public edifices within the city of Poseidonis.

As the *Blossom* nosed into its berth, those aboard could not help but notice the crowds of refugees gathered by the quay, their pitiful belongings and wailing children scattered about. The sight inspired Mystrel's feminine sympathies, and her heart went out to them.

"Those poor people!" she said. "Can nothing be done for them?"

Bogort shrugged. "They await the next transport that will take them to the more populated provinces. There the king has arranged to have them resettled."

"How long until the next ship arrives to take them away?"

Again Bogort shrugged. "Hard to tell. We didn't pass any on the way here. So it could be some time."

"Elak . . . ?" said Mystrel, a tone of pleading in her voice.

"Captain Bogort, by the authority vested in me as the king's representative, I order you to take on as many of these people as you can when you depart back to the city."

"But, Lord Elak, the *Wild Blossom* is a warship . . ."

"I care not. If there's any problem, I'll take full responsibility. Furthermore, I'd like to see those other ships take on refugees as well when they head back with their cargoes."

"As you will," replied Bogort with a slight bow of acknowledgment.

In quick order, once their belongings were piled ashore, Elak and Mystrel watched with satisfaction as the refugees began to go aboard the *Blossom.*

"Do you think they'll all be able to go?" asked Mystrel.

"It'll be a tight squeeze," said Elak. "But I think so."

Just then, a tall, spare man appeared on the dock. Dressed in workman's tunic and trousers with a broad-brimmed hat on his head and sturdy sandals whose straps wound to his knees, he introduced himself.

"The Lord Elak," I presume?"

"I am. You must be the royal geographer."

"Kivar is my name. At your service."

"Good to make your acquaintance, Kivar," said Elak. "How long do you estimate it will take to reach Zhondarf?"

"Quick and to the point," responded Kivar. "I like that. Well, should there be no delays, and the weather holds out, we should be there well inside of two months. However, if we're slowed . . ." Here he eyed Mystrel. "Frankly, your lordship, I didn't expect to have a woman along."

"Forgive me," said Elak. "This is my wife, Mystrel."

"Fear not, Kivar," said Mystrel. "I won't slow anyone down."

"Well, we can't travel any faster than the slowest mule," said Kivar, approving of Mystrel's somewhat masculine travel attire. "And I trust you can walk faster than that if need be. But you need not worry about that. We'll find something you can ride.

"I've bought forty mules for our pack train," said Kivar, turning to Elak. "Let me show them to you. We can send someone back for your belongings from there."

Kivar led them through the dusty streets of Uloodna where the stone and mortar houses crowded close together. By the time they reached its outskirts, there was a commanding view of the town's major source of income and employment: the massive cliffs of a distant hill where marble was quarried.

"Quite an impressive operation," noted Elak.

"It is. Most of the stones quarried here will be used in construction of public buildings and repairing the city walls," said Kivar. "But the stone is also popular with sculptors. And of course, a by-product of marble are gemstones such as ruby and sapphire. But, naturally, the king has a monopoly on those."

"Too bad," said Mystrel upon hearing this information. "I would've liked to take home a souvenir!"

"Don't try it," cautioned Kivar. "I hear the court is very jealous of its prerogatives."

As they watched, a steady train of heavy carts carrying smaller stones trundled slowly toward the docks while a number of truly massive stones were transported using thick wooden rollers with hundreds of men and animals pulling and pushing. A firmly packed road allowed for easier passage than rough ground would have.

"At least there won't be any lack of employment for any refugees seeking work," noted Elak.

"Indeed," agreed Kivar. "Many already have found employment. The only problem, as it always is in Uloodna, is the lack of quarters to accommodate everyone."

"I'll have to bring the conditions here to the king's notice when I return," said a grim Elak.

"Ah, here we are," said Kivar presently.

They were faced with a large enclosure made of wooden rails holding a small herd of mules.

"These are the animals I've acquired for the journey," said Kivar. "Our supplies are bundled and protected in that storage shed."

Just then a wagon arrived from the docks bearing Elak's and Mystrel's belongings.

"Place them in the shed, please," Kivar instructed the driver.

A moment later, an unsavory-looking man walked boldly up to the little party. His squinty eyes flashed when they caught sight of Mystrel, something that did not escape the notice of Elak. He did not mind, and in fact expected it, when men stared when his wife passed by. She was uncommonly beautiful. Yes, that was to be expected. It was those stares that lingered that concerned him.

"We lost two animals to the equine fever," reported the man. "If we don't want to lose more, we have to get them going and out of this pestilential hole."

Kivar cleared his throat nervously. "My lord, may I present Brusus Hilarit, our muleteer. Brusus, this is Lord Elak and the Lady Mystrel. Elak is the king's agent and has supreme authority over all aspects of the expedition."

Brusus grunted and spat. "I'm not one for the formalities, my lord," he said. "Especially on the trail. You'll have to pardon my ignorance of the latest court manners."

Bristling at the man's arrogance, Elak controlled himself. "So long as you know your job, and Kivar assures me that you do, we'll get along."

"It'll be no place for a woman, I can tell you that now," said Brusus, his eyes trying to bore through Mystrel's outfit. "Have to warn you. Me and my men are wont to curse frequently, words that might offend the lady."

"You tend to your affairs and pay no mind to my sensibilities," said Mystrel, smiling. "I'm not unfamiliar with the ways of working men."

Brusus nodded slightly, his eyes never leaving Mystrel. It seemed that her reply had lifted her in his estimation.

"We can leave at first light," suggested Brusus. "It'll be dark by the time we pack up the animals. Better to get started before the sun comes up in the morning."

"Very well," said Elak. "Just so long as there's no delay. I want this expedition to be conducted swiftly and efficiently. I trust you'll make sure of that."

3. *A Kidnapping in Zhondarf*

Despite his reservations about Brusus, Elak had to admit the man was efficient. By the time dawn began to lighten the sky in the east, their supplies had been secured to the mules, and the team of muleteers, through a combination of whipping and shoving, had lined them up along the road leading into the arid lands dominating the outskirts of Uloodna.

And while Elak and Kivar sat astride a pair of goodly horses, Mystrel, not without some complaint, found herself saddled on to a more sure-footed mule. "This is undignified," she said upon learning of her conveyance.

"Horses are at a premium in Uloodna," explained Kivar regretfully. "Animals are needed for the work of hauling the stones. I was lucky to acquire the two we have."

"Besides," added Elak. "A mule will be safer to ride once we enter the rougher country."

But as soon as the train began to move, Elak realized that no matter how well the muleteers did their work, travel would be slow. Mules were sure-footed creatures, but lazy, requiring constant urging by the muleteers so that by the end of the first day, they had covered only sixteen kords. A distance, he was assured by Brusus, that was the limit of a mule's ability when fully loaded.

"It was good time," confirmed Kivar that night around a small campfire. "If we can keep up this pace, we'll eat the kords and reach Zhondarf inside of a month."

"Doesn't sound so bad," said Mystrel, content after a meal prepared by a cook that Kivar had also employed.

"Easy for you to say," said Elak with a wink to Kivar. "While everyone else sleeps on the ground, you have your pavilion stuffed with all those cushions you took from the palace."

"I told you I didn't need the pavilion," insisted Mystrel. "I could've slept on the ground with the rest of you."

Elak rolled his eyes.

In truth, the first day did pass pleasantly, if one disregarded sore backsides. The dry country was picturesque with its colorful shale outcroppings, drifting sands, giant cacti, and wild flowers that particularly delighted Mystrel who had gathered enough to decorate her pavilion, giving it a feminine touch.

"I'm surprised there didn't seem to be any attempt at quarrying out here," said Elak.

"The hill from which Uloodna retrieves its marble is a geographic anomaly," explained Kivar. "The rest of the country roundabout is low and dry. I speculate that it was once part of the sea bed before its waters receded."

"You think so?" asked Mystrel.

"I know so," said Kivar, reaching into the bag where he kept rock samples. "What do you think of this?"

"A sea shell?" guessed Mystrel, handing the object to Elak.

"Exactly right," said Kivar. "I found that along the trail. They're not uncommon in this area. How do you suppose a sea shell ended up here, so far from the ocean?"

Mystrel was at a loss for an answer.

"My thinking is that Atlantis rose from the waves many thousands of years ago and, as it rose, the water drained away, leaving sea beds like this . . ." he gestured around them ". . . to dry and become deserts. It suggests to me that there could come a time when Atlantis could sink back into the sea as well."

"Surely that's not possible," insisted Mystrel, not a little frightened at the prospect.

Kivar laughed. "Well, not for a long time at least!"

The next several days passed without incident as the mule train continued its steady pace. Then, on the western horizon, something new had appeared.

"What's that strip of green up ahead?" asked Mystrel, shading her eyes against the lowering sun.

"The forest of Toscador," said Kivar. "A coniferous band of trees that marks the end of the dry lands and the start of a gradual incline to the Montarcus Ridge. The ridge is a divide between the eastern and western portions of Atlantis. On this side of the divide, the rivers flow eastward and on the other side they all flow westward."

"Fascinating!"

"What's more," continued Kivar, encouraged by Mystrel's interest, "the opposite side of the ridge presents a completely different environment. The climate there becomes wet and hot. That's where we'll enter the jungles of Quanthee Province."

"Will we be able to see the Madmollon Mountains from there?" asked Elak.

Kivar nodded. "Normally, we should be able to see their snowcapped peaks, but if reports by the refugees are correct, those might be gone."

Kivar's reminder of the purpose of the expedition sobered both Elak and Mystrel, and the conversation lapsed into silence.

They passed another few days traveling amid the scent of pine and towering trees whose boles were larger in circumference than the average home back in Mondresori, then crossed the ridge and came into sight of the vast jungle in the steaming lowlands below. In the distance, the mountains failed to make an appearance. Instead, only a brown smudge hung over the horizon like dirty storm clouds. Occasionally, their nights were lit by pulses of light in the far distance and Elak, at least, could not help but feel a sense of oppression and foreboding.

"It could be volcanic activity," commented Kivar when asked about the phenomenon. "The refugees did confirm such. But when they claimed that all the peaks in the range blew off at once . . . well, it's not likely."

"So what's your guess?" asked Elak.

"A single peak, perhaps with some accompanying earthquake activity, and of course, lava flows. That alone would be enough to panic the population and distort their observations."

"Well, I don't mind saying that something about the sight of that sky in the distance frightens me," said Mystrel, rising to give Elak a peck goodnight. "I fear it will give me nightmares tonight."

"Don't let it disturb you, my lady," said Kivar. "It's all a very natural phenomenon, I'm sure. Just a normal process of the earth."

Mystrel nodded her thanks for the reassurance and retired to her pavilion. But her movement did not go unnoticed. In the darkness beyond the campfire, Brusus lingered, watching her with hungry eyes. It was not often he saw a real lady of the court with her refined ways. In fact, he'd never seen one before, but Mystrel fulfilled all of his imaginings of such. He found himself drawn to her like a moth to a flame. And now, seeing her silhouette against the side of the pavilion, he found himself consumed by an unreasoning desire.

There followed many days of more tedious travel than previously as the party made its way along miasmic swamps, turgid streams, and vine-hung trees that twisted and reached for sunlight made dim in the steamy air. If it had not been for the trail left by fleeing refugees, their progress would have been a good deal slower, if not nearly impossible. As it was, every day was a battle with the jungle's insects and even less savory denizens that crawled and squirmed in the brush. Again, Mystrel's heart was torn at the sight of the refugees' belongings scattered along the trail, given up in exhaustion and haste. Worst of all were the hasty graves dug alongside the trail, many marking the tragic deaths of infants and children from the many ways the jungle can kill.

At last, however, they reached the limits of the jungle and the land began to rise again. They had arrived at the foothills of the Madmollon Mountains. Now the devastation that had chased away the inhabitants of a once happy valley was made clear. Indeed, every mountain within sight had blasted away its peak, leaving cone-shaped remnants that still smoked and bubbled and spewed the occasional molten debris. A low, smoky haze lay over the valley lit by the occasional flash from the volcanic mounds. And everywhere, like black snow, lay a coating of ash, some of which still lingered in the air. The sight was altogether depressing but one that Elak, for one, was somewhat relieved to see. It was all natural after all, as confirmed by Kivar, at least from a superficial observation. The geographer expressed his eagerness to begin his formal study of the abnormal situation as soon as possible.

"We'll pitch camp here on the ridge, in the protection of these rocks," he said. "We can unload what supplies we'll need for a few days and send the men and animals back to the bottom of the far slope."

Elak agreed, having already noted the skittishness of the superstitious muleteers who constantly looked over their shoulders and longingly back down the trail from which they had come. It was feared that if they were forced to stay in the valley, they would bolt during the night, taking the supplies with them. The only question was whether Brusus could be trusted to control his men and keep them in place until their work was done.

But later that night, sensing danger in the valley, Brusus connived to visit Mystrel in her pavilion.

"My lady," he began. "I've come to warn you of danger."

"Brusus!" exclaimed Mystrel, who had been preparing for bed.

"There is danger in the valley below," said Brusus again, advancing a step into the pavilion. "The gods have placed it under a curse and to go further is to risk their wrath."

"I trust the judgment of my husband and Kivar that no malign gods are involved," replied Mystrel. "It is only a natural phenomenon. Now I suggest you go."

"I hope your trust has not been misplaced," said Brusus, advancing another step. "But should you change your mind, I'm prepared to help you."

Mystrel retreated a step. "Thank you, Brusus. Now, if you'll take your leave . . . ?"

With a last, hungry look, Brusus bowed himself out and disappeared in the night, leaving Mystrel wondering if she should report the visit to Elak.

It was after the moon had set, when the night was darkest, that Mystrel was awakened from her slumber by rough hands. Before she had completely come to her senses, she felt bearded lips crush her own. Awakened by peril, she struggled, but her assailant was the stronger, pulling her from the pavilion. A hand clamped tight over her mouth.

"What goes on here?" said a voice. "Brusus! Is that you?"

It was Kivar, returning from the latrine. When he saw what the muleteer was about, he ran instinctively to Mystrel's defense, but Brusus was the stronger by far. With his free hand, he brushed the geographer aside and, hoisting his captive, clad only in the flimsiest of pantaloons, moved quickly to the top of the ridge.

But the commotion was enough to awaken Elak who, taking up his rapier, dashed for the high ground with the intention of cutting off Brusus from the ridge.

"You'll die for this!" snarled Elak, brandishing his sword. "Release my wife, blackguard, and defend yourself!"

Throwing Mystrel to the ground, Brusus drew his own sword from a scabbard at his side. It was a short, thrusting blade, old and worn, but showed definite usage.

"Come on ahead, you damn court fop!" he cried. "I'll carve you like a holiday torqus bird!"

Instantly, any reservations Elak may have had about fighting a man with a shorter blade vanished. With a quick feint to make it appear he was about to slash at his opponent's head, Elak shifted his stance and prepared for a quick stab to the man's belly.

"Mystrel," called Elak. "Return to your pavilion!"

Considering her state of undress, Mystrel raised no objection.

Now, without Mystrel to concern him, Elak could concentrate on his foe, who managed to avoid his first thrust.

Giving Elak no time to regain his balance, Brusus slashed his blade downward, forcing Elak's rapier nearly into the ground. Then, keeping his heavier blade atop the other, Brusus threw his shoulder into Elak, throwing him onto his haunches. Seeing his advantage, the muleteer lifted his short sword over his head, preparing a two-handed slash that, if it had succeeded, would have cut Elak in half.

But the move was sufficiently telegraphed that Elak had plenty of time to roll aside and spring back to his feet. Now it was the muleteer's turn to be off balance, as his downward slash left him open for a counter thrust.

Seeing his chance, Elak wasted no time, and a moment later blood was oozing from a puncture in Brusus' side.

Enraged and in pain, Brusus knew that he had to finish the fight quickly before loss of blood weakened him to the point that he could not no longer defend himself. Growing desperate, he embarked on a series of thrusts, forehand and backhand slashes that forced Elak back and out of the muleteer's reach.

Elak knew as well as Brusus that time was on his side and it was in his interest simply to stay on the defensive until the muleteer was too weak to defend himself. But such was not Elak's way. Instead, as he dodged yet another clumsy thrust, he caught his opponent's sword between his left arm and side even as he lunged with his right, piercing Brusus through a lung and up into his heart. The big man froze, an unbelieving look in his wide, staring eyes, before he slumped to the ground, dead.

But Elak had no time to consider his victory as a scream filled the night!

Whirling in the direction of Mystrel's pavilion, he observed its canvas sides throbbing and straining against a struggle inside. The candle that usually afforded Mystrel some dim light inside had been overturned and extinguished so that it was impossible to see what was the cause of her distress. Then, suddenly, the pavilion was ripped aside, its interior accouterments scattered, and Elak was confronted by an incredible, unexpected sight: a man-like creature had its scaly arms wrapped around a supine Mystrel, still clad only in her filmy pantaloons. In a moment it glared back at him before spreading its leathern wings and taking to the night air.

With a roar of anger and frustration, Elak charged forward, his rapier reaching for the creature through the sooty atmosphere but to no avail. The demon was quickly out of reach and soon disappeared into the darkness. So overwhelmed was Elak with the sudden turn of events that he failed to notice a second demon remaining amid the wreckage of the pavilion.

"What is it? What's happening?" Elak heard Kivar ask from where he still sprawled on the ground. He paid no heed, focusing all his attention on the second demon which now advanced, exuding a palpable sense of arrogance that Elak heartily wished to wipe off of its leering face.

Then, still at some distance, the creature stopped . . . and spoke!

4. *Compelled to Serve*

"Hail, Elak, son of Cyrena!" mocked the demon, its wings straining over its back.

"You know my name?"

"So my master has informed me," replied the demon. "He commands your presence in his dwelling thither."

The creature lifted its long arm and pointed up the valley.

"Never mind that! What of the woman, my wife! What have you done with her?" growled Elak, taking a threatening step in the direction of the demon.

But the other appeared unimpressed.

"She has been taken to my master's dwelling, there to remain as his guest pending your arrival."

With these words, Elak calmed a little, but only a little. His guard remained up and his rapier pointed at the demon.

"You do not reply," noted the demon, "indicating that you are considering my words. I urge you to consider them well, and accept them. Otherwise, my master bids me tell you that the woman will surely die."

Swallowing his pride along with his anger, Elak nodded and lowered his sword.

"I have no choice, it seems," he said.

"A wise choice. Now send the others away. My master deems them unnecessary."

"Why must they leave?" asked Elak suspiciously. "They'll be needed to accompany us on the return journey."

The demon's yellow eyes narrowed. "It is my master's condition. It must be obeyed, otherwise . . ."

"Enough!"

Sheathing his sword, Elak turned to Kivar, who stood by struck dumb by the rush of events.

"Kivar," began Elak, but with no immediate response by the geographer, he tried again, more forcefully. "Kivar!"

Startled from his trance-like state, the geographer turned to face him.

"Kivar, you're to pack up our gear and lead the others back over to the far side of the ridge. There, bury enough supplies for Mystrel and me to be able to make our way back to Uloodna. Leave a pair of mules as well. Hopefully they won't have wandered far by the time we come back. You're to return to Uloodna and make a report on the expedition including the reason I remained behind."

"Are you sure about this, Elak?"

"I have no choice, my friend."

"Very well," said Kivar, extending his hand. "Good luck, then. May the gods be with you."

"My thanks," replied Elak, taking the man's hand. "Now go."

After watching Kivar go about rousing the muleteers, Elak turned to the waiting demon. "Now then, lead on."

The demon stepped closer, as if he would transport Elak the way his companion had carried off Mystrel.

"Not that way," said Elak quickly.

"You would compel me to walk like any earthbound creature?"

"Yes, damn you! Walk!"

The demon stared for a moment before turning and loping off down slope to the valley below. Behind him, he left a trail in the deepening ash, one that Elak forced himself follow.

For hours, it seemed, they descended deeper and deeper into that hellish, twilit environment where the sun was but a memory and ash drifted on the air. Forced to tie a kerchief around his mouth to keep from breathing in the black flakes, Elak stumbled over hidden rocks and veered away from still-glowing chunks of molten debris dotting the once-fertile plain. All around him the mountain peaks smoldered and chugged bursts of flame; all except one. The largest of them all remained relatively quiescent, and Elak wondered about that even as they came within site of a large stone building that hugged the side of the distant ridge.

"There is the dwelling of my master," said the demon after Elak had inquired if such was their destination.

The building was farther away than it appeared, and it took some hours more to reach its entrance. A heavy gate had been lowered in anticipation of their coming, and Elak entered in the footsteps of the demon. Inside was a small courtyard with rough walls rising a number of storeys. Of the few embrasures, Elak wondered which room might contain Mystrel. As it was, they were all dark, and about them all was silent.

The demon, however, had not halted but moved on to an inner door just wide enough to permit its broad shoulders and wings to pass through. Inside, a torch hung on a wall, indicating the lower steps of a stairway that wound up into darkness. The demon squeezed its way upward, Elak close on its heels. They debouched into a large room, hung with curtains that hid the stone walls. An embrasure in the far wall looked outside to the peak that Elak had noticed lay virtually dormant. There was a rude table and chairs, in one of which sat a man who was just rising.

"I bid you welcome, Lord Elak," said the man in not unfriendly tones. "I have long planned for this occasion."

"Never mind that," growled Elak. "Where's Mystrel? Where's my woman?"

The man held up a hand, calling for patience.

"She is a guest here and will remain so until we have concluded our business."

"What business would I have with you, kidnapper?"

"I have a small task I wish you to perform for me. One suited, I think, to a fighting man such as yourself."

"How do you know anything about me? And I insist on verifying the safety of Mystrel before we discuss anything further."

"As to your first question, I learned of you in a missive sent by the king some months ago...."

"You're Jindamus!" exclaimed Elak. "The missing governor of Zhondarf Province!"

Jindamus bowed his balding head in acknowledgment. "I am he."

"Then what goes on here?" thundered Elak, advancing menacingly. "Why have you not reported the conditions here to the king? Why have you not done anything to help the people evacuate? Why didn't you make any preparations for the arrival of the expedition if you knew we were coming?"

"Oh, but I did make preparations," replied Jindamus. "I have prepared for you, Elak. You see, I need you to perform a certain service for me. One that might prove somewhat dangerous. Too dangerous for myself but not for an adventurer of your ability."

"What kind of service?"

Jindamus moved around the table and over to the embrasure at the far end of the room. Waving his arm indicating the conical mountain outside, he said, "I would like you to climb Mount Volunterique and inspect the summit. Its peak has exploded as did the other mountains in the range, but unlike those, it is not active in the same way."

"I noticed. And why is that?"

"Inside is the resting place of the god Tsathoggua, whom I wish, like you, to become my servant," said Jindamus matter of factly. "With its help, I can become ruler of all Atlantis."

"You're mad!" cried Elak. "No one can command the Old Ones!"

"There, you are wrong," replied Jindamus, returning to the table where he lifted a sheaf of scrolls. "These are the writings of the high priest Karkash-Ton which I found in the great library of Poseidonis. In them I discovered the resting place of Tsathoggua as well as the secret of bending it to my will. When I learned this, I resolved to be named the next governor of this province." He chuckled. "I was praised by the king for volunteering to serve in such a remote location!" Then, more seriously: "Zoolanguadec, the demon that led you here, is a creature I summoned and can control with the help of Klakash-Ton's writings. I will do the same with Tsathoggua."

"Then you are the one responsible for all this?" guessed Elak, indicating the ongoing destruction of the valley outside.

"Unfortunately necessary in order to release Tsathoggua," admitted Jindamus.

"You are mad!" reiterated Elak. "Your actions have resulted in uncounted deaths, in thousands made homeless."

"If my plan succeeds, it will be worth it."

"No one can control the forces you plan to unleash," insisted Elak. "Sooner or later, anyone who tries will become their victim."

For the first time, Jindamus showed signs of impatience. "Enough! You will do as I say or I will hand your woman over to my demons to do with as they will!"

Enraged, Elak jerked his sword from his belt but halted in mid-motion, remembering Mystrel.

"It is good that you control your anger," said a smiling Jindamus. "And now, before you embark on your errand, I will grant you your request to verify the safety of your woman."

Jindamus clapped his hands, and the curtain behind him parted to reveal Mystrel in the grip of the second demon, its clawed hand encircling her tender throat. The creature's other hand held her arms behind her back. She was naked but for a slim girdle at her waist from which hung ragged strips of her pantaloons that did nothing to hide her shapely legs, now scratched and bruised from her earlier struggle with the demon.

"Elak!" she cried, but the pronunciation of his name was lost in the gurgle of her near-strangled voice.

"Mystrel!" he gasped, his hands raised in helpless supplication. "Don't worry! I'll get us out of this!"

"Very true," soothed Jindamus. "After you inspect Volunterique for me."

"All right! But why don't you just send your pet demons to do the job?"

"Very simply, I don't trust them. They, too, are conjurations enabled by the scrolls of Klarkash-Ton, and, though they might follow simple commands, they do not have the intelligence for the task I have in mind."

"So what is it exactly you want from me?"

"You shall take a number of these objects," said Jindamus, indicating a small pile of star-shaped stones on the table. "At the summit, you will place them around the circumference of the cone. They have mystical properties granted them by the Elder Gods that can bind the Old Ones and make them susceptible to control."

"You really believe that?' asked Elak, doubtful.

"Klarkash-Ton has not disappointed me yet," was the reply.

"Oh, very well! Show me the way and I'll be off!"

"No need. Zoolanguadec will be your guide," said Jindamus, placing the stones in a canvas bag and handing it to Elak.

"Come, then," said Elak to Zoolanguadec. "And let's not dawdle." To Jindamus: "And see that my woman remains unharmed."

Then, hoisting the bag over his shoulder, Elak followed Zoolanguadec from the dwelling.

5. *The Elder Gods Return*

Outside it was still dark, the way forward illumined only in the glow of the various volcanic cones. Everywhere, ash still drifted on the air and settled over everything so that it was impossible for Elak to retain any appearance of cleanliness.

For its part, Zoolanguadec seemed uncaring of its surroundings, dragging its cloven feet through the ever-deepening ash. Ahead of them, looming in the gloom, was the shape of Mount Volunterique, its summit still glowing dully. And as he began to climb the lower portions of the mountain, Elak could see that the valley below was veined with dark cracks and fissures where the land had opened at the convulsions that had rocked it when the surrounding mountains exploded into volcanic life.

All around him were rumblings from deep within the earth and the explosive coughs from volcanic peaks that still held fiery life. Beneath his feet, the very mountain he climbed shuddered as if in evil anticipation of Tsathoggua's imminent release. Off to the left a stream of steaming magma rolled slowly down the mountainside. Everywhere the stench of sulfur was awful. Fearfully, Elak wondered if the legends he had heard throughout his life were true: that to gaze upon any of the Old Ones was to lose one's mind. Should he therefore screen his eyes against the sight within the cone? Should he keep his back turned as he laid the stones? But as the hours passed in climbing the increasingly vertical slope of the mountain, he steeled himself to dare the ultimate and prove to himself that the old legends were just that, stories to frighten children. He could see no circumstance in which simply facing some horrid creature could do anything to blast his mind.

Now his decision would face the test as he saw Zoolanguadec reach the rim of the cone and turn to motion him to hurry on. Elak studied the rocks before him, looking for likely hand- and footholds. He began the final climb. As he neared the summit, the ascent became more difficult. Elak unslung the bag from his shoulder and prepared to toss it up to the demon.

"Take the bag," he called, and threw it upwards with all his might.

The bag flew straight and true. The demon could have caught it with ease. Instead, it leaped back as if it had held a tangle of poisonous adders.

"You are useless to me," called up Elak, all the while wondering at the demon's behavior.

Soon enough however, he was hoisting himself up over the last barrier and a moment later stood on the ridge overlooking the wreck of the former mountain. Actually less than half its original height before the conjurings of Jindamus had blown off its crown, Volunterique was now but an open sore on the pockmarked face of the earth. The volcanic hole thus formed was large enough around that Elak could barely see to the opposite side. But within it, he could see all too well. There, amid a bubbling, viscid pool of effluvia that glowed redly with internal fires, rested Tsathoggua. It could be no other, as the thing that nestled amid the boiling, oozing mess matched precisely the stories Elak had heard: a toad-like thing with numerous, unguessable appendages and bulging eyes that, as they stared up at him, seemed to demand sustenance in the form of a sacrifice. Even as Elak continued to stare, transfixed at the otherworldly ugliness of the monster, it shifted its weight impatiently, sending a wave of the steaming effluvia over the rim of the cone and splashing down the side of the former mountain. The movement broke the spell that had fixed Elak, and he staggered back from the rim only to stumble over the bag of stones that still rested where he had thrown it when Zoolanguadec had refused to catch it.

On his hands and knees, Elak fumbled with the bag and removed one of the star stones. Placing it on the ground near the rim of the cone, he began making its circuit, laying more of the stones as he went. He had almost finished when he once more encountered Zoolanguadec.

"A fine helper you turned out to be," he shouted over the bubbling, gurgling noises generated within the pit and a growing thunder in the sky overhead where dark clouds had begun to gather.

"I am not charged by my master with the conduct of base labor," said the demon unconvincingly.

"Oh, so? Then you're not properly obeisant to the god in the cone?"

"It deserves my respect as well as my fear."

"So you do fear something after all." Then Elak had a flash of insight. "Do you also fear . . . this?"

With that, he tossed one of the star stones toward Zoolanguadec and, as he expected, the creature leaped back with the partial aid of its wings, in order to avoid any contact with the stone.

Elak moved quickly to retrieve the object and, holding it before him, herded Zoolanguadec in the direction of the pit. Then, as the turbulence in the sky overhead continued to grow, he feinted toward the demon with the stone in hand. Instantly, the creature jumped back, lost its footing, and fell back into the pit. Looking over the rim, Elak saw the demon try to spread its wings, but there was not enough time to properly deploy them. It fell into the miasmic filth that embroiled Tsathoggua to be gulped and instantly consumed by the Old One.

Elak had no time to register his disgust, however, as the sky above suddenly opened up with a mighty roar as of a thousand thunderings. The sonic blast was enough to knock him off his feet and over the topmost ledge leading back down the side of the mountain. Somehow he managed to retain his hold on the star stone he had used to frighten Zoolanguadec and, as he found some reliable footing, he looked back up and was startled to see the black clouds overhead begin to circle inward like a child's pinwheel. Lightnings flashed from amid the blackness, and everywhere around it the smoke and ash and other aerial debris scattered, leaving the slowly rotating clouds alone directly over the open wound that Volunterique had become.

And then the thing happened that very nearly did break Elak's mind!

The black clouds slowly stopped circling and began to congeal into the shape of a gigantic visage, but of a kind completely alien to Elak or indeed to any living human being. So totally alien was it that forever after, Elak, on those dark nights alone with Mystrel's arms safely about him, could barely bring himself to tell of his experience, one that he had to struggle to describe in any detail. The sole impression that remained with him was one of vast, unknowable powers to whom he, Jindamus, and even Tsathoggua itself, were as nothing. Mere insects or even less that were not worthy of the slightest attention. The enormity of that realization, that he now looked upon nothing less than one of the Elder Gods as it condigned punishment upon an upstart Old One, compelled him to retreat down the mountain with such reckless abandon that he reached the bottom in a fraction of the time it took to climb it. By the time he stumbled to the gate of the governor's dwelling, he was smeared in black ash, his clothes were a shambles, and his exposed limbs were criss-crossed with scratches and bloody scrapes.

Catching his breath, he saw that in all his panicky retreat he had somehow managed to retain his hold on the remaining star stone. With it, his clearing brain realized, he would be able to defend himself against the second demon and rescue Mystrel. A crack as of the end of the world broke his train of thought and, turning, he beheld Zoolanguadec as the colossal thing he had identified as one of the Elder Gods was completing its task, covering the open cone and rebuilding the mountain's peak taller than before, trapping Tsathoggua inside for all time. Then, slowly, the indescribable features of the Elder God retreated into clouds again, and the clouds swallowed themselves up, leaving only a full moon overhead, seen for the first time since Jindamus had triggered the volcanic activity that had exposed Tsathoggua. Looking about the valley, Elak saw that the fires within the surrounding peaks had likewise been extinguished, and the last of the ash had settled to the ground. Sharp, silver moonlight now filled the quiet valley, promising a clear day come the dawn.

But before the coming day's sunshine could be welcomed, Elak had some unfinished business to take care of.

Grimly, he stood and staggered into the stone dwelling, passed through the courtyard, and took the stairs upward. In the room where he had met Jindamus, there was no sign of the wizard. His rapier in one hand and the star stone in the other, Elak moved cautiously toward the curtains hanging behind the table. He found the place where they parted and an open archway beyond. The interior was lit by the occasional torch mounted on the walls, and he followed them one to the other.

Then he could hear it. A low sobbing whose timbre he immediately recognized as that belonging to Mystrel. His heart leaping, his mind a turmoil of imagined wrongs done to his wife, he plunged ahead into a dimly lit room. The first thing he saw was Mystrel, still with a few useless strands of filmy material hanging about her waist, her hands held by chains above her head, her toes barely brushing the cold stone floor. Her tender flesh was striped with scratches and marks of other rough handling. Her blond locks hung entangled about her head, hiding her features. But her sobs struck like a dagger into Elak's heart.

Before Mystrel, towering a full head taller and holding a whip in its scaly hand, was the second demon, who, sensing a disturbance behind him, turned to find Elak at the ready.

"Beware, manling," it growled. "lest I devour your flesh and suck the marrow from your bones!”

“Come along, then, and feast if you dare!” challenged Elak.

A crude smile creased the creature’s face as it lowered the whip and prepared to leap at its intended prey. But just as it was ready to jump, Elak tossed the star stone in its direction. Unaware of what the object was, the demon caught it in expectation of tossing it aside in contempt. Instead, it shrieked a ghastly shriek and exploded into a shambles of body parts, leaving droplets of cold blood spattered over the remnants of Elak’s jerkin.

The demon’s sudden death, jolted Mystrel into a better awareness of her surroundings, and upon noticing Elak, she called his name in delight and relief.

“Oh, Elak!” she said. “My darling! My love!”

“Hush, my dear,” said Elak, picking up a ring of bloody keys from where they had landed following the combustion of the demon. Quickly he freed Mystrel, who immediately collapsed into his arms. “There, there. It’s all over now. But can you walk? Did they do you any real harm? Did they violate you in any way? If so, I’ll . . .”

Elak felt Mysrel’s head shake from where it was buried against his shoulder.

“No. I’m all right in that regard. I think Jindamus never expected you to return. The demon kept taunting me with words about its brother feasting on you when your task was completed and was looking forward to eating me, too. But that was to wait until after Jindamus had had his way with me.”

“I’ll kill that madman,” vowed Elak, gripping his rapier the tighter. “But I thank the gods that there was not time for them to do you such harm as could not be undone afterward.”

“I know where Jindamus keeps himself,” said Mystrel, pulling herself away from Elak.

“Lead me to him!”

With growing strength, Mystrel took his hand and led him from the abatoir into another corridor and another stairway leading upward. There they found a wooden door, and Elak pushed it open revealing a bed chamber well warmed by a fire roaring in a grate.

At first, Jindamus, who had been studying the scrolls he had shown Elak earlier in the evening, looked up and noticed only Mystrel.

“My dear,” he oozed. “Your appearance is earlier than I expected, but . . .”

Then he stopped as, instead of his expected demonic servitor, Elak stepped into view, sword in hand.

"What's the meaning of this?" demanded Jindamus, confused. "Have you completed your task? I had not expected Myntorazorak to release the woman into your custody without my permission...."

At that point, the governor seemed to realize that something was not right.

"I'm here to terminate your appointment as governor, Jindamus," threatened Elak, keeping Mystrel behind him.

His mind clearing quickly, Jindamus mouthed a spell, no doubt taken from the scrolls of the revered Klarkash-Ton, and instantly there were a dozen of him filling the room.

"Come then, Elak of Cyrena," said the images in unison.

Then, as their prototype reached for a sword that hung over the grate, they all were suddenly armed and, dispersing, began to circle Elak.

"Rather difficult to discern who is the real Jindamus, is it not?" said the images, pointing their swords threateningly.

Elak lunged against the nearest of the images, only to have his rapier cut thin air. The image, however, was not canceled but continued to stand and maneuver, instantly mixing with the others so that Elak lost track of it.

"And now, I think I shall be merciful and not prolong the agony," said a confident Jindamus. "After which, I shall enjoy the company of your woman."

Just then Mystrel made a dash along the wall in an effort to seize the scrolls.

Her flashing legs and nearly nude body, disfigured as they were by physical abuse, were no less attractive to the male eye including that of Jindamus.

Instantly Elak saw his chance and lunged, piercing the real Jindamus through the torso, killing him in a moment.

Suddenly the room that had seemed so crowded a moment before, was empty.

Mystrel, who had halted her run upon the reversal of fortune, ran to Elak who encircled her waist with his arm.

"How did you guess which of the images was the real one?" she asked.

"The eyes of the real Jindamus followed you as you scampered along the wall," said Elak with a grim smile. "He wouldn't have been human if he didn't."

Then, taking the scrolls, Elak tossed them into the fire.

With Mystrel, he headed for the door, then stopped to look back. An expanding stain of blood was slowly smearing the front of Jindamus' blouse.

"But in the end, he was human after all," concluded Elak.

THE END

The Demon's Lover

Wayne Judge

1: Stories at the Inn

THE RAIN HAMMERED down in unforgiving fury from the thundering night sky. Skar's way only lit by the occasional streak of lightning which crashed through the dark swirling tempest. He considered drawing his cloak tighter around him but dismissed the idea with an audible grunt, soaked to the bone as he was it would make little difference. His horse was a sturdy one and not frightened by the peels of thunder or flashes of lightning, he would reward the stallion with a warm stable as soon as lodging could be found.

Through the incessant wet and dark a lantern could just be made out sputtering and clattering against a sturdy post some small ways ahead and even over the howling wind the faint hint of music caught the barbarians ear. An Inn at last. His purse fat with gold the warrior began to think of wine and meat and maybe even the company of a woman for the night. Spurred on by his imaginings he urged the steed towards the faint light of the just-perceived windows faster.

With his mount assured a good stable for the night Skar entered the tavern and was met with only a few stray glances even though he was wringing wet. He was tall and broad of shoulder, sinews forged in battle and the look of a man who knew his way with a blade. His eyes were dark and his shoulder length hair was silvery white. A wicked looking scar ran in a straight vertical line from his forehead to about an inch below his right eye, though the eye itself was not harmed. A mark given him as a child by the marauders who slew his family, a mark from which he took his name. Save for the broadsword that hung at his waist he was garbed only in simple leather breeches, folded jack boots and a plain doeskin tunic. There was no mistaking that this mighty warrior was from the northern hills of Tor.

Making his way to the large stone fireplace he took up a chair and flashing a gold coin called for meat and ale. The serving girls, sensing a traveler with coin to spend, were quick to oblige. As they waited dutifully the barbarian spoke between mouthfuls of beef and bread;

"I'll need a room. And someone to share it with." He eyed a comely raven-haired servant lustily with a sly smile as he gulped down a draught of ale.

"Of course my lord, we will prepare it while you warm by the fire!" The girls, giddy with thoughts of gold, jumped to their newly appointed task and hurried to prepare a room.

As Skar finished the roast beef and called for another tankard of ale he began to listen to the tales being told around him. Roadside Inns were always good for a bit of gossip or a ribald tale, local unrest or a lead to put gold in ones purse. Any seasoned traveler worth his salt knew to keep his ears open in any Inn or tavern, but the tale that met Skar's ears now intrigued him more than usual. A portly old man with a face like a dried root and the look and manner of a traveling merchant was telling of a wonder seen in his recent wanderings:

". . . The gold is there for the taking! A Kings ransom! I tell you I watched two stout men enter that strange house and neither returned, but the weird cries of whatever guards the treasure within chilled me to the bone. 'Tis like sport in that place, a crowd waits outside as if it were a game!"

Skar turned to face the old man who was weaving the tale and inquired:

"Tell you legends or what, of this gold and strange house?"

The man eyed the barbarian warily and stared for a moment at the scar across his eye, until the steely look from those piercing blue orbs made him avert his gaze to the ground rather quickly.

" 'Tis no fable stranger. The City of Corma just beyond the black hill, not a half league from here."

"And what is it that makes the house so strange in your eyes?" At this the elder balked.

"Hmf! Not just to me, the house moves in place, like a great wheel. Many have seen it."

All around the tavern flagons raised along with cries of "Aye!" Apparently this strange wonder was well known among the denizens of this area. At that the old man turned sheepishly back to his companion and continued to converse in a much more reserved tone. The story had piqued Skar's interest and he resolved to see this wonder for himself. As the bar wenches had returned and giddily began plying their attentions upon him he smiled: "After a good night's rest of course." He thought aloud as he took a goblet of Varkunian wine offered by one of the nubile girls.

2: Count Raktu's Challenge

The morning was gray with the retreat of the previous night's storm as the swordsman doled out coin to the two carnally talented women with whom he had shared his bed. As they retrieved his dried gear for him and watched as he belted on his sword and dirk they begged him to stay;

"Oh please my lord, there's hardly a real man in these lands."

The barbarian scoffed as he gave one of the girls a stinging slap to her firm, round buttocks with his hard hand as he strolled out of the chamber door;

"Would you say that if you knew my gold was all gone wench? Ha ha haa I think not!"

Dejected the girls sat down on the bed and eyed him coldly.

"Barbarian!" one called.

"I never claimed anything else my ladies." He chortled as he disappeared down to the tavern.

He retrieved his horse from the stable boy in back and eyed the low hills that lie further down the road. One hill in particular stood out from the others, a craggy jut of basalt devoid of vegetation. The aptly named "Black Hill" the pass through which would take him to the city of Corma.

It took no time at all to reach the landmark and in short order he had rounded its crest. Reigning in his horse he scanned the land below. There spread out just beyond the shadow of the scrub-covered foothills was the city of Corma. Small cottages and shops within the safety of a wall hewn from the very basalt he now crossed over. In the center stood a single tower, rising like a spire over everything else in sight. And around the tower was a curious structure indeed. A stone circle that seemed to turn slowly in a clockwise motion like a giant gear. Within the massive ring of stone was another slightly smaller circle which moved counter clockwise. And within the second was a third moving the same direction as the outermost ring. Skar stared in absolute amazement. In all his travels since leaving the mountains of Tor he had never beheld such a wonder. How it moved he could not tell. He saw no slaves to turn it, nor beasts of burden. Mayhaps underneath? He thought . . . at the stray thought of a sorcerous possibility the hairs on the back of his neck stood up. Only evil men and devils used magicks! Shaking the unpleasant thought from his head the silver haired warrior spurred his mount on to the black stone

157

city gates.

In every realm and every far flung land it seems cities are all the same. Streets filled with beggars, merchants hawking their wares, and the smell of too many people in too small a place. Always there was noise, pointless squabbling, yelling, and chattering. Skar did not care much for cities. As he made his way through the streets he came at last to his destination of choice the massive moving ring. It made no noise as it slowly turned and stirred no dust, the surface was stone but polished as smooth as glass. He cautiously extended his left hand and let his fingers glide along its surface. As he stared incredulously a voice interrupted his thoughts. The voice was loud and boisterous, powerful and commanding, yet also it held a tone of contempt.

"Ahhh my friend, you look to have a strong arm and quick leg, come for my challenge have you?"

The barbarian turned to face the voice. It belonged to a large and obscenely rotund man, bald of hair with a double chin. He wore a robe of fine red silk and gilded slippers that easily had to cost more than a good horse. His pudgy fingers were adorned with jeweled rings and he smiled too easily. His beady, black eyes devoured Skar's form from hungrily top to bottom as he looked him over approvingly. Skar dropped his hand from the strange buildings wall.

"What challenge do you speak of? I would know the name of whom I speak with."

The large man laughed a wheezing cackle:

"He-heeee, your manners are atrocious sir! This will be most splendid! Do forgive me Northman—I am Count Raktu, owner of this marvel!" with a bow of his head the Count flourished towards the Stone Ring Building.

"Strong men from all over come seeking to take up my challenge. You see", he explained, "within the center of this most strange and wonderful structure is enough gold to make any man a king!"

Skar frowned and crossed his sun bronzed, muscled arms.

"He-heeeee, Yes, yes, you are a shrewd one, there is more to it than simply waltzing in to take it! You see," The Count's face took on an almost mocking look of sadness and his tone dropped theatrically, "my home was not always this rotating wonder. Alas I was cursed by a demonic and sorcerous beast for some transgression he claims I perpetrated against him. He is terrible to look on! A monstrous creature of nightmarish form that I dare not describe! The foul thing has usurped my home."

The barbarian raised his hand to halt Raktu's speech;

"Gold there may be but 'tis the fiend you wish destroyed, aye?"

The corpulent dandy smiled widely.

"Shrewd as I said, my boy! The building rotates this way and that and the halls and rooms within are such that it forms an ever-changing maze. Six strong men have taken up the task so far and as yet none have returned. I would give all my gold to be free of this pox on my land!"

The Count eyed Skar expectantly even as the warrior sized him up in return. Doubtless the man held much wealth but the thought of some hellspawn beast that wields magicks outweighed even that. Skar was no fool. But a king's ransom . . . the empty feel of his coin purse and thoughts of wine, wenching and debaucherous revelry that demanded gold outweighed his instinctive fear of the unknown.

"Very well!" He stated, "But have your bards ready to sing my legend when next you see me Count."

Thee Count let loose his easy, sinister smile. "Well said, my strapping lad! Well said! And just in time too, as the entry way has come round to meet us!"

The silver maned barbarian followed the gesticulation of Raktu and spied an open, arched portal in the silently moving tube-like wall making its way with surprising swiftness towards where he stood. Without warning the large hand of Count Raktu shoved him through with no warning, the surprising strength of the push was inhumanly forceful! Skar hurtled into the doorway like a rag doll, his head slapping the interior wall with a crack and the white light of pain. Vision slowly blurred as the cold flagstones of the floor rushed up to greet him. Blackness claimed his senses even as the mocking laughter of the Count echoed dull and muffled from the outside. Too late the Northman knew that he had made a mistake.

3: The Living Labyrinth

Skar sat up with a start and an ache in his skull as consciousness throbbingly returned to him. Looking about he realized that he had to have been out for quite some time, an hour, a day, he knew not for sure. The slow but constantly moving floor and walls were dramatically different looking to him from what he so briefly spied on his quick and unpleasant entry and there was no way to tell how far into the structure he had been carried as he lay stunned. Thoughts of gold and treasure meant nothing to him now, the thought that burned foremost in his mind was to get out of this maze and run cold steel through that fat bastard Raktu's heart!

Skar took in his surroundings as he regained his feet. The hall was wide and curved off to front and back. It was of the same polished stone as the outside yet the interior was dimly lit by large, amber stones affixed to the ceiling. Not only did the floor slowly move but also the walls and roof, each seemingly moving opposite its parallel counterpart. Close inspection showed no visible seams denoting where wall, floor, or ceiling began or ended. In fact the more he attempted to inspect where such a seam or joint should be, the more clouded his senses became.

"Sorcery!" he spat aloud with contempt.

Rubbing the knot on his brow and gritting his teeth the adventurer sat off in the most logical direction, against the way of the floors movement. As slow as this particular movement was perhaps he thought, he would find the exit forthwith.

He walked for what seemed like hours, the moving hall was so uniform it became hard to tell if indeed he had been making progress at all. His boredom was broken at last by the sound of feet faintly padding through the hall just ahead. Picking up his pace Skar barely caught a fleeting glimpse of a silken robed female form. Just as sudden as it appeared it vanished into the very wall itself! Stopping in his tracks the barbarian shook his head in disbelief. Had his previous blow and the ceaseless monotony of this strange place caused him to hallucinate?

He started off again and spied for the first time a break in the stagnate, smooth wall. A door moved into view. It was undoubtedly the passage through which the girl must have darted. With no better options and the possibility of encountering another soul he stepped through.

Skar's eyes met at last with what seemed like a definite room. Silk tapestries depicting hunting scenes adorned the walls and overstuffed cushions lined the floor along another wall. Turning to glance back at the doorway through which he came he found it was no longer there. The movement of the walls was deceptive and although it seemed to move at a slow pace the passage had already slid by.

This room was square and the walls did not seem to move, although the Northman still felt the sensation. Leading in the same directions as the outer hall were two halls exiting the room. Thinking back to when he had first seen this incredible structure from the outside, Skar surmised he must have found his way into the second ring. Deciding to continue in the same direction as before, the warrior chose the exit to the left.

As he stepped into the hall his eyes once again beheld the inexorable turning of the floor which caused his senses to reel momentarily.

"Madness and deviltry!" He cursed aloud.

He was startled even further to hear his voice carry in an echo through the hall. And what he heard next made him wish he had kept his mouth shut. Just ahead of him and echoing through the hall as if in grim answer to his words, came a sibilant hiss like that of a snake, only far louder and stranger than any serpent he had heard before. With a metallic ring his blade left its scabbard in one smooth movement. Again as if in answer to this new noise he had made came a response, the sound of a girl crying.

4: The Demon's Lover

The entry to another chamber soon came into view. Skar approached as stealthy as a prowling panther, sword at the ready, steel corded muscles tensed to pounce like a jungle cat. A great rattle of scales met his ears accompanied by a pleading and distinctly female voice;

"No! Please, *no!*"

Reflexes honed in a hundred battles had his dagger springing into his free hand with nary a thought as the barbarian leapt into the chamber ready to face death itself! His gaze caught the serpent-like tail of an unnatural and monstrous creature as it moved like liquid lightning out the opposite door to the chamber. His eyes then fell upon the form, which lay sobbing upon the floor beside the same door. She was beautiful, dark hair held back in an ornate comb of silver, her cheeks ruddy with youth. Her body was the rival of the fairest dancers of the Desert Kingdoms, whom were known to be among the fairest in the world, and was draped in fine silks that left little to the imagination. Her skin was like fine porcelain as she lifted her face from her hands and beheld the barbarian warrior before her. He could see her full, pouty lips and enchanting green eyes. So beauteous was her countenance even in the throes of woe that Skar's breath was literally taken away for the briefest of moments. Sheathing the dagger but keeping his broadsword firmly in hand he spoke with a firm, commanding, yet reassuring tone.

"It's gone now girl. Come here and I'll keep the beast from you or die, I swear it!" He offered a strong hand to the fair creature.

"Like all the others before?" She queried in an almost sarcastic retort.

The beauty gestured to the corner of the chamber. As the warrior followed her indication a horror unfolded before him. Stacked in the corner like firewood before a winter's storm were the rotting corpses of six men. A couple were missing the heads and another was bloated and putrid, as if poisoned by some vile venom. Those which still had faces wore a frozen mask of pain and terror. These fallen swordsmen had not prevailed against the beast and the girl obviously seemed to think that this latest "rescuer" would fare no better.

"Why has he not killed you lass? Does he keep you for some dark purpose?"

The girl hung her head in sorrow. "I . . . am Mitani, and I . . . I am his lover."

Skar's face grew hot with rage. What foul and evil beast would enslave such a woman as this and defile her so. Sheathing the mirror polished sword he pulled the girl to her feet and brushed a tear from her cheek.

"Come, we will find the monster and end your suffering!"

The girl recoiled from his touch in anger.

"No! I am his lover by choice! He is no monster!"

"Witch!" The barbarian backhanded the girl knocking her to the pillows roughly and bruising her soft cheek.

"HHSSsssSSSS!!" came the voice of the monster as it shot into the room and coiled its tail around Skar's legs with hellish speed. He crashed to the floor but managed to draw his sword. Twisting his head he now saw the creature fully. It was enormous, a gigantic serpent that moved upright like a man but was twice the size of even the muscled barbarian it now faced. Other than its size and manner of movement it was all snake save for the two scaly, humanoid arms in which it held twin curved scimitars. The fiery luminescent eyes of the beast showed anger as its jaws stretched opened, exposing two fangs the size of carving knives which dripped with noxious, acidic venom.

Skar fought the instinctive fear which rose within him and swung his sword at the snake man's reptilian flank. With a rasp the shock of the blow reverberated up the barbarians arm as the scales remained proof against steel. The beast clashed its blades like a butcher ready to carve meat and readied himself for the killing blow.

"No my love! No more! You give the Count more pleasure with each killing!" Mitani threw her lovely arms around the rough body of the demon and pressed her head to its chest. "Please . . ."

The demon released Skar's legs at the same moment effortlessly knocking the sword from the warrior's hand with a whip of his tail. The creature then lowered its head to gaze at the girl. Its eyes seemed to round into a look of profound sadness as a scaled hand tenderly caressed the girl's bruised cheek. She took the hand in hers and kissed it lovingly then turned quickly to regard the barbarian;

"Stay your hand and you will not be harmed. Please."

Stepping out of range of the beast's tail Skar eyed the pair in disbelief.

"What madness is this? What does that bastard Count Raktu have to do with all of this?"

The girl hung her head sadly.

"If you will listen, barbarian, I will tell you a tragic story."

5: A Jealous Spell

The Serpent man coiled its lower half into a spiral upon which Mitani sat to tell her tale. The whole time Skar noticed the beast kept a vigilant eye on him.

"Seven winters past, Count Raktu came to Corma a travelling sorcerer of ill reputation and no small skill. Unable to sell his abilities to the leader of our city, Lord Dane, he grew bitter. It was then that he saw the betrothed of Lord Dane and desired her.

"The wizard tried his best to dazzle the girl with tricks and conjurings that would doubtless delight most any naïve, young woman, but his inherent cruel nature showed through and made the sweet promises he proffered ring with an air of dishonesty and hidden intent. The girl spurned his advances and unwittingly raised his ire.

"Knowing full well that his conquest was impossible and that he would never have the girl he decided that the rightful lover would also not have her. His petty curse was powerful and filled with jealousy and envy! It was terrible to behold! All but the central tower of the Lords Keep was transformed into this maddening labyrinth which imprisoned the two people who were the targets of the Counts enmity. The crux of the curse was simple enough: The girl and her lover would be forever trapped in the maze, eternally together yet eternally apart. For Lord Dane was transformed into a monster incapable of human speech or touch!"

As the girl choked out the last sentence she began to cry and the snake man lowered his head in what seemed to be grief. It was clear now. These were the ill-fated lovers. The snake demon the cities rightful ruler, Lord Dane and Mitani his betrothed and beloved. Skar calmly retrieved his blade from the floor and sheathed it;

"Magicks that are made can be unmade as well."

"You . . . you would deign to help us?" The girl looked hopeful, the Serpent eyed the warrior suspiciously.

"I've had the misfortune of dealing with a wizard or two." Grunted the barbarian, "In my experience the things they conjure die with them at the end of a sword."

Mitani grew hopeful as she rose from the coils of her slithering lover.

"We two cannot leave here. The spell prevents us. But at the same time we are able to move about the maze unaffected by its enchantment. If you will kill Raktu we can show you the way out of here."

"Aye, woman, I have no love for the man myself and plan to kill him regardless for sending me into this trap. Show me the way and Count Raktu will taste my steel before the dawn!"

Lord Dane laid down now as a true serpent would and the barbarian sat astride his shoulders. Bidding farewell to the Lady Mitani he rode his strange mount through the moving halls with speed faster than any horse. Twisting and winding through the passages towards the center of the structure they soon arrived at a circular room in the dead center of the living labyrinth. Stepping from the colossal snake Skar looked up to see a wooden plank trap door with an iron latch set into the ceiling. As he stood upon a stair that led to the door and reached to open it a scaly hand rested firmly on his shoulder. He turned and looked at the cursed figure of Lord Dane before him. The creatures' eyes peered into his own and with supreme effort from a throat that was never meant for human words came a rattling hiss. The barbarian knew what the beast was trying to say and clapped a hand onto its scaly shoulder in return. With that he turned the latch and stepped up into the central Spire of the City of Corma.

6: Might & Magic

Skar padded up the steps of the tower with the practiced silence of a thief. He thought it strange that the residence of the Count contained no guards or servants, a testimony to the arrogance and overconfidence of the sorcerer. Making his way into the central main chamber he strode into the center of the mirror like, black marble floor and bellowed out a challenge in rage:

"Raktu, I am free from your circle and your snake, show yourself!"

The room was decorated with columns from which hung tapestries bearing the crest of the false ruler. At the forefront of the room was a chair such as where a city leader might take council. Skar turned slowly scanning each and every shadow of the great chamber. The torches in the room fluttered and the tapestries blew, from the great chair where a moment before had been no one now came the voice of the wizard Raktu:

"Barbarian Dog! I don't know how you got out but I'll see you put back in to feed my snake!" He pounded his fist into the arm of the chair and the noise echoed through the grand room like a gavel crashing down its judgement.

Skar wheeled to face him, steel gleaming in each hand wickedly:

"Lord Dane sends his regards wizard." The bulbous man's face distorted in sudden surprise and shock at the mention of the name.

"And Mitani sends you a kiss!"

Taking advantage of the surprise the warrior threw his perfectly balanced dagger with expert skill. It found its mark sinking to the hilt into the wizards' heart with a meaty finality.

Raktu looked even more surprised now as he slowly gazed down at the bronze hilt which had sprouted from his chest. And then . . . he laughed.

"He-heeee-hee! You didn't think it would be that easy did you?"

With a mildly annoyed tug he pulled the blade from his form and tossed it aside casually. Skar's hair stood up on the back of his neck and he stared in disbelief as the dagger clattered bloody to the floor. Raktu rose and began to approach him.

"Idiot," he snorted.

"Devil!" cried Skar, bringing his glinting sword to the ready.

A flash of steel sliced the rotund magician from shoulder to thigh at an angle and bit an inch deep. The Counts robe was flayed open but incredibly only a minor amount of blood issued from the wound and seemed to stop just as quickly. With an elephantine roar and a quickness that belied his size, the wizard's bizarrely large fist slammed into the barbarian's body. The muscled warrior flew backward through the air like a ragdoll and landed in a heap on the floor sliding across its surface another few feet. Staggering up on legs of thick muscle Skar coughed up a spray of blood and stared at the fat man in astonishment.

"You see Northman," Raktu began; "Part of my spell was that for each life taken by the cursed Lord Dane, I received their strength! When you face me you face one with the power of seven!"

As the Count bragged Skar eyed his surroundings looking for anything to aid him in his battle. The fiend did bleed, though not much, but if he could bleed he could die! He moved in cautiously as Raktu merely smiled in supreme confidence. His blade struck out fast and the warrior darted away faster, again he moved in and then away, again and again he laid a deep cut and darted away until the floor was slick with blood. No use it seemed, as the wounds closed almost instantly.

"What are you playing at dog? Come here and I'll end it quickly."

As The Count stepped forward the barbarians failed assault had an unexpected effect. The blood under the large man's feet had made the polished marble floor as slick as ice and Raktu soon found himself crashing onto his back as his feet flew out from under him. His head hit the floor with a loud crack and served to stun him momentarily.

Skar leapt upon the corpulent sorcerer, blade in the air;

"And now you die . . . GGKK!!" His sentence ended in a choke as the wizards' huge hand shot up and clenched around his throat in a squeeze.

"And so do you fool!"

As his eyes bulged from the pressure of the giant clutching grasp and his vision began to spot, the mighty warrior brought his sword up with both hands and sliced the Counts offending hand off at the wrist. With an anguished howl Raktu stumbled backwards clutching the bloody stump even as Skar fell to the ground and removed the severed hand from his bruised neck.

Before his eyes the wizard seemed to lose a good deal of his bulk, he shrunk to almost half his enormous girth. Was it just the lack of oxygen from being choked or were the three rings on the severed hand actually giving off a faint glow? The pieces of the puzzle fell into place within the barbarian's head. Six men, six rings. The conjurer stared at the savage swordsman with a burning hatred now;

"What have you done?!"

Skar smiled wickedly as he slipped the rings from the dead hand onto his own. With a surge of power and a euphoric rush unlike anything he had ever felt his already prodigious strength and size swelled immensely!

"Evened the odds I think."

For the first time in too long Count Raktu knew fear. He was no fighter by training or nature and the barbarian with the strength of three added to his own was easily more than his match. The remainder of the battle was short indeed. Skar's sword quickly removed not just the other bejeweled hand but the whole arm at the shoulder in a spray of blood that spattered the columns. The mirror blade lashed out one final time and with a vicious hack took the head of his foe which tumbled through the air even as the transformation of the rings wore off. When at last it smacked the cold stones like a wet piece of meat it was thin and wore a horrified look of surprise upon its bloody countenance.

As predicted the moment the wizard's life was extinguished so too did his magicks begin to unravel. The earth trembled as if in the throes of a great earthquake which shook the warrior from his feet and brought him to the floor. The jewels on each of the six rings grew hot and Skar tore them from his fingers quickly even as he saw them turn black as coal. Regaining his legs as the shaking and rumbling subsided he found his way to a small slit of a window and stared out where the great ring structure should have been. Instead his gaze fell upon the parapets of a small keep where once the wondrous spectacle rotated.

7: The Nature of a Man

Skar looked on approvingly as the heavy satchels of gold were packed onto his horse. Enough to keep him in women and wine for many a long night to come. A strong hand clasped his shoulder and he turned to see the smiling and grateful face of Lord Dane, restored once more to the form of a man.

"I would make you comfortable in Corma my friend; I am forever in your debt."

The Lady Mitani, resplendent in her fine gown offered the warrior her hand in gratitude. "We owe you our lives, Skar. Tell me, where will you go if you will not stay with us?"

The barbarian looked off to the mountains which loomed farther West. Beyond that he knew was the Barakai Sea, rich in adventure.

"Perhaps I will buy a ship and a few good men to sail her. There's a world out there that begs for someone to discover it."

With that he offered the two lovers a smile and swung up into the saddle with the graceful ease of an expert horseman. Without looking back he spurred his steed into a gallop and rode out of the City of Corma, steering his mount towards the majesty of the distant, snow-capped peaks.

Mitani gripped Dane's arm and stared at the barbarian as he disappeared in the distance;

"What drives such a man? Living under the sky and surviving only so long as your blade strikes first. Such a man lives only for the thrill of combat and the call of adventure. How could he ever know love?"

With a kiss on her Lords cheek she turned and walked towards the town bazaar. Lord Dane stayed and stared at the distant mountains himself and almost inaudibly he answered his betrothed's query:

"The ring of steel on steel, the open sky as your roof. Skar isn't lacking in love, a man such as he lives it!"

With a sigh and a faint smile the Lord of Corma pushed such thoughts from his mind and turned to catch up with his woman.

END

The City Without Name

Glen M. Usher

BOSCASTLE GUIDED THE stolen stallion along the edge of the sea of dunes. He was too fearful of crossing it directly: this would mean a slow and lingering death from parching; such an end he would not even consider; he would sooner go down fighting, cleft in twain by the fearsome scimitar of Mustafa bin Hazred.

Here the great rocky spires of these majestic and craggy mountains reached for the pale azure of the firmament, like the teeth on the jawbone of an unimaginably huge dragon jutting out from the eternal dusty shroud of the sands. Their upper peaks were partially shrouded in billowing banks of clouds; they were glazed with a coating of snow.

He knew that bin Hazred, the Moorish slaver, could be only about half a day's ride behind him; added to this bin Hazred was familiar with these dusty tracks in this parched and hellish landscape and rode with vengeance in his heart. Two days before, Boscastle had killed his brother Abdul; a more perverse and degenerate fiend in human form would be difficult to imagine. Big and shaven of pate and with a long, crooked nose, Abdul had taken the greatest of sadistic pleasure in the whipping and rape of slave girls. Boscastle had been on the wrong end of his sadistic efficiency whilst chained to the oars of the xebec galleys for close on two years. His back bore the scars as testimony.

Two days earlier the opportunity of escape had presented itself when the pin in the fetters that held him captive had finally yielded to his efforts of many days and his hands were free at last. He had struck Abdul with the most vengeful of blows with the length of chain as the torturer sat astride his magnificent black stallion. Gore and brains had splattered in all directions as the fiend crashed to the paving stones of the street in this stinking harbour town. Boscastle was able to snatch the keys from the corpse, which was by this time leaking brains and bone fragments from its shattered head, blood now running in gruesome channels of crimson through the gaps in the paving stones.

Boscastle appropriated the horse and the contents of the saddle bag and made like the wind for the hinterland before his crime could be discovered. He found some strips of cloth to cover his conspicuous yellow locks, much out of place among the dusky folk of this land.

He was free for now, it was true. But for how long? He was now the quarry of a ruthless and vengeful hunter in the shape of bin Hazred.

Boscastle reflected upon the irony of his situation as the sun at its zenith beat down upon his head and arms. He was some twenty years of age, broad of shoulder with eyes of emerald green. Son of a wealthy Bristol wine merchant, he had a misspent youth besotted and debauched. His family fortune had kept solvent many a tavern and house of ill-repute.

All this had come to an end two years ago when the Arabs had raided that dismal, dank coast town, taking him along with several others. He had been too drunk to do anything about it at the time, and had languished in chains ever since.

He was no weakling, it was true; his father had bought him a commission in the King's navy at one point; he was good with a sword, but his weakness for strong drink and harlots had seen to it that this tenure of employment did not end well for him. Wars raged in the wider world, the upstart Corsican Napoleon constantly adding to his conquests.

None of this mattered any longer to Boscastle as his new home became the rock-walled, stinking fortress town on this sun-blasted shore. Usually he was shackled like an animal on the rowing decks of the xebecs of the Sultan's pirate vessels; other times he was assigned back-breaking labour on work crews under the cruel lashing of the whip.

Upon his escape he had made inland, thinking there would be less chance of a successful pursuit by the vengeful sibling. As he penetrated further inland, the lush fields of olive groves gave way to barren, scrubby rockiness and sun-parched hills with few signs of human settlement. As he followed the barely discernible road over the rise of a large hill, he looked over his shoulder. His sharp eyes could make out a figure in the haze of the distance following the path he had taken; without a doubt it was Mustafa bin Hazred.

How had the merciless slaver managed to make up the missing time and gain on him so quickly? He must have driven his steed to the utmost limits of its endurance, the Huguenot mused to himself.

Before long the rocky expanses gave way to the high mountains; here and there a stream trickled down from the melting snow of the highlands, from which Boscastle was able to fill his water skins and refresh the horse, but he dared not tarry too long with the vengeful scimitar of bin Hazred so eager to imbibe the blood of the infidel.

Off in the distance he spied approaching trouble, a fearsome *khamsin* or desert storm inflaming the graceful sand of the dunes into billowing clouds hundreds of feet in the air. He would need to find shelter fast. Should he take his rapidly wearying steed up and try to find some route of escape? Perhaps a gap between the foothills of the stone sentinels that stood eternally watchful over the border of this massive expanse of sand? Or maybe try to find some point of sanctuary whilst the storm abated its fury.

Before long, things had been whipped up to a frenzy, and he could scarcely gaze in front of him as the stinging sand blasts struck his face. It was then that he saw it, a short distance out, in among the sea of dunes. Ancient pillars and columns comprising some sort of structure, somehow exposed by the fierce action of the storm. Could he find sanctuary here? Respite from the fierce *khamsin* that raged all around him?

He led the now-terrified and whinnying steed towards the ruins. Upon reaching them he realised the extent of them as they were far larger than he had at first thought. He entered a huge domed structure with ornate pillars of marble and some other darker stone types he was not able to identify.

Below the level of this structure, one of the few points protruding above the level of the sand dunes, a massive chamber spread out in all directions, fading into the black distance. There appeared to be many annexes and side chambers. In many a place the roof had given in under the pressing mass of the sand above. Here and there a collapsed minaret or spire allowed some ingress of light into this otherwise eternal twilight.

The walls and columns of this temple were decorated with ornate inscriptions and murals; in the twilight of this vast chamber Boscastle could not make them out. The horse had calmed somewhat in the comforting embrace of this vast womb-like chamber, so the Huguenot tethered him to one of the columns and stroked his nose, proffering soothing and gentle sounds to ease the burden of fear that lay upon the beast. "Tush, my friend, this place fills me with fear, too. Can't think it's played host to many a lord or lady in quite some time, only rats and spiders by the look of it."

Something struck Boscastle as odd in the extreme about this place: here and there the roof had caved in, and huge piles of sand had seeped in from above, yet it held. Why had not the encroaching sands completely crushed this long-abandoned fastness? How had it managed to resist the unimaginable weight of the creeping and almost sentient mass of sand? Boscastle's sandaled foot scraped at the floor of the chamber. He looked around and noticed that in a number of places what looked to be stairwells led downwards to where he surmised lay another vast and similar chamber. The light was fast dwindling now. He looked around and spied what he took to be torches attached to some of the walls and columns.

Upon inspection he saw that the oil-impregnated cloth core of them was still moist. Some rummaging in the saddle bag soon procured him some flint, and he was able to light the torch.

This place must still have some occupants, he mused to himself. Or at the very least *did* until some time recently. If he could find them, he could maybe negotiate, trade Abdul's bejewelled dagger and some other items from the saddle bag for food and water, even feed for the horse.

The illuminating torch brought the carvings and murals of the chamber to vivid life, revealing scenes of great strangeness. Depictions of beings that had the married form of men and serpents, with similar beings seated in thrones. Scenes of oceans and carven images of tentacled creatures of many eyes; engravings of beings with long conical skulls and eyes set aslant like the folk of the Orient, long spindly beings. Boscastle knew not what to make of this and could not decipher the weird hieroglyphs that punctuated these murals that told their phantasmic tale like some diabolical missive from the depths of Hades itself. Despite his feeling of ill-boding, Boscastle elected to descend one of the stairwells into the chamber below.

"I'll return, beast, fret not," he cooed in the twitching ear of the tethered horse that snorted and rasped its hoofs gratingly on the sand and stone of the chamber floor.

By the light of his torch Boscastle could see that this downward passage had been bored through the very bedrock granite of the earth itself. Crystalline fragments gleamed and glistened. At frequent intervals there were unlit torches on fittings in the wall, and he used his torch to ignite them in order to facilitate his journey back upwards once he had completed his exploration of the lower chamber.

Who had built this strange complex? This question vexed Boscastle's mind. He was reasonably well-schooled coming from his wealthy background, schooled enough to know these ruins were neither Greek nor Roman. Neither Minoan nor Carthaginian, not even a distant colony of Egypt.

To him it seemed these passages, though of archaic antiquity, were still in use: there was a singular lack of dust, and the torches all seemed fuelled and tended along the entire length of these dank passages. Mohammedans could certainly not have built it; he was well familiar with their culture and styles of building, thus whoever had built this structure must by the dictates of logic predate these others . . . these questions.

He called out greetings to any who might be in earshot, in English, in French, and in the language of his Arab captors that he had crudely mastered during his captivity. The only reply was the reverberation of his own words in the chilling dankness, and he fancied that shapes slithered and hissed just beyond the glow of his torch, things about man-height encrypted among the stygian and stifling blackness. He fingered the sheathed dagger in his gordel reassuringly.

After what he judged hundreds of feet of descent, the stairway levelled off into a long chamber that stretched way off into darkness beyond the gleam of his torch. In alcoves in the wall at regular intervals were what seemed to be ornate sarcophagi. The passage terminated when he reached a huge sarcophagus made from some shining crystalline stone he was unable to identify. Upon its lid was the moulded likeness of a woman, tall and slender, with fine and pointed features and slitted eyes; her hands crossed over her ample bosom; at seven points along the length of her body were differently hued jewels. Boscastle stood gazing admiringly upon this image of unimaginable beauty.

He lost track of time, mesmerized into some reverie from which he was not able to extricate himself. Only when the torch burnt itself out did he manage to snap awake once again. He took another of the lit torches from its cradle along the wall. It was time to head back to the upper chamber.

The horse was still grating its hoof at something on the floor upon his return. "Still at it, are you, my friend?" he remarked.

Night had fallen outside; it appeared that the storm had abated somewhat, but still it raged, howled and wailed like a legion of banshees. But whatever nameless evil lurked in this place or in the unknown depths beneath, it still offered sanctuary from the storm.

He had settled down into a slumber among some makeshift items from the saddle bag that he used in the stead of a blanket.

His mind drifted away, heedless of the howling winds outside, beyond the star-strewn firmament, across the vast sidereal gulf. His shade flew above a dry and desiccated world, cold, barren, and red, but in a heartbeat his shade saw this world as it formerly was; a world of pale blue firmament; tossing and heaving azure oceans where mer-folk frolicked and disported themselves in the waves. Twin pale and golden orbs of moons raced through its skies, the greater and lesser, moving like tethered chariots.

Majestic cites of marble rose from its shores atop steep granite cliffs against which the pounding surf crashed; inland vast forests and orchards bloomed, unearthly trees reaching to great height, defying the weight constraints of our heavier world. His attention was drawn to the city that clung to the shore of this alien ocean, an opulent cliff-top palace, and he was there in the twinkling of an eye.

The girl from the sarcophagus lid! She was clad in silken robes of strange colouring and adorned with jewelled sandals. She gazed with yearning across the alien ocean with its swells and tides sighing like star-crossed sweethearts; the golden orbs of the moons reflecting like mournful faces on the ocean's surface.

She turned and faced him, and somewhere within, a spark of recognition illuminated her feline eyes and pale, wan, but beautiful features. She held out her arms as if to beckon him to her. As he walked towards her, a sense of the familiar crept over him, and a name came to him like a flash on the Damascus road: *Oxafia, Oxafia!*

He jolted into instant wakefulness. It was light outside. The horse was once again scraping its hoof on the same spot on the floor. Attention drawn, Boscastle found an indent in the hollow of the floor. Embedded within it was some kind of strange tablet. His dagger pried it loose without difficulty. It was covered with runes and hieroglyphs. He packed it into a sack and stowed it in his saddle bag. He decided his time among these ancient ruins was at an end.

Outside and among the sweeping sands as the storm was blowing itself out, an unpleasant surprise awaited him. On the crest of the highest dune facing the mountains was Mustafa bin Hazred mounted on his magnificent white stallion. He grinned as he saw Boscastle and his black steed cross his field of vision. He drew his long and bejewelled musket from his saddle pack. On it were some crude flip sights that he adjusted to get the bead on his target. As he grinned, his white teeth shone out from his perfectly kept beard.

Bin Hazred drew back the hammer on his musket, it crashed forward, flint igniting powder, the resultant explosion propelling the musket ball towards its quarry. The ball shattered the rear left leg of his steed and sent Boscastle sprawling forward in an eruption of sand. The Huegenot was pinned beneath the stricken beast, and the contents of the saddle bag were strewn everywhere over the dune.

Bin Hazred drew his scimitar, perfectly balanced and honed beyond razor sharpness. By this time Boscastle had managed to pull himself free from beneath the stricken and now screaming beast and was attempting to limp over the rise of the next dune. Bin Hazred judged that he would be able to decapitate the infidel cleanly at a gallop. He and his mighty stallion charged.

Boscastle heard the sound of the hoofs on the sand behind him as he tried to cross the closest dune, but it was hopeless; he might as well face it, his dagger was lost somewhere in the sand. At least it would be over quickly. He turned. Bin Hazred was closing in on him fast and emitting a blood-curdling yell; then he remembered the heavy stone tablet in the sack, reaching for it just as bin Hazred was upon him. He threw it full at the oncoming rider, the force of it dislodging bin Hazred from his steed, which continued racing to the rise of the next dune.

The rider hit the sand, which sprayed in all directions. He was recovering his stance when Boscastle was on him with the sack containing the tablet; he swung it crushingly down on bin Hazred's skull, once, twice, thrice . . .

He managed to coax bin Hazred's horse back from the crest of the next dune and give the beast some water, and some reassuring. He examined the saddle packs and saw that they were well-provisioned and that there was water in the skins.

The pitiful wailing of the faithful black steed drew his attention. He stroked the beast's nose reassuringly but was in no doubt as to what needed doing, he retrieved the long musket from the sand and sought out the powder horn . . .

There were two dead beings in this clearing amid the dunes. Bin Hazred's corpse lay sprawled in the sand, its skull caved in. The rapidly heating sands seemed to be eagerly sucking in the brains and gore that issued forth from it. Yes, two dead beings but only one worth mourning, he thought to himself as his gaze fell upon his faithful horse.

The carrion birds circled overhead from their perches in the lower crags in the foothills close by. Soon they would feed. Where was the nobility or justice in being food for vultures? Boscastle set about covering the body of his horse as best he could, fetching broken pieces of marble paving and columns, masonry and whatever else he was able to. It was long and arduous work, and by its completion the sun was close to setting upon the western horizon below the line of dunes where the sky now grew a crimson hue.

A cairn of broken marble and stone snow marked the resting place of his steed, and he placed the saddle pack on the top. Moisture issued from almost every pore in the completion of this task. Some of it seemed to issue from his eyes and, as he wiped it away with the back of his hand, he assuaged himself with the thought that this must be due to the irritation of the stinging sands that blew around him.

He mounted bin Hazred's white stallion and headed west across the dune sea towards the setting sun, away from the lost city without name.

Soon even the tracks left in the endless sands were erased by the wind as the figure was lost in the distance.

FIN

... SHE WAS A FOUNDLING, ABANDONED ONLY HOURS AFTER HER BIRTH, TAKEN IN BY A MYSTERIOUS WITCH-WOMAN — AT 15 SHE WAS ABDUCTED BY PIRATES AND SOLD INTO SLAVERY, DURING WHICH TIME TONGA OF LEMURIA CAME OF AGE... IT WAS THE TIME SHE ALWAYS REGARDED AS HER...

GLADIATOR DAYS

THE BLAZING SUN OF OLD LEMURIA BEATS DOWN ON THE SANDS OF THE ARENA! THE GLADITORIAL GAMES ARE EVERYTHING IN TSARGOL, THE SCARLET CITY, AND TONGA IS THE CITY'S CURRENT SUPER-STAR GLADIATOR...

THE CROWD ROARS ITS ACCLAIM AS IT HAS FOR THE PAST TWO YEARS DURING TONGA'S METEORIC RISE TO FAME!

SHE DOES NOT KNOW HER OPPONENT, ONLY THAT HE IS EXTREMELY FORMIDABLE, AND IS THE SLAVE OF VENDRA POM, HIGH DRUID OF YAMATH IN TSARGOL...

... A FORTNIGHT AGO...

... AND THIS YOUNG FEMALE GLADIATOR, THIS BEAUTY, AGAINST WHOM NONE CAN PREVAIL, THIS TONGA, SHE WILL FIGHT? BY YAMATH'S ALL-CONSUMING FLAME, SHE IS A LOVELY CREATURE — BUT, YOU DO MEAN TO FIGHT HER IN THESE UPCOMING GAMES, EH ZHU ZHARVIS?

BY
CLAYTON L. HINKLE

* TONGA'S LEMURIA IS ALSO THONGOR'S LEMURIA, AND IS USED WITH KIND PERMISSION FROM THE ESTATE OF LIN CARTER!

... REASON ENOUGH TO BE WARY! VENDRA POM WAS KNOWN TO BE A POWERFUL SORCERER, HIGHLY RESPECTED, EVEN FEARED, IN THE ROYAL COURT, WHERE...

ZHU ZHARVIS, LEADING GLADIATOR MASTER AND FIGHT PROMOTER OF TSARGOL, AND TONGA'S OWNER, HAD BEEN SUMMONED TO THE PALACE OF EUKIGOS KHOR, THE SARK...
OH, OF COURSE YOUR REVERANCE, FOR IS SHE NOT THE CITY'S FAVORITE?
SHE IS WELL DESERVED OF FAVOR, EVERY MAGNIFICENT INCH OF HER! ER, HEH, I FIND MYSELF MOST INTERESTED IN HER, YOU SEE...
IN THAT YOU ARE NOT ALONE, YOUR EMINENCE. WHO COULD NOT BE 'INTERESTED' IN SUCH BEAUTY COUPLED WITH SUCH INCREDIBLE TALENT AND ABILITIES?
BUT YOURS IS NO CASUAL INTEREST, I'LL WAGER, VENDRA FOM! FOR WHO KNOWS WHAT REALLY 'INTERESTS A SORCERER LIKE YOU...
...I MUST TREAD CAREFULLY AROUND YOU, THIS I KNOW! EVEN OUR MIGHTY SARK HERE, EUKIGOS KHOR HIMSELF, IS RUMORED TO FEAR YOU...
A WONDER IT IS THAT I WAS NOT AWARE OF THIS INTEREST OF YOURS, VENDRA, BUT THEN I AM CONTINUALLY BUSY WITH MATTERS OF STATE!
OF COURSE, SIRE, MATTERS OF STATE!
BUT WHILE YOU PONDER THE MUNDANE, BUT IMPORTANT, MATTERS OF STATE, I CONCERN MYSELF WITH THE ESOTERIC MATTERS OF THE COSMIC AND SPIRITUAL REALMS - HOW COULD YOU, AFTER ALL, BE AWARE OF MY INTERESTS?

THOUGH OF COURSE, WE ALL KNOW THE MUNDANE WORLD HAS ITS DELIGHTS,

SUCH DELIGHTS AS MAY EVEN TEMPT ONE SUCH AS I.... I, WHOSE LOFTY GAZE IS SO OFTEN FIXED UPON MATTERS OF COSMIC PORTENT, EVEN I TAKE PLEASURE IN THE EXCITEMENT OF THE GAMES! AND YOUR TONGA, ZHU ZHARVIS! BEAUTIFUL! MAGNIFICENT! THAT BODY! I, I MUST CONFESS — IT IS SHE WHO IS REALLY THE FOCUS OF MY, AH, INFATUATION WITH, ER, GLADITORIAL SPORT!

I HAVE NOTED THAT SHE SEEMS TO HAVE YET TO MEET A WORTHY OPPONENT — TO SEE SUCH AS SHE EXTEND HERSELF TO HER VERY LIMITS WOULD INDEED MAKE AN ENTERTAINING SPECTACLE, YES? THUS, A PROPOSAL: I WILL, AH, FIELD, AN OPPONENT FOR HER, AND SET YOU A WAGER...

IF YOUR LOVELY TONGA WINS, YOU, AS HER OWNER, WILL RECEIVE TEN HUNDRED-WEIGHTS IN GOLD — SHOULD MY FIGHTER WIN, I SHALL RECEIVE... TONGA HERSELF!

TEN HUNDRED-WEIGHTS! GORM! I TRUST NOT ANY SORCERER, BUT I DARE NOT REFUSE...

AH, WELL, I — I ACCEPT YOUR WAGER, EMINENCE!

BUT, I MUST ASK THIS QUESTION: WHAT IF TONGA SHOULD LOSE, AND DIE IN THE LOSING? WILL YOU NOT HAVE LOST YOUR WINNINGS BY WINNING THE FIGHT?

AH! NO NEED TO WORRY —

YOU SEE, I'LL STILL POSSESS HER BODY, NOT TOO TERRIBLY DAMAGED, I'LL TRUST! THAT'S ALL I REALLY NEED, ANYWAY!

BACK TO THE PRESENT - TONGA SALUTES THE ROYAL BOX ...
THERE IS THE SARK, LIFTING A LAZY HAND IN REPLY, AND THERE IS VENDRA POM, LEERING, STARING ...
WITH A SNORT OF DISGUST SHE TURNS TOWARD A RISING PORT-CULLIS, FROM WHICH ISSUES A FRIGHTFUL SOUND!
CLANKLANKLANKLANK
BLARG!
BLARG!
THE INHUMAN ROAR QUIETS THE ARENA, AND WHAT LUMBERS OUT OF THE DARK TUNNEL WITH ANOTHER ROAR IS A HORROR, A NIGHTMARE OF MERGED METAL AND FLESH!

BACK TO THE PRESENT — TONGA SALUTES THE ROYAL BOX...
THERE IS THE SARK, LIFTING A LAZY HAND IN REPLY, AND THERE IS VENDRA DOM, LEERING, STARING...
WITH A SNORT OF DISGUST SHE TURNS TOWARD A RISING PORTCULLIS, FROM WHICH ISSUES A FRIGHTFUL SOUND!
CLANK LANK LANK KLANK
BLARG!
BLARG!
THE INHUMAN ROAR QUIETS THE ARENA, AND WHAT LUMBERS OUT OF THE DARK TUNNEL WITH ANOTHER ROAR IS A HORROR, A NIGHTMARE OF MERGED METAL AND FLESH!

A COLLECTIVE GASP ECHOES ABOUT THE ARENA, FOLLOWED BY THE CONFUSED GABBLE OF SURPRISE — AND NO DIFFERENT IS THE ROYAL BOX!
BY GORM!! WHAT IN ALL THE NINE HELLS IS THAT THING!?
OH, MY LORD, WHAT MONSTER APPEARS BEFORE US?
OH!
GORM!
NOW, YOUR MAJESTY KNOWS I SWEAR ONLY BY BLESSED YAMATH! HEE HEE HEE
THAT 'MONSTER' IS MY CREATION, AND HIS NAME IS BLARG!
LONG WERE MY LABORS, UTTERLY INCONCEIVABLE TO MORTALS THE... SPELLS AND MAGICS USED, BUT THEY SUCCEEDED, AND HERE HE IS! HEE HEE HEE HEE HEE HEE
NOR IS THE FIGHTER'S BOX UNAFFECTED BY THE SIGHT...
GORM'S BALLS! D'YOU SEE THAT THING, ZHU ZHARVIS?
THAT BASTARD POM TRICKED ME! NOW I'LL LOSE TONGA, AND EVEN WORSE — TEN HUNDRED-WEIGHTS OF GOLD!! GAAAAH!!!
BLARG!
HAHOO, WHAT'S THIS? ZHU TOLD ME TO BE READY FOR ANYTHING, BUT...
TOOMF
TOOMF TOOMF
TOOOMF TOOMF
TOOMF TOOOMF

A MONSTER MADE OF METAL AND FLESH? BY GORM, WHAT SORCERY IS THIS?!
BLARG!
CHONK
POWERFUL YOU MAY BE, BUT SLOW, CLUMSY AND STUPID TOO! AH! I SEE YOU ARE NOT METAL EVERY WHERE, AT LEAST NOT...
CHT
BL GG
SHLLLLKK
G-G-ARG
...WHERE IT COUNTS!
7

GG-GR-GLGG
THE YOUNG GLADIATRIX MUSES THAT THOUGH A MONSTER, 'BLARG'S' BLOOD IS AS RED AS ANY MAN'S! HE STAGGERS, DESPERATELY TRYING TO KEEP HIS FEET, STUMBLING, BLEEDING...
BGLGUG-GGG
CHUF
CHUF
CHUF
...IN HIS HORRID GURGLING ONE LAST ATTEMPT AT A "BLARG!", HE AT LAST CRASHES TO THE SANDS, DEAD, OR APPARENTLY SO!
GFFFF
THUMP

THE ARENA ERUPTS IN APPLAUSE!
VENDRA POM IS BOLT UPRIGHT, QUIVERING, TWITCHING...
HE WATCHES AS TONGA BOWS MOCKINGLY...
HE WATCHES AS SHE GLIMPSES HIS OWN FACE, AND STARTS TO LAUGH...
TONGA'S LAUGHTER SETS THE SARK TO LAUGHING, SO OF COURSE THE WHOLE ROYAL BOX STARTS LAUGHING...
THE TSARGOLIAN MOB FOLLOWS SUIT, A RUMBLE GROWING INTO A ROAR...
AT THE FIGHTER'S BOX, BORTHUS AND ZHU ZHARVIS HOWL WITH GLEE...
AND WORST OF ALL FOR VENDRA POM IS THE LAUGHTER OF TONGA, THE FOCUS OF HIS LONG-LAID PLANS, HIS LONG-HELD FANTASIES, AND THE ARCHITECT OF HIS DEFEAT! HIS FACE TAKES ON AN ALARMING HUE - VEINS CRAWL AND BULGE...

GAAK!
VENDRA PON'S TWITCHINGS TERMINATE IN A CONVULSIVE JERK, THEN...
CCRUMP
TONGA'S LAUGHTER TERMINATES AS ABRUPTLY, WHILE SHE GAZES IN WIDE-EYED ASTONISHMENT!
THE SARK AND OTHERS IN THE ROYAL BOX ALSO STARE IN SHOCK...
THE MOB'S LAUGHTER SUBSIDES INTO A CONFUSED MURMER AS THEY POINT AND GESTICULATE--AND ZHU ZHARVIS FEELS SUDDENLY COLD...
HIS HEAD LOOKS LIKE A BUSTED KROTER EGG, SIRE! HE'S DEAD AS YESTERDAY'S BREAKFAST!

—THE LEMURIAN SUN BEATS DOWN ON THE SWEATING GLADIATORS IN ZHU ZHARVIS'S TRAINING YARD, AS BORTHUS WORKS HIS WHIPPING ARM...
ALRIGHT PUS-HEADS, KEEP MOVIN'! THOSE BAGS ARE LIGHT! YA CAN'T SHARPEN SWORDS ON BUTTER, BY GORM!
CRAK
GRRRR
AARRAAHH!!
YAAH!! GORM'S BALLS, TONGA GIRL! THATS NO WAY TA TREAT YER LOVING, KINDLY OVERSEER!
DAMN YOU BORTHUS! IF YOU WANT THAT WHIP WRAPPED AROUND YOUR THROAT AND STUCK UP YOUR BUNG-HOLE AT THE SAME TIME, CRACK IT AT ME AGAIN!
PROOM

DID I NOT WIN MY FIGHT IN SPECTACULAR FASHION? DID NOT OUR SCHOOL WIN ALL OF IT'S FIGHTS? YES, YES? THEN WHAT'S WITH THIS WHIP-CRACKING BOUPHAR CRAP?!
SORRY, TONGA LASS — ORDERS FROM OL' ZHU HISSELF!
YA SEE, VENDRA POM BET ZHU TEN HUNDRED-WEIGHTS O' GOLD, AGAINST YOU — IF YOU'DA LOST, VENDRA'D GET YOU — OR YOUR BODY! WEIRD, HUH? BUT SINCE HE DIED, ACCORDING TO THE SARK, ALL HIS PROPERTY REVERTS TO THE CROWN, EVEN AND ESPECIALLY THE TEN HUNDRED-WEIGHTS! ZHU'S TEN HUNDRED-WEIGHTS!
AND WHOSE FAULT WAS IT?
YOURS! THE WAY ZHU FIGURES IT, ANYWAY! HE WAS SO MAD HE TOLD ME TA WORK ALLA YEZ 'TIL YA DROPPED, AND IF ANYBODY COMPLAINED, TA TAKE THE WHIP TO 'EM — SO, I GOTTA DO WHAT I GOTTA DO — TAKE THAT!
ALRIGHT MY LOVLIES! NOW YOU'VE RESTED, LINE IT UP FOR BURPEES! BURPEES UNTIL I'M TIRED! C'MON LOVLIES! LET'S GO!
END

9 798988 957584